Praise for
Alan Dean Foster
and *Reunion*,
a Pip & Flinx Adventure

"Bestseller Foster has created yet another entertaining adventure story in the far-flung reaches of a
far-future outer space. . . . Using the traditional cliff-
hangers and narrow escapes of classic SF adventure
page-turners, and propelling Flinx from one crisis to
another, from moral dilemma to deus ex machina,
Foster enlists multiple formulas for a surefire . . .
reading experience that should appeal to space-
opera fans."

—*Publishers Weekly*

"Flinx's trek through the deadly desert and his en-
counters with the AAnn make for a good read."

—*Locus*

BY ALAN DEAN FOSTER

Published by The Random House Publishing Group

The Black Hole
Cachalot
Dark Star
The Metrognome and Other Stories
Midworld
Nor Crystal Tears
Sentenced to Prism
Splinter of the Mind's Eye
Star Trek® Logs One–Ten
Voyage to the City of the Dead
. . . Who Needs Enemies?
With Friends Like These . . .
Mad Amos
The Howling Stones
Parallelities

THE ICERIGGER TRILOGY
Icerigger
Mission to Moulokin
The Deluge Drivers

THE ADVENTURES OF FLINX OF THE
  COMMONWEALTH
For Love of Mother-Not
The Tar-Aiym-Krang

Orphan Star
The End of the Matter
Bloodhype
Mid-Flinx
Flinx's Folly
Sliding Scales
Running from the Deity

THE DAMNED
Book One: A Call to Arms
Book Two: The False Mirror
Book Three: The Spoils of War

THE FOUNDING OF THE COMMONWEALTH
Phylogenesis
Dirge
Diuturnity's Dawn

THE TAKEN TRILOGY
Lost and Found
The Light-Years Beneath My Feet

Books published by The Random House Publishing Group
are available at quantity discounts on bulk purchases for
premium, educational, fund-raising, and special sales use.
For details, please call 1-800-733-3000.

SLIDING SCALES

A PIP & FLINX ADVENTURE

ALAN DEAN FOSTER

BALLANTINE BOOKS • NEW YORK

Sale of this book without a front cover may be unauthorized. If this book is coverless, it may have been reported to the publisher as "unsold or destroyed" and neither the author nor the publisher may have received payment for it.

Sliding Scales is a work of fiction. Names, places, and incidents either are products of the author's imagination or are used fictitiously.

2005 Del Rey Books Mass Market Edition

Copyright © 2004 by Thranx, Inc.
Excerpt from *Running from the Deity* copyright © 2005 by Thranx, Inc.

All rights reserved.

Published in the United States by Del Rey Books, an imprint of The Random House Publishing Group, a division of Random House, Inc., New York.

DEL REY is a registered trademark and the Del Rey colophon is a trademark of Random House, Inc.

Originally published in hardcover in the United States by Del Rey Books, an imprint of The Random House Publishing Group, a division of Random House, Inc., in 2004.

This book contains an excerpt from the forthcoming book *Running from the Deity* by Alan Dean Foster. This excerpt has been set for this edition only and may not reflect the final content of the forthcoming edition.

ISBN 0-345-46158-4

Printed in the United States of America

www.delreybooks.com

OPM 9 8 7 6 5 4 3 2 1

For my nephew, Matthew Aaron Hedish.
Something for later.

I am in danger of becoming permanently, irrevocably, and unrescuably moody, Flinx found himself thinking. He knew *unrescuably* wasn't a word, but the mangled syntax fit his melancholic state of mind. Forced to leave a badly injured Clarity Held behind on New Riviera in the care of Bran Tse-Mallory and Truzenzuzex, pursued now by a newly revealed clutch of fatalistic end-of-the-universe fanatics who called themselves the Order of Null (whose existence he might be responsible for), sought by Commonwealth authorities and others for reasons multifarious and diverse, he could be forgiven for sinking into a mood as black as the space that enveloped the *Teacher*.

Sensing his mood, Pip did what she could to cheer him. The flying snake whizzed effortlessly among the garden and fountains of the lounge, occasionally darting out from behind leaves or bushes in an attempt to startle her master—or at least rouse him from the lethargy that had settled on his soul ever since their forced flight from Nur. Recognizing the effort she was making on his behalf, he smiled and stroked her. But he could no more hide his frame of mind from the empathetic minidrag than he could from himself. Emotionally, she knew him better than anyone, Clarity Held included.

Clarity, Clarity, Clarity, he murmured softly to himself. When will I be able to see you again? After years of wandering, to have finally found someone he felt truly understood him and he might be able to spend the rest of his life with only to lose so soon was almost more than he could bear. Instead of having her to comfort him, he had agreed to spend who knew how long and how much precious time searching for an ancient weapons platform fabricated by an extinct race that might not even prove useful or usable in diverting an oncoming peril of incalculable dimensions and intent.

If that wasn't enough to depress someone, he could not imagine what was. At least his recurring headaches had not bothered him for a while.

Even some of the live plants in the relaxation chamber seemed to sense his melancholy, brushing his seated form with branches and flowers. The exotic scents of several blossoms refreshed but did not inspire him. The striking foliage could touch, even caress, but could not converse. That ability remained the province of the *Teacher's* shipmind. To its credit, in its limited, formalized, electron-shunting fashion, it tried to help.

"My medical programming informs me that extended periods of depression can affect the health of a human as seriously as a bacterial infection."

"Go infect yourself," Flinx snapped irritably.

"It also," the ship continued briskly, "is detrimental to the well-being of any unlucky sentients who are compelled to function in the vicinity of the one so depressed."

Slumped in the lounge chair, Flinx glanced sideways in the direction of the nearest visual pickup. "Are you saying that my mood is contagious?"

"I am saying that anything that affects you also affects me. Your continuing mental condition is not conducive to the efficient functioning of this vessel."

"Not to mention myself, eh?" He sat up a little straighter, brushing leaves and the tips of small branches away from his legs and sides. Several of them, very subtly, retracted without having to be touched. "You know, ship, I've been thinking about everything Bran and Tru told me, about all that we discussed, and the longer I ponder on it, the more my inclination is to say the hell with it, the hell with everything. Except for Clarity, of course."

"I sense that this energetic verbal response is not an indication of a lightening of mood."

"Damn right it isn't. Give me one good reason why I shouldn't do exactly that?"

The ship did not hesitate. "Because if you do nothing, there is a strong likelihood that everything and everyone in this galaxy will perish, with the concomitant possibility that the ultimate responsibility will be yours."

He rolled his eyes. "All right—give me another reason."

Surprisingly, the ship did not respond. Advanced AI circuitry notwithstanding, there were still occasional matters that required a certain modicum of cybernetic reflection. This, apparently, was one of them. Or else, he told himself, it was simply pausing for dramatic effect, something it was quite capable of doing.

"You are not thinking with your usual clarity—if you will pardon my use of that word in this context. I have been meditating on this situation for some days now, and I believe I may have, in the course of researching and studying the matter, come to a possible solution."

For the first time all day, Flinx showed some real interest. "You don't say? What have you been studying? Human psychoanalysis?"

"Nothing so imprecise. Human behavior can be slotted, albeit with variations, into specific categories. Analysis of yours suggests that you have been laboring under immense mental pressure for some time now."

The tone of his reply was sardonic. "That's hardly a

news bulletin, ship. Tell me: what prescribed remedy have you uncovered?"

The ship could not keep a note of—artificial?—accomplishment from creeping into its dulcet electronic tones. "Philip Lynx—you need a vacation. That one quick recent visit to Moth was not nearly what is required. You need a vacation from your concerns, your worries, your fears. From trying to see and learn and study. From the immense threat that looms over the galaxy. From yourself."

It was not the response he had expected. Initially cynical, he found himself more than a little intrigued. "You mean I need to spend time on a beach somewhere, or go for extended hikes in some woods? I've done all that."

"No. It's true you have been to such places and done those things, but it was always with some specific purpose in mind. You need to go somewhere and do some things to no purpose. You need to just 'be' for a while. This is a necessity for the health of any human. The library of me says so."

He considered thoughtfully before finally responding, "I don't know if I can do that, ship. I never have."

"Then," declared the ship conclusively, "it is time you did so. Every one of my relevant stored medical texts attests to the therapeutic value of such an undertaking. You need to go somewhere interesting and expend some energy in doing nothing. It is necessary for your health."

Could he? he found himself wondering. Could he set everything aside: thoughts of Clarity, of Bran Tse-Mallory, and Truzenzuzex and the steadily approaching evil that lurked behind the Great Emptiness, of the Tar-Aiym weapons platform and all those who sought him, and really do *nothing* for any appreciable period of time? Could he, dare he, attempt the seemingly impossible? A vacation? Of everything he had done in his short but full life, that struck him as being among the most alien. Even as a child he had not been able to engage in such non-activity. He had been too busy stealing, to keep himself and Mother Mastiff alive.

He had been on the verge of saying to hell with everything. Here was his ship advising him to do essentially that, only without the attendant rancor. For a little while, at least. But where to seek such mental and physical succor? He asked as much of the *Teacher.*

"I have devoted almost a full minute of thought to the matter," the synthetic voice replied, clearly gratified by Flinx's decision. "Given the inauspicious interest in your person by everyone from several independent inimical organizations to the Commonwealth authority itself, it is clear that you would not be able to relax and refresh yourself on any developed world within the Commonwealth."

Now there's an understatement, Flinx thought.

"Persisting with this line of reasoning," ship continued, "it is also plain that if you are forced to spend time on an undeveloped, unexplored world, you will similarly be unable to unwind, as all your mental acuity will perforce be focused on staying alive. This would seem to leave you with few options."

"Indeed it would." Flinx watched as Pip coiled around a dark-sided shrub and slid sinuously down the oddly patterned bark. It did not appear to bother the bush.

"What is required is a comfortably habitable world that lies not only beyond the reach of Commonwealth authority but of those other groups that seek to incommode you. A world where you can move about without, as humans like to put it, having to constantly peer over your shoulder. I do not have any shoulders to peer over, but I am able to grasp the philosophical conceit."

"I always said you were full of conceit," Flinx riposted.

His heart wasn't really in the verbal sparring, though. He was, as ship had persisted in pointing out, very tired. "You're going to tell me that you've found such a refuge?" Near the pond, Pip was bobbing and weaving like a serpentine boxer as a thorny flower struck reflexively in her direction.

"I do not possess sufficient information to so categorize it, but the world I have settled upon seems a promising candidate. Certainly it appears to fulfill the requisite conditions."

With a sigh he sat up straight on the edge of the lounge, trying hard not to think of Clarity Held and whether she was recovered from her injuries. He refused to countenance the possibility that she might not have survived. Without a doubt he needed to find something to divert himself from incessantly dwelling on such dark possibilities.

"What's the name of this handy haven you've found?" he asked dubiously.

"The planet is called Jast."

"Just Jast?" he queried flippantly. "Never heard of it."

"There is no reason why you should. It is not part of the Commonwealth and in fact does not even lie within the vast reach of the Orion Arm considered Commonwealth space."

Remembering that he was supposed to be searching for the vanished Tar-Aiym weapons platform, he experienced a sudden flicker of interest. "It's not within the Blight, is it?"

"No. Quite the opposite direction, actually." Just as well, he mused. Ship was proposing that he go to this world to relax. "Where, then?"

Much compacted in scope, a three-dimensional star map materialized helpfully in front of him. So far off the familiar space-plus vectors was the blinking yellow indicator within that it took a moment before his eyes found it. His brow furrowed.

"You're right. That is outside Commonwealth space."

"Jast lies in the region claimed by both the Commonwealth and that of the AAnn Empire," ship informed him. Flinx could see that for himself. The flashing indicator was located in a vast unclaimed area approximately halfway between Rhyinpine and the AAnn capital of Blasusarr. A long ways from anywhere, he reflected.

Maybe just what he needed.

"It's certainly off the beaten path," he admitted, increasingly intrigued. Pleased by her master's interest, Pip abandoned her shadowboxing with the long-suffering flower to flit back and settle herself in his lap. "What besides its isolation makes it suitable for a safe respite?"

"Gravity is somewhat less than t-standard, which should make for ease of locomotion. The atmosphere is reported to be heavy with organic contaminants, but nothing dangerous. The dominant sentient species, the Vssey, are cordial enough toward visitors and have achieved a high level of technological and social development. Their physical configuration renders them generally, though not exclusively, pacific by nature. Politically, they are an independent system allied with the Empire. While some Vssey have adapted AAnn ways and subscribe to the AAnn outlook, this acclimatization is far from universal."

Flinx made a face. "That doesn't sound very relaxing to me. The place is likely to be full of AAnn."

"Records relating to Jast are understandably sparse, but insist that all non-Imperial visitors are welcome. Although your concern may be somewhat justified, Flinx, the corollary is that while sojourning on Jast you are certain to be free of scrutiny from any Commonwealth organization or independent hostile group, official or otherwise."

It was a valid point. In return for exposing himself to the curiosity of potentially confrontational AAnn, he would not have to worry about dealing with the attention of those who had recently been pursuing him with ever greater enthusiasm.

"What's Jast itself like?" He was halfway convinced that the ship had made a sensible choice.

"According to the most recent galographics of related but non-integrated systems, it is very much what you would expect of a place that would draw the attention of the AAnn. Dry and desert-like, though with considerably more widely scattered rainfall than is to be found on ecologically similar Commonwealth worlds such as Comagrave, for example. One might think of it as a particularly wet desert. Though fully adapted to hot, dry conditions, the native flora and fauna is abundant and varied."

"And the Vssey themselves?"

"An unusual biotic type."

An image promptly appeared in the air in front of Flinx. Lifting her head, Pip regarded it with casual interest. The synchronized synthetic aroma that accompanied the likeness was new to her. If anything, he thought as he studied the three-dimensional alien portrayal, the ship was yet again given to understatement. The Vssey was like nothing he had encountered before in any of his extensive travels. At least, he corrected himself, like nothing intelligent he had encountered.

On the included, integrated dimensional scale, the animated Vssey stood somewhat under a meter and a half in height. Roughly cylindrical in shape, its lower body, or stem, was perhaps two-thirds of a meter in diameter. At its base, this spread out and separated into four short, stubby, opposing, toe-like flaps of flesh. The body itself was ridged with ligaments and muscles.

At the upper end, the body expanded out into a meter-wide flattened dome that resembled an ancient umbrella. The overhanging, circular edge was fringed with a sufficiency of prehensile tentacles to suggest that the Vssey were an especially dexterous species. There was no neck. Near the crown of the dome a pair of eyes emerged on short, independently swiveling stalks. As the animation proceeded, Flinx saw that this arrangement allowed the Vssey to see in any direction, as well as in any two directions at once. Located above the flexing tentacles but well below the eyes, in place of readily recognizable ears there flashed a narrow comb-like ribbon of erect, dull orange membrane that ran around the entire circumference of the dome, making up in extent what it lacked in height. Below the eyes was a slit of a mouth that, when opened, revealed two sets of flat grinding plates for chewing food.

Though exceedingly odd-looking, it was evident that the Vssey had the necessary tools to see, hear, and effectively manipulate their immediate environment. What they could not do, Flinx immediately suspected as he continued to examine the detailed depiction, was get around very well.

"How do they move?" he murmured, fascinated as always by the sight of an entirely new sentient body style.

"Notice the significant musculature lining the central body core," the ship instructed him. "Observe."

The lowermost portion of the body and its quadruple flaps promptly contracted and released, causing the image of the Vssey to leap a few centimeters forward. The process repeated itself until Flinx, adequately educated, called a halt to the display. As a method of locomotion suitable to what was essentially a one-footed creature, the technique was admirable and efficient. It did not, however, compensate for the fact that the Vssey were compelled to explore their surroundings literally one step at a time. Flinx found himself smiling. A Vssey in forward motion resembled nothing so much as a hopping mushroom.

"Is that as fast as they can go?"

"My records do not extend to the inclusion of a compilation of Vsseyan athletic accomplishments, Flinx. But I would venture to say that even a moderately active human would easily be able to run circles around any Vssey."

"Or any AAnn would," Flinx added somberly. Visions of the nimble, fleet-footed reptiloids tormenting slow-moving Vssey sprang unbidden into Flinx's mind. It was not a pleasant picture, and he could only hope that the reality on Jast and the relationship between the two species were more amenable than his imaginings.

"Certainly so," the ship readily agreed. "Podal agility is likely not to be accounted among the foremost abilities of the Vssey. Like any intelligent species confronted with an inherent physiological impediment, I am sure they have found ways and means to compensate. For one thing, they are asexual and reproduce by budding. Not having to search for a mate greatly reduces the need to move about repeatedly and rapidly, with concurrent consequences for related evolutionary development."

"No doubt," agreed Flinx more somberly, losing the smile. "Tentacles—or those tentacles—don't look very strong."

"They apparently are not," the ship agreed. "However, they must be adequate to the shaping of an advanced civilization, which the Vssey have done. And there are many of them. Perhaps forty or fifty weak fingers are the equal, or even the superior, to ten stronger ones. Or to sixteen, in the case of the thranx."

"They must be descended from an ancestor that was originally permanently sedentary." Flinx was taken with the possibilities of the Vssey body design. "Like Terran anemones."

"Perhaps. The information I have on the species does not extend to details of their racial pedigree."

Flinx leaned back in the lounge and continued to study the image of the Vssey as the recording ran through to its conclusion. When it began to loop, he waved it away.

"Your description of Jast doesn't sound very inviting. I don't much care for dry places. As you know, during our recent visit to Pyrassis I 'enjoyed' more than enough forced desert sightseeing to last me a long, long time. Not to mention a similar experience years ago on Moth, in the company of an old reprobate named Knigta Yakus." His tone softened. "But the Vssey—*they* intrigue me. One might almost call them charming."

"That is not a biologically accurate categorization," said the ship in a voice that was mildly reproving.

"I know. It's a silly subjective human categorization. One I think happens to fit the sentients under discussion." He waved a hand grandly. "Set course for this Jast. I'm taking your advice, ship. I'm going to make a strenuous attempt to unwind among the mushrooms."

"*Strenuous* and *unwind* should not be used tangentially in the context of a proposed vacation, Flinx, as the meaning and intent of one seriously contravenes the meaning and intent of the other. And the Vssey are not taxonomically related to any individual family of the fungi, irrespective of—"

"Ship?"

"Yes, Flinx."

"Shut up and navigate."

As always, the *Teacher* complied. If it felt disrespected

by the abruptness of its master's command, it kept any such reaction entirely to itself. Besides, Flinx had taken its advice, both as to what to do next and where to carry out the doing of it.

No more than that could an AI ask for.

2

Takuuna VBXLLW didn't particularly want to kill the two Vssey juveniles. But he did not particularly mind the prospect of doing so, either. It was not as if his schedule was full. As it was, his duties as a secondary administrator for the outer Vsseyan provinces of Qwal-Dihn and Tual-Sihb left him too much time to think. Too much time to dwell on the dead-end nature of both his assignment and his life. Still young and adventurous, like any ambitious AAnn adult he desperately wished for an opportunity to present itself that would allow for substantial personal advancement. Only then could he change his name to Takuuna VBXLL and hope to ascend within the formal hierarchy that was the Empire.

Jast was not the sort of place, nor his assignment the kind of work, where one was likely to encounter such a ready prospect. This was a drawback he shared in common with millions of his fellow nye. As he was only concerned for himself, he did not reflect on the fact that behind the AAnn Empire's continued steady expansion stood this collective racial impatience that was reflected in every individual's desire to get ahead. Executing the two miserable young Vssey would likely neither advance nor slow his personal progress. It was just part of the job.

Letting out a soft hiss of resignation, he glanced skyward. The choluub were already ascending. Small, limbless nocturnal grazers on Jast's surprisingly luxuriant and varied desert flora, they ate and defecated pretty much where they lay. In addition to eating, they spent the night regenerating membranous sacs from a special organ on their slightly humped backs. As a by-product of their consumption of Jast's nourishing plant life, they produced methane gas. Instead of voiding it anally, the gas was diverted inside the cholub's body to the freshly extruded membrane, slowly filling it.

As the sun rose, it heated the gas inside the membranes. Now, hundreds of sleepy cholub, elevated by these slowly expanding balloons, were rising into the air from the surrounding terrain. In contrast to the dull brown and dark green bodies of the cholub themselves, the transparent membranes that provided their lift were strikingly iridescent. All around the open courtyard of the local AAnn administrative compound, hundreds of glistening, multi-hued bubbles were rising majestically skyward. After filling their bellies during the night, the hovering cholub would rest and travel with the wind. By late afternoon they would begin to vent gas and sink slowly surfaceward, to gently touch down anew in fresh grazing grounds.

It was a process of aerial wandering that took place every day across much of the planet. Many other species—some larger, some smaller, some day-sleepers like the cholub, others diurnal, and a few who were unabashedly carnivorous—utilized similar methods of locomotion to get around without the need for legs or tentacles, wings or fins. Furthermore, migrating to new feeding grounds while asleep was highly efficient, a fine way to conserve energy.

Srrsstt! Everything on this world moves slowly, Takuuna growled to himself. In a naturally sluggish environment, the Vssey had distinguished themselves not only by developing intelligence, but also by evolving a method of comparatively rapid locomotion. But only comparatively. Any healthy AAnn, even one aged and sloughing scales, could beat the fastest Vsseyan sprinter, and probably do it while running backwards. The minds of the stolid Vssey, however, were as sharp as those of any other sentient—which left them, like everyone else, the administrator knew, at least one cut below the average AAnn.

A sudden warm downdraft threatened to fill the elegant parquet courtyard with its tinkling fountain and fine tile work and writhing Vsseyan sculptures with globs of bulbous, drifting choluub. Irritated, Takuuna swatted at one that came floating toward his face. Unintentionally, the sharp, short claws on the fingers of his right hand sliced into the lifting membrane. There was a whiff of escaping stink, the punctured balloon collapsed, and the softly squeaking choluub fell the rest of the way to the ground. Startled awake and stunned by the fall, it lay there motionless and mewling softly, bewildered by its surroundings. Takuuna could have lifted up a wide, sandaled foot and stomped it flat, but chose to ignore it. Unable to reach anything edible in the spotlessly clean courtyard, it would soon go silent and likely expire before nightfall.

The two condemned Vssey waited at the far end of the courtyard, mumbling to each other in the local dialect of their mellifluous language. Occasionally, a bubble or two would emerge from a mouth to rise into the rapidly warming air of morning, only to pop into nothingness before it had traveled more than a single body length. Instead of utilizing hand and arm gestures like the AAnn, for emphasis the Vssey blew bubbles to underscore or stress certain words or phrases. It struck Takuuna as a childish means of expression. One that was eminently suitable to the species as a whole, he reflected.

The two accused were not alone. They were flanked by several armed Vssey. Ordinarily, a simple crime like thievery would be dealt with by local authorities and would not even involve the AAnn. But the theft had occurred at an AAnn scientific station and had involved AAnn property. Therefore, according to Vsseyan law, it was the right of the affronted to pronounce and carry out sentence.

The AAnn could have dismissed the charges entirely, or requested sociality counseling and treatment for the offenders, or simply ignored the case altogether. But the head of the station, having suffered from such thievery previously and tired of having to fill out the relevant reports, had chosen to make an example this time. The local Vssey had been left shocked by his decision, but with no choice except to follow the letter, if not the spirit, of the law.

Which was why secondary administrator Takuuna, brought over from his comfortable office in Skokosas, had been asked to personally carry out the sentence. Sharpclawed devil, that station head Muurindi, he mused. Make an example of the thieves, but import someone else to deliver the punishment that had been decreed. That way all the local opprobrium would fall on Takuuna, giving the station head what he wanted but sparing him the anger of the locals.

Takuuna saw no way to manipulate the situation to his personal advantage. He could not turn down the request because fulfilling such requests from outlying AAnn communities and stations was part of his job. Perhaps, he thought, he was making too much of it. As soon as he had concluded the business he would climb back into his waiting aircar and zip back to Skokosas. It was just that he did not look forward to doing work that he could not turn to his benefit. As to the guilt or innocence of the two young Vssey he was about to kill, he gave not a thought. Like the doing of the killing itself, he did not really much care one way or the other.

The two Vssey certainly cared. It was evident in the way their eyestalks retracted flush against their wide, flattened heads and their rippling hearing organs lay almost flat against the upper, domed portion of their bodies. As Takuuna approached, the two sets of guards flanking the prisoners hopped off to opposite sides. Only one, unarmed and identified as an Elder by the disgusting flaking of his epidermis, advanced in slow, deliberate hops to intercept the oncoming AAnn. By way of cordial preliminaries, a couple of bubbles emerged from its mouth.

"I am Awn-Bween, senior judiciary of eastern Tual-Sihb." Several of the tentacles that lined the upper, dome-like part of the Elder's body extended themselves in the AAnn's direction. Takuuna took an indifferent swipe at them with one hand. There were no claws to make point-to-point contact with, and he did not much like the dry, wormy feel of Vsseyan appendages. His attention remained focused on the two cowering detainees.

"*Tsslk*—let uss get thiss business over with," he hissed impatiently.

Like a large, upturned brown bowl, the Elder's upper body tilted in the administrator's direction. "If I may be permitte', administrator, I woul' like to point out that it be possible for you, as presiding official in this instance, to grant clemency to offenders."

Pweetasst, Takuuna thought angrily. As if his position wasn't sufficiently awkward already. The senior judiciary's associates looked on thoughtfully. As they did so, Takuuna experienced a powerful urge to slice through their eyeball stalks with a single swipe of one clawed hand.

A wayward thought, he admonished himself. These are allies. They support the Empire and therefore my work here. They are not thranx.

Such realities notwithstanding, he saw no reason to

commute a sentence that had already been handed down, and said so. The colorful tentacles that encircled the upper portion of Awn-Bween's body fluttered in the bright sunshine. His eyes dipped slightly, the stalks inclining toward the visitor.

"Then we await the carrying out of sentence. Though my companions an' I think it unduly harsh, as the offense was committe' against your property, it is your right to judge. We will not interfere."

As if you could, Takuuna thought. Reaching down, he drew the pistol he always carried with him. An unarmed AAnn was a naked AAnn. The sidearm was floridly decorated, as befitted an official instrument of justice. It was also fully functional. As the senior judiciary and the others hopped clear, Takuuna raised the muzzle of the pistol. Since the Vssey possessed nothing like a central heart, there was no point in aiming anywhere at the thick stump of a lower body. But the brain was easily located. It lay in the center of the upper cap, between the eyes.

Two quick shots and it was all over. Though not a veteran soldier, at such close range even a youngster could have done the work efficiently. Small craters smoking from the apex of their rounded upper bodies, tentacles twitching violently, first one thief and then the other toppled over onto the smooth tile of the courtyard. Those curious AAnn who had been watching from a distance turned back to their work. A new group of Vssey came forward to remove the bodies. Since their tentacles were too weak for the purpose, they employed clever mechanical devices to lift the corpses into a waiting, self-propelled container.

Awn-Bween chose to walk Takuuna back to his temporary quarters. Feeling some slight sympathy for the Vssey official, who doubtless was charged with the task of informing the relatives of the recently deceased of their actual demise, Takuuna slowed his walk to a crawl to enable the laboriously hopping judiciary to keep pace.

"Imperial justice is as swift as it is harsh." The Vsseyan language was so liquid that it reminded Takuuna of an infant's contented hissing. The occasionally emitted punctuational bubbles only reinforced the impression.

"It workss," Takuuna replied brusquely. "Had I been the one to have committed the specified offensse, againsst your property, you would have been granted the right to sshoot me."

Except that your manipulative digits aren't strong enough to hold a proper weapon, he thought. A hovering naqueep materialized in front of him. It was smaller and more robustly built than a choluub, and rode the air by means of not one but three gas bladders. He could easily have killed it or sent it crashing to earth. Instead, he brushed it out of his path with a back sweep of his hand. It hooted querulously as it struggled to find a breeze on which to flee.

With waves of hands and tail he acknowledged the polite salutations of fellow AAnn as well as the occasional Vssey he knew from previous visits to this eastern Imperial outpost of Tual-Sihb. Exiting the courtyard, he found himself in the narrow avenue that ran parallel to the central administrative complex. Paid for by the government, his rooms were in the better of the town's two hotels. He was looking forward to a nice sand bath in the desiccated atmosphere of his quarters. Then a meal, a good sleep, and first thing in the morning it would be back to far more heavily urbanized Skokosas, where real work awaited him.

Awn-Bween bid him farewell outside the complex. "I myself have studie' a goo' deal of AAnn law. Though I disagree with some things, there is much in it to admire. I understan' what you say."

"Truly," Takuuna agreed indifferently. He could already feel the heated imported sand against his skin, the delicious caress of fine silicaceous grains abrading dead scales and dirt from his body. "It must be ssaid that your people have been very ssensible and cooperative in allowing uss to establissh our few outpostss on your world."

"I personally revere the Empire and look forwar' to the day when Jast is officially include' in it." Tentacles rippled like a breaking wave by way of a farewell salute. "Not all are so enthusiastic, but many very much are."

And the rest can be dealt with appropriately, as has been done elsewhere on other worlds, Takuuna knew. While it was not his place to measure or facilitate that eventual formal integration, he could see it coming. So could his fellow nye. Another world to swell the boundaries of the Empire. One more small expansion of Imperial space. Despite their physical handicaps and unpleasant appearance, the Vssey would be welcome. Outstanding engineers, builders, and artisans, they had a very real contribution to make. Though not noted as innovators, they were superb mimics, able to reproduce in their factories any device or apparatus that was presented to them. Given such promise, their displeasing physical appearance could be overlooked.

They parted amiably, AAnn administrator and Vsseyan judiciary. Gratefully, Takuuna resumed a more normal stride, his long, powerful legs carrying him past and around busy Vssey as if they were standing still. None envied him his forward velocity. They were quite comfortable proceeding at their own speed, one methodical hop at a time. Never having had legs, they did not miss them.

Only once did he have to slow, when a vast flock of low-drifting satubvwo blocked the street. Caught by a shifting, unusually strong breeze, they had been blown in and down. A change in the wind would carry them up and away easily, since no building in town was more than two stories tall. Although they possessed an excellent sense of balance, like any monoped the Vssey lived in fear of falling—the more so because their small tentacles did not provide a means for easily returning themselves to an upright position. A Vssey who fell and was not equipped with a mechanical means for righting itself had to rely on the assistance of others in order to return to a vertical stance, or else look forward to perhaps an hour of hard struggle with both its tentacles and the bracing edge of its flexible dome.

So it was that Takuuna found himself fuming impotently at the swirling, confused, and incredibly dense flock of satubwo that blocked the street in front of him. It was small consolation that the crowd of busy Vssey over which he towered by a head were equally frustrated. Despite the flock's density there was very little smell. Vertical travel allowed them to leave clinging dirt, vegetative matter, and individual waste products behind. Unlike the smaller, softer-voiced choluub, however, the satubwo did make quite a lot of noise. With each one generating a steady wail from its conical mouth, the siren-like collective howl tended to overwhelm the polite murmuring of the Vssey.

Crowded together, the locals dealt with the situation in the traditional manner: they began to discuss it among themselves. Looking down at them, Takuuna marveled that they had ever been able to advance beyond the tribal stage. Nothing was done swiftly. Any action involving more than one Vssey required the attainment of consensus, usually arrived at after interminable discussion of every possible ramification of even the least confrontational issues. This inherent cultural trait, no doubt evolved from when the ancestral Vssey existed as fixed individuals incapable of movement, made for great philosophers and deep thinkers, for fine musicians and authors, but it was no way to conquer the next hill, much less vast swaths of space. Those accomplishments were to remain the province of more active, energetic species, he knew, and of one in particular. Reaching for his sidearm, he prepared to yet again underline the reality of that conviction. But before he could do so, the conundrum of the airborne roadblock was resolved by the nature of Jast itself.

A large intruder came drifting down into the closely packed flock of satubvwo. That it was not a peaceful nocturnal herbivore like the choluub was made immediately apparent by the flock's rapid switch from confused wail to frantic whining. Seeing that the newcomer was a blohkbaa, Takuuna left his sidearm holstered. The local carnivore would soon have the flock cleared away.

Descended from active, hungry predators himself, it was always instructive to watch another carnivore feeding. Like the choluub and the satubvwo, the blohkbaa was kept airborne by a gas-filled sac attached to its back. The difference was that the carnivore's serpentine form was lined with not one, not three, but more than two dozen such sacs, arranged in double rows along its widely separated upper ridges. By venting or adding gas to these it gained far greater maneuverability than its harmless drifting relations, who traveled solely at the mercy of the wind and weather.

Its method of consumption was straightforward. Positioning itself beneath chosen prey, it extended a single flexible, sharply pointed tendril upward. Ignoring its quarry's frantic twitching and futile efforts to escape, it utilized this tool to puncture the prey's supporting gas sac. Deprived of lift, the quarry would immediately begin to sink downward—directly into the yawning orifice that occupied much of the blohkbaa's dorsal expanse.

In this efficient manner it proceeded to munch its way at a surprisingly rapid pace through at least a third of the satubvwo flock. It completely ignored the busy Vssey who, relieved of the need to make a decision on how to deal with the temporary obstacle, used the steadily widening gap in the helpless flock to continue on their way up the street. Borne along on two highly capable limbs instead of one, Takuuna impatiently pushed his way to the front and soon outdistanced the crowd. Continuing back to his rooms he was forced to dodge numerous Vssey who were unable to hop out of his way. Unlike the roadblocking flock, however, this caused the administrator no undue distress. Having been assigned to Jast for several years, he was used to it by now. One could not allow oneself to become frustrated by individual pedestrians when their entire species was a constant source of frustration.

He did not dwell on the execution of the two Vsseyan thieves. He could not. He had paperwork to attend to.

Lwo-Dvuum eyed the gathering of friends glumly. Without a formal, pre-agreed-upon agenda, they could not properly be labeled conspirators. Without a declared manifesto, they could not be condemned as rebels. And without weapons, they could hardly be considered dangerous.

What they *could* do was talk and, perhaps more significantly, commiserate. It had not taken long for news of the execution of the two unfortunate young thieves in rural Tual-Sihb to reach metropolitan Skokosas. That the sentence had been carried out by a local AAnn administrator instead of by the Vssey themselves did not particularly concern the members of the group. What did trouble them, what had troubled them enough to bring them together in the first place, was that it had been done according to AAnn law that had been adapted for Vsseyan use.

"We have always ha' our own laws," Mua-Briiv was saying. As a senior member of the circle, the Elder had assumed a stance with his back to the setting sun. Behind him, silhouetted against the fading light, a mixed flock of jwoyourn and pwalakum were settling down for the night, sifting to earth as lazily as fine flour as their airsacs lost buoyancy. "Then these right swift AAnn come, promising all manner of goo' things if only we will welcome them and their needs, and those of our own kin' we truste' to look after our interests turn into mindless spore sacs."

Next to the Elder, Bno-Cassaul fluttered those tentacles that were not presently interlocked with those of the young historian's immediate neighbors. Like everyone else who had gathered on the outskirts of the city, ostensibly to observe the sunset ritual, Bno-Cassaul formed part of the circle of close friends. Originally a defensive posture that in olden days gone by enabled a group of Vssey to hold off attackers larger and quicker than themselves, the circle had evolved to serve numerous cultural and commercial purposes. It would have astonished the members of the other, similar circles who had also gathered on the ancient wall for the purpose of contemplating the evening sunset that the avowed aim of the one currently occupying the far corner of the revered ramparts was sedition.

"Somehow we must regain control of our culture," Bno-Cassaul was saying, "an' expel these fast-moving, fast-talking guests."

"How?" wondered a seemingly resigned Tvr-Vheequa. "It cannot be denie' that these AAnn have brought many wondrous things to Jast. As a result, the government is comfortable with the present arrangement and alliance."

"Too comfortable by a long hop," declared Bno-Cassaul.

Lwo-Dvuum knew that Bno-Cassaul could be counted on to do whatever was necessary to help expel the domineering AAnn. The trouble was that, while there existed among the circle of friends many who were inclined in that direction, Bno-Cassaul was the only one who could be counted on. Before any serious moves could be contemplated, the two coconspirators needed the support and cooperation of some of the Elders. Support that needed to take the form of something more substantial than encouraging platitudes.

Among the Elders who had gathered to converse, Mua-Briiv seemed the most likely to lend serious backing. But even that aged worthy, patches of whose trunk-like torso were exfoliating with age, remained far from convinced. Nwi-Pwaal gave voice to such concerns.

"Even if the majority of Vssey wishe' to oust the AAnn, how could such a thing be accomplishe'? The AAnn are skille' in the arts of war, while we Vssey are a peaceable people."

"Our ancestors invente' and built many powerful machines to defen' themselves against the predators of Jast," Bno-Cassaul pointed out. "While physically we are slow and almost helpless against such as the AAnn, our machines are not." Reflecting deeply felt passion, the speaker's eyestalks were fully erect and many bubbles accompanied his earnest word-speaking. "It is true that the AAnn are agile, but no AAnn can outrun a heat drill. Their flesh fries as astringently as that of any Vssey."

Tvr-Vheequa's tentacles rippled with distress as the orange-hued hearing comb twitched. "Talk of frying flesh unsettles my central digestive system." By way of supplying visual confirmation, the upper edge of the speaker's listening comb flushed a pale pink. "In this I believe the majority of Vssey would agree with me."

"Which is why we must strive harder than ever to convince them of the nee' to make such sacrifices." Lwo-Dvuum was adamant to the point of bouncing slightly up and down for emphasis, the four protruding fleshy pads at the base of the body contracting forcefully to propel the speaker straight up into the air—albeit only for a couple of dozen centimeters. Still, it was a vigorous physical exhibition of commitment.

Tvr-Vheequa rotated to contemplate the last rays of the setting sun. The ancestors of modern-day spectators had gathered here for hundreds of years, ever since the great city of Skokosas had been founded by the Pandur Mwu-Umool IV at the height of the Guluu Dynasty, blessings be unto its buddings. The direction the circle's conversation was taking made Tvr-Vheequa uncomfortable. Yet in the venous cavities that pumped blood through Tvr-Vheequa's system, the reluctant one saw the wisdom in the words of Lwo-Dvuum and Bno-Cassaul. They were rash, in the manner of those not long full-grown from buds. Tvr-Vheequa was more inclined to listen to the admonitions of fellow Elders such as Mua-Briiv.

Yes, the Vssey possessed advanced devices and modern weapons. But so did the AAnn. And over the centuries the AAnn had used them not to defend against charging pluead or acid-spilling dvojebai, but to build an empire. Tvr-Vheequa had studied their history. The AAnn did not *need* an empire. They simply wanted one. You could cooperate with them, join with them, and enjoy all the benefits of Imperial membership. Or you could resist, as some had, and find your kind subdued through subterfuge, manipulation, corruption, or, if all the other multifarious means at their disposal failed the clawed ones, force.

Unless you joined the other, even greater galactic confluence of species called the Commonwealth. Tvr-Vheequa knew far less about the Commonwealth. Only a handful of its representatives had ever visited Jast, and they had not stayed long. From all accounts, they were as impatient as the AAnn and found the slow-moving Vssey and their ways not much to their liking.

Located between two such vastly more powerful associations of worlds, the independent Vssey had been largely left to themselves until it had been decided to ally informally with the AAnn. Hence the present presence on the planet of AAnn scientific outposts, AAnn forward military bases, AAnn commercial interests, AAnn touristic enterprises, and AAnn governmental agencies and aid programs. For much of this the Vssey were grateful, and found the arrangement to their advantage without having to commit to formal integration with the Empire.

Except, Tvr-Vheequa reminded himself, for the occasional disquieting incident when Vsseyan niceties found themselves suborned to AAnn insistence, and a couple of recently budded thieves shot for their trouble instead of reeducated, which would have been the Vsseyan way.

"Tvr-Vheequa?" Tentacle-tips moved gently against the tentacles that lined the rear semicircle of the thoughtful one as Lwo-Dvuum sought to bring a drifting associate back from contemplation of the sunset—and other things.

Tvr-Vheequa pivoted. "These are such meaningful matters. Clearly they require much more thought before any sort of serious response can be considere'. I myself will broach the matter to an additional triplet of high worthies and report back to you the nature of their reaction."

"Another study group. More talking, more consideration, more thought! But no action." Bno-Cassaul's impatience was atypical for a Vssey. "Jast will be absorbe' wholly into the AAnn Empire while well-meaning, thoughtful individuals are still discussing the prospective ramifications of possible resistance. When they finally awaken, an independent Jast will be a distant memory suitable only for the casual amusement of curious archivists!"

Seeing that friend Bno-Cassaul had hopped too far, Lwo-Dvuum hastened to intervene. "Wisdom lies between

haste and torpor. You all speak worthwhile thoughts."
One eye swiveled to regard the quietly seething Bno-
Cassaul. "We are not nearly strong enough to move
against the AAnn in any significant fashion. Indee', we
are barely strong enough to organize these meetings."
The other eye rotated to focus on Tvr-Vheequa. "Talk
then to your eminent triplets. With luck you will there
find sympathy for our position as well as insight." Having
soothed the situation, Lwo-Dvuum used a dozen tentacles to gesture meaningfully in the direction of the other
spectators. Having observed and enjoyed the sunset, the
viewing circles were now breaking up and making prepa-
rations to return to the city proper.

"Until the next agree'-upon meeting time and place, it
is best we are not seen together in more than a casual
pairing. I do not think the AAnn know of our faction or
its philosophical bent. It is desirable to maintain that useful anonymity. Meanwhile, each of us will continue to advance the aims of our faction in any way that they can."

The circle was re-formed. Tentacles were entwined.
Eyestalks withdrew into concave upper bodies until only
the glimmer of the eyes themselves were visible. Mua-
Briiv recited the Kwolal liturgy. That helped to banish any
lingering feelings of stress, whereupon they all went their
separate ways: friends united behind a common idea as
yet devoid of the slightest means of implementing it.

Tvr-Vheequa and Bno-Cassaul chose to return to their
dwellings by means of the latest type of air-repulsion vehicle. Three other members of the circle who had not spoken, who had only listened, utilized other mechanical
means of transport. Only Mua-Briiv and, somewhat surprisingly to the others, Lwo-Dvuum chose to ride traditional ouvomum.

Both were tethered near the very end of the old city
wall. As was only courteous and proper, Lwo-Dvuum

waited until Mua-Briiv had slipped into the other riding sling and departed before approaching the remaining mount.

Five times the length but weighing less than the average Vssey, the ouvomum browsed contentedly at the public feeding trough to which it had been secured. Long and flat, mottled brown and green on top and blue on its underside, the creature chewed cut grass and grain with a wide, flattened protrusion of a mouth. Working against the feed, the grinding plates inside the mouth masticated it to a pulp before swallowing.

The ouvomum had four limbs that were neither arms nor legs. Instead, the quadruple projections that extended from each corner of its roughly rectangular body curved upward instead of down. Their tips terminated in muscular, cylindrical tubes that expanded into four huge, colorful, membranous balloons. If not for the strong artificial leather tether that kept it secured to the feeding trough, the ouvomum would have rapidly and contentedly drifted off into the evening sky.

The elegant, embossed harness that encircled its body formed a kind of conical sack beneath the central stomach, with the base of the harness resting on the smooth stone pavement of the old city wall. A single well-practiced high hop landed Lwo-Dvuum's four-sided base perfectly in the center of the harness. Leaning forward, the rider used several tentacles to release the mount's tether and pull it in. As it was secured to one side, four reins dangling from above were gripped confidently in two other sets of tentacles. The ouvomum let out a melancholy moan as it drifted away from the feeding trough. When it started to deflate its two fore gas bladders in an attempt to descend back toward the food, Lwo-Dvuum tugged firmly on the rearward reins.

Within a couple of moments the well-trained ouvomum

responded to the controlling tugs on the four reins. Alternately deflating and inflating its bladders, it turned back toward the city proper as it rose. As mount and rider soared gracefully over the city's outskirts, Lwo-Dvuum reflected that even if they were neither long nor particularly strong individually, having more than two dozen manipulating limbs had its advantages. It was possible to keep a double grip on each of the four reins while simultaneously steadying oneself in the harness by holding on to several of the enclosing straps.

In an age of modern conveniences, flying an ouvomum was a stylish and fashionable way to get around. The only drawback was a lack of speed. The ouvomum was anything but swift. But soaring along beneath one gave a rider time to think, something the Vssey had always prized. The AAnn felt that the Vssey already spent too much time thinking. Lwo-Dvuum did not care what the AAnn thought, so long as they did not discover what the circle of friends was thinking.

Difficult as it was to admit it, there was no question that Tvr-Vheequa's caution was well founded. Weapons alone, even allowing for a sufficiency of those willing to employ them, offered no guarantee of being able to expel the AAnn. Masters of the conciliatory phrase and cunning proclamation those swift-running, sharp-toothed warriors might be, but when words failed them, Lwo-Dvuum knew that they would not hesitate to butcher any who stood in their way. Knew this because much AAnn history had passed in perusal before the teacher's intensely curious eyestalks. On the whole, it had not made for pleasant reading.

What we need, Lwo-Dvuum thought as the ouvomum dipped toward the conical structure whose topmost level was home to its rider, is something to spark the wider interest of the otherwise contented and disengaged Vssey.

Something to shake them from their communal lethargy. Something to stiffen their eyestalks and open their eyes to the true intentions of the seemingly benevolent long-legs. An incident. A diversion. An event. In the continuing absence of anything palpable, could one perhaps be manufactured?

If nothing else, it was, his mind insisted as busy tentacles directed the mount to void gas from its bladders and descend homeward, something to think about.

3

That the shuttle was granted permission to land at all was due in no small part to the fact that the entire staff of Skokosas port operations was composed of Vssey. By the time the local AAnn representatives found out about and learned the true nature of the unanticipated arrival, the visitor was already on the ground and it was too late to do anything about it. Nor could they blow it up out of hand, its crew having followed proper procedure in requesting and being granted permission and concurrent directions on how and where to set down.

That did not mean that the AAnn authority on Jast was happy about this unexpected development. Captain Qerrudd VXXDLM in particular was distressed. As liaison to the Vssey Ministry of Transportation, it was she who was ultimately responsible for any untoward visitation that might impair Imperial influence among the natives. The fact that a Commonwealth vessel had managed to arrive and settle unnoticed into orbit around Jast was embarrassing enough. She knew that the fact that it had arrived unannounced, alone, and without a formal preceding request from the Commonwealth government, unlike every Commonwealth craft that had come before it, would not be sufficient to excuse the oversight.

Hoping to minimize any damage—especially to her career—she hastened from her workplace within the AAnn

Authority complex inside the city to the main shuttleport that was located on a flat, rocky plain not far to the south. Pushing the compact aircar to its limits, she took the risk of annihilating any leisurely Vssey who might be unlucky enough to get in her way. Those traveling in modern conveniences such as her own, either of local or imported AAnn manufacture, would be perfectly safe. Their onboard avoidance systems would prevent any collision. Regrettably, there were still Vssey who preferred to travel around and outside the metropolitan sector utilizing more traditional means of transportation.

Though the aircar's passing was low and swift enough to rock pebbles and arthropods from their resting places as it rocketed madly toward the shuttleport, no bladder-lifting individuals, either domesticated, wild, or of voting age, splattered themselves against its transparent dome. By the time she arrived, tense, out of breath, and struggling to adjust the coiling straps of her right sandal, the crew of the shuttle was already being debriefed by local Vssey authorities. Hurrying to keep up with her, one of the AAnn soldiers assigned to the shuttleport supplied yet another surprise. Apparently, the crew of the shuttle consisted of a single individual. A single individual and his (it was apparently a male human, though the soldier was not sure, having never in his life encountered a human in the flesh) pet.

She finally slowed as she reached the room where the unwanted arrival was being debriefed by Immigration. Two Vssey stood behind a curving counter festooned with built-in instrumentation. There were no chairs, no seats. The Vssey had no use for seats, their bodies boasting nothing to put in them. They could stand in one place for hours, even for days, at a time, doing nothing but contemplating their surroundings. In contrast, a sane AAnn forced to remain motionless in one place for any length of time would quickly go crazy, Qerrudd knew.

There was no question that the arrival was a human. To her additional surprise, it was conversing with the Vssey not in symbospeech but in extraordinarily fluid AAnn. That immediately roused the captain's suspicions. While many of the softskins could speak the language of the Empire, few did so with any fluency. This tall young male's enunciation was superb. Idly she noted that his pet, some sort of colorful but otherwise unimpressive limbless, winged creature, was sheathed in scales not unlike her own, albeit far smaller and different in shape. Whoever the strange visitor was, he at least showed some taste in his choice of companionship.

She was startled when he glanced unexpectedly in her direction. Since she and the soldier who was accompanying her were standing behind a privacy screen and could not be seen from the immigration room, the glance had to be coincidental. Still, she found it hard to escape the feeling that he had been looking directly at her.

"I am going insside," she informed her subordinate, adding a third-degree gesture of insistence.

"Do you wissh me to firsst clear your arrival with the authoritiess?" the soldier inquired.

She brushed him off with a simple gesture. "I have no time to wasste on the ussual interminable Vsseyan procedure. They sshould have no objection. I intend only to obsserve, not to interfere."

The human barely took notice of her when she entered. It was as if he had already seen and appraised her. Nor did the presence of the large sidearm prominently displayed on her belt appear to unsettle him. The Vssey officials, of course, were not armed.

Without moving its body, the nearest swiveled one eyeball to regard her. "We welcome the presence of Captain Qerru". You have come to greet our visitor?"

Double eyelids half closed over slitted pupils as she studied the imperturbable human. He smiled back at her.

"I have come to ponder him. Greetingss I leave to you. Thiss iss your world. It would be impolite of me to contemplate ussurping any of your official functionss."

"That's very gracious of you," the human responded. His command of her language really was impressive, the captain decided—exactly what would be expected of someone sent to spy on Imperial operations. What operations? The Commonwealth had expressed no special, distinctive interest in or plans for Jast. Why do so now? And if that was the case, why send only a single observer? Could the human be nothing more than a casual visitor? A lone casual visitor? Or were, even now, as they chatted coolly but amiably in the pleasantly warm room, dozens of skilled, heavily armed fighters listening and waiting in his vessel high in orbit, waiting for the right moment to descend and wreak havoc with the limited AAnn operations on Jast?

What operations? she had to ask herself again. Jast was not an Imperial colony, or even an outpost. It was a developed, technologically sophisticated world whose inhabitants had shown an interest in ongoing AAnn overtures. She was being paranoid.

Lone representatives of hostile species who dropped from nowhere tended to do that to one, she reminded herself.

Maintaining her vow to remain aloof from the actual questioning, she positioned herself off to one side and tried to still the steady back-and-forth switching of her long tail. Occasionally reaching up to stroke the head of his quiescent pet, the human proceeded to answer with quiet aplomb every question the Vssey immigration officers put to him.

"Very few of your kin have visited Jast," the nearest one commented aloud. "Those who have done so have all been official representatives of your Commonwealth government or United Church." The Vssey hesitated. "Yet you insist you are not a representative of your government or your principal religious institution?"

"That's right."

"You have come alone? There are no other organic sentients on your orbiting vessel?"

"Yes. No."

"Then why are you here?" the other immigration officer asked.

The human bared his teeth in a slight curve. "As you have already observed. To pay a visit."

"Commercial?" inquired the first immigration officer. Its tentacles were fluttering irregularly, a clear indication of uncertainty. "Scientific? Historical research?"

"Just a visit," the human replied placidly. There being no word in AAnn that translated precisely as *vacation*, Flinx added helpfully, "For a period of hopefully recuperative non-workingness."

Truly alien were the softskins, mused Captain Qerrudd. Unable to restrain herself further she asked, in a voice notably more brusque than that of the more soft-spoken Vssey, "Why Jasst? No humanss come here without a sspecific program in hand."

Undaunted by her tone, the human turned to face her. "That's why I've come. Because no humanss come here."

Disgusted with this uninformative response, she eyed the two officials. If it was up to her she would have simply shot the human and been done with it. If he was here on his own, without the encouragement or protection of Commonwealth authorities, then that meant there would be no one to object to his sudden demise. Probably no one would even know.

But what if he *had* come burdened with such imponderables, and someone *would* know if anything untoward happened to him? Faced with an unexpected crisis, the AAnn could move swiftly. They could also step back and evaluate. Captain Qerrudd elected to step back. Caution, care, cogency: always caution first.

She could always shoot him later, she knew.

Or perhaps even leave him alone. If he was telling the truth about his reasons for coming to Jast, then maybe he was harmless enough. He would uncover no secrets (not that there were any secrets to uncover), cause no trouble (not that the present situation on Jast was trouble-prone), incite no awkward questions (not that there were awkward questions to be asked). His visit might even be some sort of deliberate provocation, designed specifically to test AAnn reaction to a human's unplanned arrival. If that was the case, then she could best defeat him by ignoring him.

Clearly, the Vssey officials were as unsure as to how to treat this visitor and what to do with him as she was. The opportunity to gain merit by making a constructive suggestion could not be disregarded.

"Truly, it iss apparent this human means no harm to Jasst. The AAnn also recognize the need to interrupt working with periodss of non-working. Iss thiss not a mosst Jasstian concept?"

The Vssey officials agreed that it was. Still, they hesitated. They would have much preferred to report the arrival to their superiors, who would call a conclave where everyone with even a remote interest in such an unexpected occurrence would enjoy the chance to have their say. There would then follow an extended period of discussion, at the conclusion of which a decision would be rendered and then implemented. By which time, for all they knew of its alien biology, the smooth-skinned bipedal arrival might be a dead of old age. One of the officials thought there might be a possible solution. If nothing else, it might absolve them of the responsibility of having to reach a verdict.

"As this is something of a unique situation, some latitude must be allowed for lack of precedence." Eyes on slowly weaving stalks exchanged a look of understanding. "While the human presents no visible threat to Jast or Vssey, we are too ignorant of its kin to properly evaluate any potential for trouble." One eye swiveled around to focus on the tail-twitching captain. "In contrast, it is well known that the AAnn are quite familiar with humankin', with their mannerisms and needs. If Captain Qerru' woul' be willing to assign one of her own to accompany and guide the visitor during his stay on Jast, we believe this would be sufficient to allay any concerns of the relevant governmental agencies."

Her intervention had paid off. She couldn't have come up with a better solution to the discomfiting state of affairs had she proposed it herself. As she prepared herself for refusal or argument, the last thing she expected was for the human to readily agree to the idea.

"I'd be delighted to have a guide," Flinx avowed when the suggestion was put to him. "Until I learn my way around, anyway."

Which, if things went well, might never happen, Qerrudd reflected. "We are pleased to be able to offer our assistance to one insspired to travel sso great a disstance for sso little." If the cavalier insult offended the two Vssey officials, they chose not to comment on it, not even when she added a gesture of second-degree assertion. "I mysself would introduce you to what vissual and other pleassures Sskokossass hass to offer, but truly, I am consstrained by my dutiess as an Imperial military attaché." When the human exhibited no reaction to this revelation of her martial credentials, she did not know whether to be relieved, pleased, or disappointed. Perhaps, after all, he was no more than what he claimed, and his purpose in traveling all the way to Jast no more than what he had declared it to be.

"I'm sorry to hear it." To her ears, the human sounded genuinely disappointed.

"However," she added, "I do know of one on the Imperial staff who not only possessess wide knowledge of the entire province and in the course of hiss work hass traveled extensively through Qwal-Dihn, Abuv-Dwan, and Tual-Sihb, but who may alsso be ssomewhat knowledgeable of human dessires and requirementss."

"My requirements are very slight," Flinx informed her, "and my desires easily satisfied."

"Excellent," she declared. What could have been an awkward confrontation had been resolved in a highly satisfactory manner. "Then while you conclude the landing and arrival formalitiess with thesse good representatives of Sskokossass, I will make hasste to secure the sservices of the individual I have in mind to assist you."

Surprising her yet again, the human responded with a second-degree gesture of thanks. It could not, of course, punctuate the gesticulation with the appropriate corresponding tail swipe. Setting her instinctive dislike for his softskinned species aside, she found that there was much to admire in the way he was handling himself before not one but two different alien inquisitors, albeit an inquisition that was as mild as it was polite. She rather hoped he was just what he claimed to be and that he was *not* some kind of spy or agent provocateur.

Graft some proper scales over that revoltingly flexible and pulpy flesh, enlarge the eyes, and equip the rest with some decent teeth and claws and the visitor might even have made a decent AAnn. She hoped that the official she had in mind to serve as minder—no, as *guide*, she corrected herself with a slight internal flush of amusement—to the human would similarly appreciate the softskin's qualities, so lacking in others of his kind. In any event, no matter what eventuated, she was safely out of it.

Feeling very good about herself, she left the Vssey immigration officials to conclude their interview with the human.

Takuuna was fuming. That is, he was fuming more than was usual for him. Nursemaid to an alien! And to a human, at that. While part of him was undeniably intrigued (he had never encountered a human in person; only in the form of material representations), the rest was outraged that he was to be drawn away from his assigned duties. They would pile up in anticipation of his return, burying him beneath work that ordinarily was dealt with on a daily basis. Subordinates in his department could deal with a portion of the backlog, but not all of it.

Nor had he been consulted. That was what galled him most. To be ordered around by a simpleton like Qerrudd, may her ovaries shrivel and be voided through her alimentary canal! But there was nothing he could do about it. Qerrudd had invoked clauses relating to matters military. Before these, even a high-ranking administrator like himself had to submit.

He would retaliate. He would get back at that domineering, supercilious, self-centered—he ran out of expletives. He had no idea how he would do these things, but accomplish them he vowed to do. Meanwhile, he was as stuck with the situation as a juvenile who had forgotten to retract its own tongue while eating and had accidentally chomped down on that sensitive appendage.

His studies, common to all AAnn who entered the Service, did not prepare him for the height of the human. While AAnn varied considerably less in individual physical dimensions than did the softskins, they tended to see eye to eye with a goodly number of them. That was not the case with this specimen. It gazed down at Takuuna from a considerable, if not commanding, height. Takuuna guessed its weight at a hundred kuyster or less. The administrator was not intimidated, only surprised. Of additional interest was the small winged creature that lay across the human's shoulders like a decorative insignia. Though not sapient, it was scale-skinned and quite colorful. It eyed the administrator intently, almost as if sensing his irritation.

Turning from the window through which he was contemplating the city, the human took notice of the administrator's gaze. Reaching up and out with one spongy hand, he smiled. Takuuna recognized the expression from his lessons. It was one of an extensive range of expressions the softskins could produce with their disgustingly flexible, soft facial features.

"This is Pip." Though he had been told that the human could speak the civilized language, Takuuna was still startled by the human's glibness and lack of accent. Well, fluency would simplify things.

"I am Ssecondary Administrator Takuuna. I am to be your esscort during your sstay on Jasst." He saluted, simultaneously sheathing his claws, bowing slightly, and turning his head to the right to expose his jugular. Adding to his astonishment, the human proceeded to replicate the gesture, though he had no claws worthy of the designation to sheathe. Instead, he curled the tips of his fingers slightly inward.

The impressive showing only enhanced Takuuna's suspicions. How came a human who professed to be traveling alone, on his own private business, and having nothing to do with either the Commonwealth military or diplomatic service, to have such knowledge of AAnn language and ways? In the straightforward AAnn manner, he asked as much.

"The gaining of knowledge is a hobby of mine," the human replied. "In some ways, it's my life. By the way, you can call me Flinx."

At least that was pronounceable, the administrator appreciated. Not the usual barbaric multiplicity of vowels that made so many human names and words sound like their user existed in a state of perpetual drowning. In fact, he found it easier to enunciate than the great majority of Vssey names.

"I am told you have come to Jasst to do nothing."

"More or less." The human smiled anew. With a couple of modest exceptions, Takuuna noted, every one of its teeth was as flat as the soles of an infant's feet. As useless in a fight as Vsseyan grinding plates, he mused. It did not make him less wary. Humans, he knew from his studies, could fight well without having to resort to biting. He glanced down at the equally hopeless excuses for proper claws that tipped each of the softskin's fingers. Or scratching.

Too soon to think of fighting, Rationale first. Meanwhile, the softskin was not the only one capable of learning from new experiences.

"And you have come alone. There is no one else on your sship? No crew?"

"The onboard AI takes care of everything," Flinx assured him. "I came here because few do. I like places like that. They help me think." The human seemed to pause.

"Although while I'm here I'm not supposed to do any more thinking than is absolutely necessary."

Was the softskin mentally addled? Takuuna found himself wondering. No, he decided. The creature was too alert for that. Too aware, too quick, and too logical with its responses. There was something else. Something he could not put a claw on. That he would eventually isolate this puzzling component of the softskin, Takuuna had no doubt. Until then, he would do as he had been ordered, while subtly seeking out the visitor's secrets—and weaknesses.

Both sets of eyelids blinked twice. "It sseemss that I have been placed at your disspossal, worthy guesst Flinx. What would you like to ssee firsst?"

The human lifted its shoulders slightly and then dropped them in a gesture Takuuna did not recognize. He found himself wishing he had paid more attention to the relevant studies. As was only natural, during his matriculation period he had focused his attention far more on the thranx, humankind's close allies and the AAnn's ancient irritants. Humans, he now saw, were nothing like the thranx.

"What would you suggest?"

The administrator considered. "Without knowing more about you or your perssonal tasstess, it iss difficult to resspond to ssuch a query." The human did not rise to the bait, but merely waited patiently. It had been worth a try, Takuuna felt. "I am an administtrator, not a guide. You ssay that you are interessted in gaining knowledge. What do you know of Jasst's ecology?"

"Very little," Flinx replied honestly.

Takuuna hissed softly. "It hass one prevailing characterisstic. Sslowness. Nothing here movess quickly. Certainly not the dominant sspeciess, the Vssey."

"I've already noticed that. It's hard to move fast in the absence of legs."

"Truly." With a start, Takuna realized that the human was making an attempt at humor. It was an effort that fell well within the restricted parameters of what the AAnn regarded as amusing. "The great majority of advanced life-formss on Jasst are either ssedentary, as the Vssey themsselvess once were, or incapable of rapid movement. A ssingle kravune from my homeworld could make a hundred of them prey each and every day without ssacrificing sso much as one of itss own sscaless."

"That would explain the vigilance of the immigration officials at the porr."

He misses nothing, Takuna thought. He comes here claiming to be in search of nothing, but sees everything. A trained observer, or merely an enthusiastic one?

"Come. I will introduce you to the sslowness that iss Jasst." Raising up on the balls of both sandaled feet, he pivoted ceremoniously and started for the door.

As Flinx followed, he sensed Pip's continuing unease. She had been restless ever since they had entered the administrator's presence. Flinx did his best to calm her. Attacking their official escort would be a poor way to convince the local authorities that he meant no harm.

Besides, he had also perceived the antagonism that was being directed toward him. Unlike Pip, he thought little of it. It was no more than one would expect from any AAnn. They were instinctively and unremittingly hostile to any-one not of their own kind—and often to those as well. As he knew from long experience, this very consistency of enmity made it difficult to guess their intentions. How could you tell when someone was really angry at you when they existed in a state of perpetual animosity?

There *were* degrees of anger, though. So far, the one called Takuna had emitted little more than the usual nervous unfriendliness. A Vsseyan guide would have been more agreeable. On the other hand, he reflected as he followed the AAnn through the doorway, given the average pace at which things Vssey moved, he suspected that seeing anything substantial in their company would require a minimal commitment of a year or two.

Once in the aircar and outside the city, Takuuna seemed to relax. While hardly what one would call a convivial conversationalist, he at least deigned to engage in some interspecies small talk. Flinx's fluency in the AAnn language, with its multiple honorifics and stylized grammar, continued to surprise the administrator. Unlike many individuals who had spent time in Flinx's company, Takuuna showed no fear of Pip. Maybe it was the scales they shared, Flinx mused.

It was midday before he thought to dip into the food supplies that had thoughtfully been provided—not by the AAnn, but by the Vsseyan authorities. As it sampled a bit of each, the analyzer on his belt told him what was edible, what was poisonous, and what was likely to make a good solvent. Some of it was nutritious, little of it was tasty. Vsseyan food, apparently, was as bland as those who had supplied it. Though she nibbled on what was offered to her, Pip plainly shared his opinion.

Water had also been provided. As for Takuuna, he did not offer to share any of his own provisions. Flinx would have been shocked had his guide volunteered to do so. Such a generous gesture would have been most un-AAnn.

Chewing determinedly on a squarish loaf of something with the consistency of heat-softened plastic and a faint flavor of spoiled cheese, he debated whether to extract a piece of compressed chocolate from the emergency pack that was also secured to his belt. Once popped into his mouth, it would expand into something substantial and filling. He held off. They had traveled a good distance already, and he had no idea where they were going. The landscape, with its fantastical twisted growths and dense but neatly spaced vegetation, had engaged the majority of his attention. Eating, and the need to forget what he was eating, induced him to reengage his host in conversation.

"Is this meant to be a general tour of the countryside, or do you have some specific destination in mind?" Flinx squirmed in his seat. He was too tall for the curving protective dome, and the sharply down-angled slope of the chair seat caused his knees to come close to eye level with his face. Furthermore, part of his backside kept trying to push out through the slot in the back of the seat that was designed to accommodate the AAnn tail.

Sitting opposite him in the other front chair, Takuuna took no note of his guest's discomfort. "We are traveling to Saudaunn Chasm. It iss a bit remote, but home to a unique biological phenomenon that well exemplifiess the uniqueness of Jasstian fauna. One such as yoursself who collectss knowledge will appreciate it." He added a third-degree gesture of curiosity, tempered with mild irritation. "Meanwhile, iss not this a fasscinating and beautiful place?"

It would be to the AAnn, Flinx reflected as he gazed out through the dome. No wonder they were so protective of their rights here. Since his arrival, he had noted that the native people, the Vssey, were very much in charge of their own world. Flinx doubted they even realized the kind of danger to their sovereignty the AAnn represented. And while the AAnn could move very rapidly when they wanted to, they could also be very patient in the pursuit of their aims.

It was none of his business, he reminded himself firmly. He was here on vacation, to relax and do nothing of consequence. Interstellar politics, interstellar disputes—he had left that all behind, along with the situation on New

Riviera and the search he was supposed to be making for a certain strayed weapons platform. He should be, needed to be, drinking in the beauty of the local landscape.

"What's that?" he asked, pointing in the direction of a tree that looked like it had swallowed live explosives. Its branches grew in every direction according to no discernible pattern. The ends expanded and flattened out until they were as thin as paper.

Takuuna hissed sibilantly at the control panel on his left, and the aircar changed direction by a fraction of a degree, still heading steadily northeastward.

"Fwellen tree. Like a great deal of Jasstian flora, it hass no leavess. The flattened tipss of itss branchess collect moissture from the air and convey it through hollow spacess in the branches all the way to the main trunk. Itss root ssysstem is very disspersse and sshallow and barely sstrong enough to keep it from toppling over."

Flinx nodded appreciatively. "You like this world, don't you?"

Pausing in his chewing of a spongy, dat-flavored snack ball, the administrator looked over sharply at his unwanted guest. "In what sspirit iss the quesstion assked?"

"I just meant that from your gestures and the brightness of your eyes when you describe something, it suggests that you're very comfortable here." He looked on idly as Pip explored a corner of the front console, her tongue poking in and out of hollows, looking for dropped tidbits.

"We are guesstss here. The Empire hass no dessignss on Jasst, and we enjoy an excellent relationship with our hosstss, the Vssey. Ssince you assk, it iss a bit cooler and a bit damper than what we prefer, but yess, we like it here. What are you implying?"

Keeping an eye on Pip, Flinx smiled easily. "I wasn't implying anything. And I didn't ask whether the Empire likes Jast, or even if your kind does. I was asking the question of you, and you alone."

He is either very shrewd, a thoroughly annoyed Takuuna reflected, or else entirely ingenuous. If the former, then there is nothing to worry about. If the latter, then I am acting the fool. That could not be allowed to continue. And there were his other considerations.

Administrator Takuuna began to plot-weave.

"This Saudaunn Chasm we're going to see," Pip had returned to his lap. "What's so special about it? I've seen many canyons."

"Not one like thiss," his host assured him. "We are not going there for the canyon itsself sso much as we are for fauna it hosstss."

"What kind of fauna?" asked his guest, newly curious.

"Vsstisst, you will ssee."

It was evening before they arrived in the vicinity of Saudaunn, and darkness had settled in tightly around the aircar before Takuuna finally located what he felt would be a propitious place to spend the evening. Another traveler might have balked at the prospect of spending a night in a strange locale with only an insensitive AAnn for company. Not Flinx. He had spent many alien nights on many alien worlds in far more unpredictable company. Besides, he wasn't alone, as Pip promptly reminded him. The instant they emerged from the confines of the aircar into the crisp, dry, and increasingly chill night air of the Jastian plateau, she wriggled straightaway down his shirt collar and huddled against his torso.

"Don't worry," he told her, stroking her through his shirt. "We'll just have a quick look around and then you and I will sleep the night in the aircar." He glanced over at Takuuna, who was striding with typical AAnn fluidity and grace toward a rocky promontory. "We are going to sleep in the aircar, right?"

His escort glanced back at him. Moonlight from one of Jast's two satellites glinted off narrowing eyes as he responded with a gesture of—well, suffice to say it was not polite. "I am charged with sserving as your guide. I am neither hotelier nor concierge. I intend to ssleep insside the aircar, yess. You may take your resst wherever you wissh."

Flinx eyed the ground underfoot. It was mostly tormented, eroded red-and-white granite. "I'm sorry there's not enough sand here to make a decent bed."

The AAnn's double eyelids blinked as he rejoined his charge. "You know much about The People. Truly, I miss the warm ssand of my ressting place in the city." The administrator seemed to hesitate. "I have never heard of humanss ssleeping within ssand."

Flinx smiled as they strolled back to their vehicle. "Sleeping under it, no. But if the beach is nice, we're quite happy to burrow in for a while."

" Beach." "Takuuna's tail whipped agitatedly from side to side. "*Damp* ssand. That does not make for a proper bedding. That doess not even make for a proper thought— for a civilized being."

Flinx glanced back the way the AAnn had come. What had he seen beyond the small promontory he had climbed? What lay beyond? The canyon, no doubt—and perhaps something more. There had to be something more, he decided. Otherwise, this long journey out from Skokosas was going to prove disappointing.

Lying on his stomach on the floor of the aircar, his arms spraddled out in front of him, Takuuna marveled at the human's indifference. The softskin slept soundlessly on his side, utterly indifferent to his AAnn escort, his colorful pet curled up alongside the red fur of the rounded mammalian skull. With a single double kick and slash of claws, Takuuna could simultaneously cut the sleeping human's throat and disembowel him. Sick of wasting time wondering and puzzling, he was sorely tempted to do just that. An accident, in the hinterlands of Jast. No one would know, no one would care.

Or would they? Might the human's demise cause difficulties for him with the Vsseyan authorities? After all, the softskin's arrival had been duly noted and officially processed by Immigration. Other than the pure pleasure the killing would provide, and perhaps a curious sampling of meat whose taste he had previously appreciated only via rumor and hearsay, was there any other reason for risking potential trouble?

It occurred then to Takuuna that it would mean a big-time burnishing of his facial scales if he could somehow prove that the softskin was no innocent tourist, as he appeared and claimed to be, but instead had traveled to Jast with the intent of doing his best to damage Imperial interests there. The fact that the human had thus far done nothing to suggest that he was anything of the sort was not necessarily an impediment to proving the contrary. Or what if it could be proven that the visitor was in fact a spy, sent alone to Jast in the hope that the work of a single agent would be overlooked?

The fact that so far he *had* been "overlooked" could only add to Takuuna's glory in exposing the subterfuge. This would in turn have the added benefit of undermining Captain Qerrudd, who had not officially protested to the Jastian authorities who had permitted the softskin's admittance. Takuuna foresaw favorable consequences: perhaps even promotion within the hierarchy above the infuriating captain. Only one significant obstacle blocked this tongue-warming scenario: the human himself, who thus far had shown himself to be guilty of nothing but persistent curiosity.

Very well, then. Administrator Takuuna was nothing if

not inventive, especially for a bureaucrat. If no transgression could be discerned, he would have to manufacture one.

Truly, but how? Lying prone on the floor of the silent aircar, shielded by its tight insulation from the night sounds rising from the nearby canyon, Takuuna pondered ritual maliciousness. He could simply shoot or eviscerate the human and subsequently claim to have been attacked. No, he decided. The young human's height notwithstanding, it would require a more physically imposing opponent to rationalize a claim of self-defense. What then? Something less blatant and more obtuse was in order. Something less amenable to close inspection and the questions that would inevitably arise from his peers.

Zealous thinking brought to mind the reports that had occasionally passed before him of the half-documented, half-rumored circles of dissident and disaffected Vssey who were adamantly opposed to the AAnn presence on their world. Suppose he could construct a suitable scenario wherein the human "tourist" had arrived to establish preliminary contact with one or more of such groups? That would constitute a credible threat to AAnn interests in this part of space. One sufficient to justify a claim of self-defense in the event that the stratagem was discovered by a bold interrogator such as himself, who was then forced to defend himself against the enraged and desperate spy. Yess, truly!

If pressed, he could then point the claw of accusation at one of the several comparatively harmless known dissident circles, accusing them of conspiring with the human and the humanx Commonwealth. Their protestations of innocence would not be believed. Before their blamelessness could be validated, he himself would generously suggest they be exonerated, innocents lured into sin by one of the always nefarious, ever cunning humans. Such munificence of spirit would serve to raise his status among the Vssey. Concomitantly, his own kind would grant him credit for great perspicacity, and no harm done.

Except to the human, of course. One lone human, on "vacation," far from the Commonwealth and friends. His presence, like his fate, would quickly be forgotten. By the time anyone came looking for him—if anyone did—the entire incident would be little more than a middling memory among both AAnn and Vssey. Who would care?

He knew he had to proceed with caution. Career-killing mistakes were usually made by those who had not carefully thought through their actions. The solution was simple enough.

He would sleep on it.

Across the floor, on the other side of the aircar, Flinx lay with his back to his host. Though he appeared asleep, he was in fact awake, his eyes closed. Though he was facing away from the AAnn, he could still perceive him. Though its dozing exhalations filled the aircar's compartment with soft, sibilant hisses, Flinx knew his host was only feigning sleep, that he was in fact awake and brooding furiously.

About what, Flinx knew not. Only when his talent was functioning could he sense emotions, not complex thought. What he sensed was open antipathy. Nothing less could be expected from an AAnn, even from one appointed to act as his guide and escort. It was their nature. For them, unrelenting hostility was a way of life that extended even to members of their own species.

So Flinx was not unsettled as he shifted his position on the hard deck. Only sleep would silence the raging emotional outpourings of the scaly sentient lying nearby. He relaxed. In the event of any sudden, untoward movement in his direction, Pip would wake him. Or, if necessary, do more than that. The flying snakes of Alaspin were notoriously light sleepers.

Among the long litany of Bad Things One Could Do In Life, startling an Alaspinian minidrag out of a sound sleep ranked very high on the list.

4

An emotive surge of uncertainty mixed with the usual enmity woke Flinx. As he rolled over, he saw that his host was just sitting up, using his strong, limber arms to push his body straight backwards. This push, combined with the counterweight provided by the ever active, switching tail, allowed the AAnn to stand erect. A glance showed that Jast's sun was just beginning to show itself on the horizon.

"It will be cold outside." Clearly, Takuuna was not looking forward to the prospect.

"I'll manage." Flinx smiled at his guide. "I've spent time on colder worlds."

The administrator let out a sharp hiss whose subtle modulations Flinx was unable to interpret. Donning his utility vest, sandals, and a heated cloak to enable him to stand the chill morning air, the AAnn braced himself. At a brush of one clawed hand over a control pad, an opening appeared in the side of the aircar. Outside air entered like a coquette's slap. Flinx sucked it in, alien aromas and all, and followed his guide outside. Unlike the heat-loving AAnn, he needed no extra clothing to enable him to cope with sunrise temperatures. He wondered if his offhand comment about having spent time on colder worlds had been taken by his host for an ambiguous slight.

In moments they were standing on the rim of the

54

canyon, and then there was no more time to analyze AAnn reactions. Or, for that matter, much of anything else. He was too busy looking, and marveling.

As the first rays of the rising sun penetrated the depths of Saudaunn Chasm, they began to warm the air that had settled within. In addition to the atmosphere, the slowly rising temperature caused the various gases contained within the lifting bladders of creatures that had made their homes on ridges and ledges, in cracks and caves within the canyon, to expand. Though this daily heating and expanding was a common occurrence everywhere on Jast, at Saudaunn the phenomenon took on particular resonance.

Because the canyon depths were home to not several, not dozens, not even hundreds but to thousands of diurnal herbivorous grazers. Twiloulds and semasamps, torokwal and bederuntt, they began to rise in their thousands from their traditional dwelling and breeding grounds deep within the canyon and its walls. Watching the mass ascension, Flinx was enchanted. Pip darted delightedly above and around him, pleased to sense her master so enthralled by the sight of so much natural beauty. Whenever he felt particularly good, the feeling was instantly perceived by her.

Close beside him, the AAnn administrator hissed softly. The unrelenting hostility he projected was submerged by an appreciation for a phenomenon unrelated to personal advancement or the demotion of another. For once, he shared something with his unwanted charge besides distaste. The claws of his left hand clicked together rhythmically.

"Truly, iss it not a beautiful thing, ssoftsskin?"

Flinx could only agree. Squawking or hooting or whistling melodiously to one another, the massed flocks of Jastian fauna came rising from the deep shadows of the chasm up into the sharp bright sunlight of morning, borne aloft by their expanding sacs of self-generated methane or hydrogen. Some creatures were elevated by only a single balloon-like pouch while others boasted as many as half a dozen. While arms and tentacles dangled from several species, none had even the most rudimentary legs. None had need for such superfluous limbs. Why try to walk when your kind had evolved to float, to hover and soar at the expense of the wind?

The wind. The thought and the image it engendered produced a question.

"If they're blown around by the breeze of the day, how do they all find their way back here, to this particular canyon?"

Takuna was no pause-thinker. He knew the answer. One did not dwell on Jast for more than a few cycles without learning such things.

"Every creature on Jasst that utilizess thiss method of travel hass wayss of adjussting coursse and direction. Lifting gassess can be vented, or added to, or jetted off to one sside or another to maneuver the animal up, down, or in different directionss." Intermittent, short hisses indicated AAnn amusement. "It iss fasscinating to watch the local predatorss in action, and the effortss of their intended prey to evade being conssumed."

Exactly the sort of natural behavior the AAnn would find entertaining, Flinx knew. He had another question to ask, but was forestalled by the sight before him.

The barrunou were coming out of the canyon.

He did not try to count them. When he asked Takuna if a census had ever been taken on the local population of the particular species, the AAnn gestured a negative. Not many non-Vssey even knew of this place, he explained.

"Of the barrunou there are perhapss a few hundred thoussand. Perhapss a million." His tail was not switching edgily from side to side now. It lay relaxed, muscles at ease, the tip resting on the ground.

Blinded by the sight, Flinx wished for the special goggles stored in his backpack. But he did not jog back to the aircar to dig them out. He was afraid he might miss something. So he stood and shielded his eyes as best he could, shadowing them with his right hand. Takuuna, he noted, frequently had to look away and wipe water from his own sharp eyes.

In their tens of thousands, the barrunou rose from their multitude of burrows and nesting places within the canyon. No bigger than an open hand, each was supported by a single gas sac that blossomed from the middle of its back. Slim and flattened, ranging in color from a striped pale brown to a mottled light blue, each individual had a fringe of cilia dangling from its wide mouth. With these, Takuuna explained, the browsing barrunou would feel of the tops of rocks and plants for the smaller growths on which they fed. Behind cilia-lined mouth rose a pair of tiny but alert eyes. Though not mounted on stalks like the oculars of the Vssey, those of the barrunou were still capable of a wide range of motion. They could not see behind them, but they had excellent peripheral vision. The soft, sweet, cheeping sounds they made reminded Flinx of a cross between a baby bird and an angry mouse. He found that he was grinning uncontrollably.

It was not their shape, however, or their varied coloration that commanded one's attention. Instead, it was the gas-filled sacs that provided their lift. Unlike that of the various air-dwellers Flinx had encountered thus far, those of the barrunou were not pale beige, or yellow, or even dappled turquoise blue. Instead, they were covered with tiny iridescent scales that caught the rays of the rising sun and flung them back at anything and everything in the vicinity. Furthermore, these idiosyncratic reflections were neither constant nor predictable, fluctuating as they did not only with the position of the barrunou but with the expansion and contraction of the lifting sac itself.

It was as if a million fist-sized spherical mirrors were rising from the depths of the canyon, each one reflecting back all the colors of the rainbow. So bright was the massed shining, so intense the aggregated shimmering, that it illuminated those corners and crannies of the canyon that the rays of the sun had not yet reached.

Side by side, human and AAnn observed the vast ascension in silence, each lost in his own thoughts, each mesmerized by the splendid aerial procession that was taking place before them. For her part, Pip ignored it. She had found something small and sweet-smelling hiding among the rocks and was doing her lethal serpentine best to coax it out of its hiding place.

As they rose higher into the morning sky, the tens of thousands of softly twittering, spherical living mirrors began to disperse, riding the east-flowing breezes. In the evening, Takuuna detailed, the wind in this part of the province of Qwal-Dihn would predictably reverse, bearing the sated and tired barrunou back to their sheltering canyon.

"The brilliantly reflective sscaless that cover their lifting ssacss did not evolve for the delectation of ssightsseerss ssuch as ourselvess," the AAnn went on to explain. "Individually, they are flasshed to attract matess. Collectively, they function to dissorient and confusse attacking carnivoress. As iss ussually the ssituation with predatorss, there iss one in particular, the wulup, that hass developed a way to largely counter thiss communal defensse."

"How does it do that?" Flinx found that he still had to shield his eyes from the glare in order to be able to look at the slowly scattering flock.

Takuuna drew a clawed hand over his face. It gave Flinx the opportunity to study the delicate engravings that had been etched into the knuckle scales of his guide's fingers. "Through the use of sspecial chromatophoress, the wulup hass the ability to darken or lighten itss eye-coveringss as necessary. Thiss allowss it to purssue the barrunou without being blinded. And they have other predatorss as well." Teeth flashed. "A food ssource of thiss ssize would not be long ignored by the evolving car-nivoress of any world."

Flinx nodded to himself. "It's spectacular. Truly spec-tacular. Thank you, Takuuna, for bringing me out here to see it." The AAnn said nothing. Moving nearer to the edge, Flinx leaned forward slightly to peer into the depths of the chasm. "There's so much to see here, so much to learn. What are their nesting sites like? How do all the different species that live down there get along with one another? Is there ongoing competition for the best resting places? Are there predators who specialize in hunting the canyon-dwellers at night, when they're sleeping? Or is predation on Jast strictly limited to the sunlit hours, when most of the fauna is airborne?"

Questions, questions, the administrator thought. And not one of them that interested him. Perhaps because a single question continued to dominate his thoughts. What was he to do? Continue to play guide and driver to this disagreeable human? Give up in disgust, return to Sko-kosas, and defy the directive he had been given ordering him to do just that? Or follow through on his thinking of the night before? And if the latter, then when, and how? He had yet to resolve in his mind the matter of whether this human was guilty of anything save being human, or if that small detail should be allowed to affect his inten-tions.

The wind changed slightly, bringing to the AAnn's

sensitive nostrils the full, undiluted scent of the creature standing before him. It was a thick, pungent, wholly mammalian stink, and it disgusted him. Whirling away from it, he lashed out instinctively with his tail. Whether he struck blindly or with full intent, he himself was not sure. But the result, and the consequences, were the same.

Flinx never felt it coming. Did not sense it even though his talent was functioning, because the surge in emotion he felt from his host was one of overpowering disgust, not aggression. When he did finally perceive the full force of the AAnn's underlying animus, the sense that there might be something more at work in Takuuna's mind than the usual simple straightforward animosity, it was too late.

He had excellent balance, but he was too near the rim and leaning just a little too far over the edge so that he could see better. The powerful swipe of the administrator's tail caught him behind both legs. He flailed his arms in a desperate attempt to maintain his balance—to no avail. Pip was at his side in an instant, drawn to him by the sudden fear and panic in his mind. She could do nothing but follow him down as he toppled over the edge.

For better or worse, Takuuna realized as he watched his charge plummet out of sight, a decision had been taken. He rushed to the rim in time to see the softskin land hard on the first sloping ledge below. The tall, lanky frame continued to bounce and roll until it disappeared out of sight over a sheer inner wall.

The administrator waited there for a while, his attention shifting occasionally to this or that interesting ballooning creature rising from the chasm's depths or drifting down into it. A hive of faunal activity, the canyon provided the opportunity to observe numerous interesting inhabitants of Jast, including one or two that were new to him. What he did *not* see during the course of his extended sightseeing was any further sign of the human.

Their soft bodies were not durable to begin with, he knew. He decided that there was no way, above or below the sand-that-shelters-life, that the softskin could have survived such a fall. Even if it somehow could have managed to do so, it would be broken and severely damaged. Unable to crawl, much less climb, out of the steep-sided, rubble-strewn canyon. He felt badly for the gullible and trusting human. This feeling did not last long.

A pity, he thought as he rose on powerful legs and turned back to the waiting aircar. But such was the fate that awaited spies and agents determined to undermine the peaceful objectives of the Empire. His superiors, he knew, would understand everything once he had explained it all to them, and would praise him for his quick and decisive action.

The aircar hummed to life without hesitation, rose, and turned back toward distant Skokosas. Within minutes it was lost to sight from the canyon's edge. From beneath a pile of broken rock and the dull orange houluwub bush that sheltered it, a hesitant and curious vopolpa emerged. The strange and frightening long-winged thing that had been hunting it had gone. Inflating the pair of thumbnail-sized airsacs attached to its back end, the black-and-purple vopolpa wept its urine and, relieved, drifted off in a direction that would take it away from the canyon.

Below the rim, all was quiet. Shattered stones that had been broken loose from their resting places lay still. Venting the last cool of the night, fecund soil began to vomit forth small, migrating spores. Those small creatures incapable of flight crept furtively from stone to shadow, bush to jaleeb vine. A finger-long wonudu stole out from beneath the shelter of a multi-trunked but dead sarobbis. Eyeing the ripe, grape-sized molk buds nearby, it scrabbled on its dozen legs in the direction of a hearty, pale pink breakfast. From above, the wonudu looked like a large, dead twig blowing in the wind.

That did not fool the patrolling jolahoh. Spotting the movement on the rocky slope below, it instantly voided the gas contained within all four of its lifting sacs. Dropping like a stone, it landed directly on top of the skittering wonudu, slamming into the tiny herbivore hard enough to break its back. The thick, fleshy pad that ran the length of the jolahoh's belly cushioned the impact, as did the layers of fat surrounding its internal organs. Legs kicking spasmodically, the mortally injured wonudu struggled to bring its sucking mouthparts to bear on its attacker. Pinned beneath the weighty mass of the jolahoh, it was unable to do so. Ignoring the feebly striking head, the jolahoh proceeded to feed on its still-living victim. As a predator it needed neither fang nor claw nor poisonous stinger to hunt and kill: it simply fell out of the sky to land crushingly on top of its prey.

Both quarry and killer ignored the much larger motionless form that lay nearby. A small flock of yobulbul, their single gas sacs each no larger than a thumbnail, hovered above the pool of blood that trickled from the body's forehead, their long, needle-like proboses allowing them to feed on the crimson puddle without landing. Striking from the other side of the body, a furious serpentine shape inhaled several of them before they could scatter, the dwarf nozzles located at the rear of their tiny forms venting gas as rapidly as their panicked, miniscule muscular contractions could manage it.

Sharp eyes searching for any other threat to her master, Pip relaxed her pleated wings and settled down on his back. Though she sensed no emotions emanating from Flinx, she could feel his heart pumping beneath her scales. He was still alive. Unconscious and bleeding, his clothing torn and his survival belt ripped away and gone, but alive.

Frantic with concern, she had been unable to do anything to break his fall, could only parallel his uncontrolled descent as he crashed and bounced from one ledge to another. Perhaps it was just as well he was insensible. It kept him from seeing that one booted foot dangled over a sheer drop of several hundred meters. Another bounce, another roll, and Pip would no longer have a companion to keen over.

Perched on his back, the flying snake settled down. There was nothing more she could do. She was empathetic, but not sentient. She could not go for help, or conjure up the emergency medical kit that filled one of the pouches fastened to her master's lost belt, or gather soft fur or other material to staunch his wounds. She could only lie, and wait, and wish, in the quiet but devoted manner of minidrags, for her companion to come to his senses.

She stayed that way for hours, leaving only once, and then but fleetingly, to find a natural cistern in the rocks and drink her fill. As she was returning, she noticed movement around her master's body. He himself was not moving, but several large, ominous shapes around him were.

There were four of the hasaladu. They were by far the biggest animals Pip had encountered since she and Flinx had arrived on Jast. Though even the largest weighed no more than twenty kilos, they were longer and wider than her master. Just one of them could have covered him like a pale blue blanket. That was what they were trying to do now, though their intentions had nothing to do with keeping him warm.

Three membranous protrusions, more like stiffened airfoils than wings, protruded from the sides and distal end of each body. Supported and extended by straw-like bones, these fan-like appendages allowed the predatory hasaladu to glide whereas the majority of Jastian fauna could only travel by means of their inflatable lifting sacs. So in addition to utilizing the three balloon-like spheres on their backs to rise and descend, the hasaladu could deflate them completely and glide on columns of air, allowing them to strike swiftly at potential prey.

There was no need to employ that particularly deadly maneuver now. In addition to not moving, their intended quarry lay immobile on the rocks beneath them. Footlong clawed mouthparts twitched as one flier, venting gas to slowly descend, prepared to wrap the large volume of motionless meat in its membranous embrace. Its companions crowded close, each eager to snatch a portion of the easy meal.

Her wings a blur of pink and blue, Pip spat a stream of venom at the one that was preparing to envelop the unconscious Flinx in its carnivorous clinch. An observing human might have wondered if Alaspinian neurotoxin would have any effect on the fauna of a far-distant world such as Jast. No such biological concerns restrained the flying snake. She reacted instinctively and without restrictive forethought.

Her venom might or might not have affected the hasaladu nervous system, but its corrosive effects were universal. Bending on their supporting stalks, the predator's eyes rose in time to catch the full force of the minidrag's poison. One eye dissolved instantly in a burst of hissing decomposition while the other was badly damaged. Letting out a weird, gargling yowl, the hasaladu rapidly inflated its lifting sacs and rose in panic. By then, Pip was in among the others, darting and striking.

Though far quicker and more maneuverable than the fastest hasaladu, she was still outnumbered. A pair of hooked mouthparts wrapped around her lower body and threatened to drag her down. A single sharp twist and turn pulled her free. Though strong, the hasaladu's grip suffered by comparison to that of a human's five-fingered hand.

The first predator she had struck now had disappeared over the rim into the inner canyon. Eyeless, a second now lay flopping in mortal agony not far from Flinx's head, battering its inflexible wings against the rocks. Another struggled to stay aloft, having lost one of its wings and proximate lifting pouches to Pip's caustic venom.

She did not have an unlimited supply of toxin, and in fact the poison sac inside her mouth was empty when the two surviving hasaladu decided that the edible bounty lying on the ledge was not worth further fighting with the small, superfast creature so determined to defend it. Fully inflating their airsacs, they curved their stiffened airfoils downward as far as possible and rose straight up into the sky, leaving their injured comrade to beat out the remainder of its life against the rocks below.

Utterly exhausted, Pip did not even have enough strength remaining to fly down to rejoin her comatose master. Spreading her pleated wings wide, she could only manage to glide to a landing on his shoulders. Mouth agape and tongue hanging to one side, she sought to vent excess body heat. Despite having folded her wings against her side, she was still unable to settle into a comfortable position. This doubtless had something to do with the fact that no matter how she arranged the coils of her body she could not find a stable perch. Far from unsettling her, the continuing instability set off a burst of internal exhilaration. Forcing herself to raise her wings, she rose painfully into the air long enough to flutter to one side.

Beneath her, Flinx was regaining consciousness.

5

H is head hurt. No, he corrected himself. *Everything* hurt. Sitting up required the kind of coordination between bruised brain and battered muscles he was not sure he possessed. The effort caused one particular place on his forehead to shout with pain. Wincing, he reached up and felt the abraded flesh. When he brought his fingers down he saw that they were covered with a sticky, largely dried mixture of grit, dirt, and some reddish material. From his wrist hung a shattered bracelet. What was the latter's purpose? Odd. He could not assign a name to it. As his thoughts began to unspool, he found that he could not assign names to a great many things. Himself, for example.

Who am I? he found himself wondering. The clearer his thinking became, the more that utter bewilderment replaced the aches and pains that seemed to vibrate through every part of his body. Where am I? What is this place? Strive though he might, he found only a great gray void where knowledge ought to be. Though many things around him *felt* familiar, he could not assign them specific names. He knew, for example, what a rock was, but when he searched his addled thoughts for a word to apply to the object, none was forthcoming. He knew all about rocks, he felt instinctively. He just couldn't put names to them. He even felt that he knew what was wrong with him, but he could no more call up the term than he could remember where he was, or where he had come from.

A surge of empathy filled him. Turning toward its source, he found himself gazing down at an exquisitely colored coiling shape. He did not recognize it. It was friendly, though. He could sense that, even if he could not identify the creature. Slitted green eyes gazed up at him as if imploring some additional form of recognition. Not knowing what else to do, he let it slither into his lap. It curled up there, apparently satisfied, a flood of contentment surging forth from it in waves that washed across his bemused mind like a soothing touch on his cheek. It did nothing to help him identify the creature that clearly had a close attachment to him—but it made him feel better.

He sat like that for some time, staring at the canyon at his feet, observing the strange airborne creatures that drifted back and forth along its impressive length. He could not put a name to any of them, or to the sparse but hardy growths with whom he shared the rocky ledge, or to the canyon itself. Try as he might, he could not put a name to anything.

Is this my home? he found himself wondering. No, that couldn't be right. A home was a comfortable place. He was sure of that. Whatever else he might be, he was decidedly not comfortable. Therefore, home had to lie elsewhere. Home. At least he had finally been able to name something.

Thirst. That was something else he could put a name to. He needed water. As he rose, the flying creature that had been dozing in his lap took to the sky but did not abandon him. Instead, it darted upward, returned, darted, returned again. Having no idea where he was or what to do next, it seemed sensible to follow the one being that projected feelings of affection toward him. Forcing his bruised muscles to manipulate his bones, he began to climb. That activity, at least, did not require struggling with the aching vacancy that filled his mind. He would have taken the easier way and headed down, if any accessible route had presented itself. But a quick investigation revealed only sheer cliff below him. So he was forced to go up, digging and scrabbling at the uncooperative rock.

Once, he came to a place that threatened to defeat him. Only isolated cracks in the stone marred the rock wall that threatened to halt his ascent. Carefully, unsure that he really knew what he was doing, he forced bruised and scraped fingers into shallow crevices, jammed his booted toes into cracks seemingly too slight to support his weight, and continued to work his way up.

Interesting, he mused as he struggled to pull himself up onto the next ledge. I know how to climb. Could it be that I am an interesting person?

He didn't feel very interesting. He felt as if death was climbing right behind him, just a little slower. Or perhaps patiently. Realizing that in addition to knowing how to climb he apparently also knew death, he decided without additional analysis that he preferred to put off further acquaintance with the latter for as long as he possibly could.

Then, quite unexpectedly, the next ledge he pulled himself up and over was not a ledge at all, but the rim of the canyon. Panting, his ripped and torn clothing soaked with stale sweat and dried blood, he sat there contemplating the chasm that spread out below him. He did not know the names of the bladder-borne creatures that floated in and out of the vast, shadowy depths. Some of them were pretty, in a resplendent, iridescent sort of way. Others made him smile to look at them. Some of the bigger and stronger methodically murdered some of the smaller and weaker—usually in silence, but sometimes noisily. None came near him.

On the lip of the gorge was only himself and the winged flying creature that would not leave him. As it once again coiled up in his lap, he reached down to stroke the back of its head. It extended its exquisite blue-and-pink wings fully, stretched, and seemed to shiver with pleasure.

Now how did I know to do that? he found himself wondering. Clearly, the creature was very attached to him. So, in all likelihood, he was somehow attached to it. Adrift in the midst of an emptiness that was both physical and mental, it was good to have a friend. Even one that was legless, mute, and scaly.

He wondered if it had a name. Straining mentally, he fought to recall. But where information ought to have lain waiting, there was only the same hazy vacuum. Whatever it had once contained, his storehouse of memory was presently empty.

Nor was it the only thing that troubled him. He was still thirsty. Rising, he turned to survey his surroundings. It was getting dark. That, he realized as he struggled to analyze the condition, was a consequence of the absence of light. Something told him he needed to seek shelter. From the cold, if not from—other things. But water first, his body insisted.

There would likely be water in the bottom of the canyon. It was a continuous amazement to him that he knew such things without being able to explain how he knew them. He was grateful nonetheless for the dribbles of wisdom. Where else was water likely to hide? In other low places, but the plateau that was cut by the great canyon was as flat as his spirit. Choosing a direction, he started off away from the chasm. Perhaps water would present itself. He knew he would have to go to it because it manifestly was not going to come to him.

A name, he found himself thinking furiously as he walked. I need a name, an identity. Riding on his shoulders, the flying creature flicked out a single-pointed tongue to caress his cheek. Through hurt and exhaustion, he smiled at it.

"You need a name, too. Until I can remember one, I'll call you Pip."

For reasons unknown, this plainly pleased his companion. Why he had settled on that name, he didn't know. At least it was short. Like his life was going to be if he didn't find water.

The search for something to drink kept him from dwelling on what had happened to him, on how he had come to find himself, battered and bruised and emptied of remembrance, on a ledge within the canyon. Later, he would contemplate it further. After he'd had something to drink.

It was not cold on the plateau during the day, but night was different. Huddling beneath an overhang of rock, he shivered and wished fervently for warmth. It did not come to him. Morning saw him little rested, his throat now dry, his lips beginning to turn to parchment. Groaning, he heaved himself up from his nonexistent bed and resumed walking eastward.

Was it a strange land he was walking in? It seemed so, but he could not be sure. Every odd growth, every peculiar creature that crawled or hopped or floated, might in truth be as familiar to him as his own name, if only he could remember any of it. He simply did not know. His ignorance of labels was utter and complete.

That curious green mat-creature whose ribbed back was lined with lifting bubbles, for example. What was it called? He watched while it drifted parallel to him for a while, grazing small buttons of crimson and yellow growths, rising and falling as it ate. When he turned toward it, the alarmed creature inflated the dozen or so bubbles on its back to their maximum and, forcefully undulating the edges of its body, fluttered off in the opposite direction. He could easily have chased it down, but to what purpose? He did not even know if it was good to eat.

Eat. That concept he understood. It was of primary importance, right behind drink. One emergency at a time, he told himself.

He passed through a forest of growing things that in the absence of leaves and branches flaunted deep folds and indentations to the sky to maximize their surface area. When the light struck these directly, they swelled until the sunstruck surface was perfectly smooth, minimizing surface area in order to minimize evaporation. They flexed like rubber when he pushed his way through them, springing back in his wake with little irritated humming noises. Other growths were striped or spotted. One was quite mobile, pulling its roots out of the ground at his approach and drifting away beneath a single inflated airsac to settle into fresh earth nearby. Flinx watched as its roots, corkscrewing like drunken worms, buried their way into new soil to reestablish the parent growth.

It was only later that he grew aware he was being followed.

Unlike every other living thing he had encountered over the past several days, he succeeded in putting a name to the creature that was unashamedly trailing him. It might not be the correct name, but in lieu of the right one it would certainly serve. He called it the Teeth.

The Teeth was much bigger than any other meat-eater he had seen. Long and slender, it had a spine that spread out above its entire length like an unfolding bony blossom. This spreading V-shape was no wider than his arm was long. From its attenuated surface rose a single line of ten big airsacs, each a couple of meters in diameter, which kept the animal aloft. Slim and muscular, the Teeth was a good six meters in length, of which a meter or more consisted of jaws. These were equally long and slender and filled with dozens, perhaps hundreds, of fine, needle-like teeth. Jaws and teeth were perfectly designed for sweeping from side to side to pluck small prey out of the air. He decided that they could also, if given the chance, rip him up pretty bad.

The several large, black orbs hanging from the front edge of the spread spine remained fixed on him. They had no pupils and did not move like eyes. Motion detectors, Flinx decided, or perhaps heat sensors, or both. The Teeth advanced with rippling, snake-like contortions of its flattened body. Despite its length, when viewed from head-on it would offer only a very small profile. Another useful characteristic for a large predator.

That it was focused on him, Flinx had no doubt. He lengthened his stride. Inflating its airsacs and increasing the rippling movement of its body slightly, the Teeth kept pace.

He climbed a fairly steep slope. Ignoring the more difficult terrain, the Teeth simply floated upward behind him. A handful of small, single-trunked browsers no bigger than Flinx's hand detected the approaching carnivore and erupted out of his path, exploding away frantically in all directions like so many spring-loaded buttons. Flinx wended his way though a narrow ravine. The Teeth kept pace by simply rising above it and continuing to track him from overhead. When Flinx tried to ignore it, the silent Teeth moved stealthily closer. When he paused to look back, it halted, hovering patiently while waiting for its increasingly anxious prey to break into a run, attack, or fall down dead.

What could he do? In combination with his own increasing weakness and need for water, the creature's size and persistence were beginning to unnerve Flinx. In response to his escalating agitation, Pip circled anxiously. She was not stimulated to attack the Teeth because it had yet to make a hostile gesture in her master's direction. Until it did, the exact source of Flinx's distress remained a matter of conjecture for her.

The Teeth was not going to leave him, Flinx saw. Somehow, he was going to have to try to defend himself. Emerging from the far end of the ravine, he began searching the surrounding ground for a weapon. There were rocks aplenty, but he was too weak to pick up and throw anything substantial, and the Teeth looked too big and tough to be discouraged by a flurry of flying gravel. Flinx examined the surrounding growths. Whether simple or complex, nothing offered the promise of a strong club. Furthermore, attempting to dismember a living plant might have unpleasant repercussions of its own. Vague half-memories warned him against taking such an action except as a last resort.

When he came upon the dead, desiccated tree-thing, it was as if he had stumbled on a potential arsenal. There were large, solid branches he could swing, smaller ones he could throw, and a plethora of strange, rock-hard protrusions. Already sensing the growing weakness in its intended quarry, the Teeth had moved dangerously close. Needle-lined jaws opened and closed repeatedly in silent expectation. At any moment, Flinx feared, it would test him with a quick bite he might well be unable to avoid.

Bending, he reached down to pick up one of the hard woody nodules lying on the ground. It came up a little ways before snapping right back down. Surprised, he tried to pick it up again. As if attached to an elastic cord, the nodule was yanked out of his hand. Not a cord, he saw, but some kind of long, strong fingers belonging to something hidden in the soil. They did not strike out at him, but they refused to surrender the nodule. It was the same with all the others. Each had been possessed by something whose presence was revealed only by clutching fingers.

He felt something tear at his back.

Flinging himself to one side, he fell and rolled once, twice. The Teeth was on him in an instant, propelling itself forward at unexpected speed by expelling air through a quadruple set of nozzles located just above the tip of its tail. With the previously indistinct threat now having defined itself, Pip was there in an instant, interposing herself between the carnivore and Flinx. She spat at it, once. Normally, she would have aimed for an attacker's eyes. But the Teeth had no eyes that she recognized, and she did not perceive its ebony motion/heat detectors as such.

The corrosive neurotoxin struck the Teeth just behind its head. Emitting a loud, shrill hiss, the carnivore jerked back, its long jaws snapping at the burnt place. Some of the cartilage of which its spreading back was composed dissolved under the effects of the toxin. Either none of the poison entered its nervous system, or else it was immune. Smoke rising from the burned place, it returned furiously to the attack.

Many of the dead trees' fallen branches were lined with thorns. Grabbing one, ignoring the pain of several small punctures, Flinx raised and swung the makeshift weapon just in time to block a downward bite. He scrambled to his feet as the infuriated carnivore gathered itself to strike again. Where was a vulnerable spot? Flinx wondered desperately. Nothing visible on the slender, rippling body hinted at the location of a vital organ. There was only the head. But the head was where the teeth were, and he preferred to avoid that end.

Forcing muscle-compressed air from its tail nozzles, the Teeth shot straight at him. It expected him to jump to one side or the other, or perhaps to crouch or duck. That was what prey did, usually to no avail. Instead, Flinx surprised it. And in doing so, surprised himself.

With the gaping, narrow jaws less than a meter away from chomping out a chunk of his belly, Flinx leaped. It was an instinctive reaction. I must have had some kind of combat training, he decided as he found himself soaring over the onrushing Teeth. Pain shot through him as twisting, flexing jaws tore flesh from his right calf. He landed on the Teeth's back. Heavily. The impact was considerable. Though strong and wiry, the Teeth could not have weighed more than a hundred kilos. It twisted and jerked, trying to buck him off. Wrapping his legs around its serpentine body, Flinx rode the writhing form as it thrashed wildly, sometimes rising a few meters skyward, at other times banging itself hard against the ground. Then he began to swing his club.

Thorns punctured first one, then a second, and then a third lifting sac. Fetid air escaped from the punctured bladders as the Teeth began to sink earthward. When the narrow jaws would twist around to snap at him, Flinx fended them off with the makeshift club. All the while, Pip kept buzzing the carnivore's head, continually distracting it.

All but bending itself double, the Teeth finally succeeded in throwing him off its back. Grunting as he landed on his left shoulder, Flinx managed to keep a grip on the thorn club. Rolling onto his back, he raised it defensively to ward off the questing jaws he expected to come snapping at his face. He needn't have worried.

Deprived of several of its lifting bladders, the wounded meat-eater was struggling to gain altitude. But no matter how hard it strained and how much it inflated its remaining airsacs, it could not quite muster sufficient lifting power. Squealing and hissing, it floundered off in the opposite direction from its intended prey. As it did so, several meter-long, worm-like shapes emerged from hiding places in the rocks. Flinx had been completely unaware of their presence. They had individual, sausage-like air bladders that ran the length of their backs, and single eyes set in the center of their fore ends. Beneath the solitary eye, multiple sharp-edged tentacles curled and uncurled expectantly, like barbed beards. Inflating their bladders, the creatures silently rose a couple of meters into the air and began to track the injured Teeth. They were careful to keep a respectful distance from the much larger carnivore. They were in no hurry, and had plenty of time.

It was a coarsely beautiful place in which he found himself, Flinx decided, but with the single exception of his winged traveling companion it was not a benign one. Once again he found himself wondering: from where had he conjured the name Pip? Was it the right one, or just something dredged hastily from the sludge that was his memory? Perhaps one day he would find out.

Following the fight, he discovered that he needed water more than ever. Scanning the rocky eastern horizon, he saw what he thought might be a line of deeper green off to his left. As he started in its direction, he wondered if he would last long enough to reach it.

I've been in this kind of situation before, he realized with a sudden start, and obviously he had survived it. So I have endurance.

What he did not have, he feared, was time.

Qyl-Elussab guided the cargo lifter with practiced skill. Though somewhat shorter than the Vsseyan average, the driver's ability to handle the transport was not affected. The manipulating tentacles presently hard at work were no less active or agile than those of a larger representative of the Vsseyan species. The driver was able to reach the controls easily enough. Of local Vsseyan manufacture, the lifter was one of those clever devices that enabled its designers to get around far more rapidly than by hopping. When several dozen short tentacles functioned in tandem, the driver was able to handle a dozen controls simultaneously. It was a demonstration of digital skill no human or AAnn could have equaled.

The lifter bore Qyl-Elussab and cargo deep into the AAnn complex. Making use of the transporter's built-in navigation system, the tightly focused driver turned down a corridor to the right. An armed AAnn stood guard at the end. After checking the visitor's credentials and running through the electronic manifest attached to the lifter, the guard hissed indifferently and passed both driver and cargo through. A stream of alternating large and small bubbles emerged from Qyl-Elussab's mouth. They would have meant nothing to the AAnn even if it had still been looking in the driver's direction.

The guard had barely glanced at the cargo. Not that it would likely have mattered if she had. The appended manifest had been clear enough, and the container was only one among dozens that passed daily throughout the checkpoint, virtually indistinguishable from the hundreds that had preceded it.

Arriving at the compound's food preparation facility, the lifter was halted by a particularly officious AAnn clad in attire appropriate to his position and status. Sparing a quick glance for the shipment and none for the driver, he gestured indifferently with hand and tail.

"Put it over there, with the other recent deliveriess."

Having divested himself of the directive, he turned away and moved off to converse with several other AAnn. His attitude toward the lifter's driver, a local, was typically dismissive. When working with their Vssey hosts, the AAnn were formally polite, but rarely more than that.

Expecting nothing in the way of a salutation, of anything beyond the curt order, Qyl-Elussab was not disappointed.

Working quickly, the lifter's automatic manipulators deposited the load in the designated place, finding an empty slot among numerous ranks of high, crowded shelves. The unloading completed within a few minutes, Qyl-Elussab backed the lifter out of the warehousing area and headed for the compound's exit as rapidly as was prudent. Only when safely outside did the Vssey abandon the lifter in the external staging zone. A couple of the other Vssey working there eyed the stranger uncertainly. Neither remembered the newcomer from previous workdays. But they were not sufficiently moved to ask questions. Local staff at the AAnn compound changed all the time.

Qyl-Elussab wanted to confront them anyway. To tell them to stay out of the complex, to take the rest of the morning off from work, to form a circle of contemplating and ponder the wind and the sky for a while. But the departing driver dared not. The organization to which Qyl-Elussab belonged was still quite small, and its opinion very much a minority one. The delivery to the AAnn support compound this morning was intended to make a statement somewhat out of proportion to the organization's size and numbers. So the driver was forced to withhold both words and bubbles as a steady series of hops brought the heavily monitored exit ever nearer. The guard there did not even check Qyl-Elussab's work permit as the visitor departed.

The rest of the morning passed peacefully. So did the following day. Within the compound, work went on as always, performed to the usual high AAnn standards of efficiency. On the third day subsequent to Qyl-Elussab's visit, a food preparatory specialist moved twenty loaves of prepacked protein stretcher from the relevant warehouse section into the main kitchen. There they were placed at the disposal of the waiting preparers. Two of them manipulated loaf after loaf into the mass cooker, where premeasured spices and condiments were added to the imported base material. Each loaf was identical to the one that preceded it into the cooker. Only the eleventh loaf was different. Its differences not being immediately visible, it was opened in its turn by a small mechanical device designed for the purpose of automatically divesting it of its airtight packaging.

It took a moment for oxygen in the room to make contact with the injected material that had been skillfully blended with the protein expander. When catalyst met contents, energy was released. Rather violently. The resulting conflagration made quite a mess of the food preparation facility, the food storage area, and the cafeteria-style eating chamber located nearby. Twenty-two AAnn were killed instantly, and dozens more were injured.

Following the screaming, hissing, stress-filled aftermath, highly efficient specialists combed through the wreckage. They found traces of the explosive that had been concealed in the protein pack. The distinctive chemical signature pointed accusingly to material that was unpretentious in origin but devastating in its consequences. A report was issued. Security was tightened at every AAnn outpost on the planet. There was no general alarm. The AAnn were not given to panic. Both their own administrators and the pertinent local officials were confident that the perpetrators of the outrage would be found, and dealt with. Suitably horrified by the unprovoked carnage, the Vsseyan authorities offered full cooperation.

Certain steps were taken.

Breathing hard, claws curled inward, tail extended fully out behind him for balance, a crouching, unclothed Takuuna pivoted slowly in one place while keeping a wary eye on his opponent. She, too, was respiring heavily, her eyes following his every movement. To the inexperienced, it would appear as if the two of them were engaged in serious, if not mortal, combat. To understand what was really happening, one would have to know that their labored breathing was not entirely due to an excessive expenditure of combative energy.

When she leaped at him, he was ready. Using his slightly longer arms, he ducked instead of dodging sideways and struck out to the left, catching her behind her knees while avoiding the claws on her bare feet. She lost her balance and fell forward. He was on her in an instant, pinning her arms while lying far enough forward on her back to avoid the thrashing tail. Words were exchanged. Her initial fury subsided into muttered, grudging admiration for his agility. An indication of willing concession, her tail slumped to one side as she fully acquiesced.

It was important if not necessary for him to win the precoital fight. The ultimate result would have been the same no matter which of them had won the right to secure the dominant position, but no AAnn worth his or her second eyelid would have simply conceded it merely for the purpose of facilitating a mating. From a social standpoint, it would have been unforgivable. Had he, for example, simply rolled and dropped his tail, she would have, despite her readiness to breed, probably spat on him and stalked out of the chamber. No AAnn got to mate unless they proved themselves worthy, and the proof lay in the customary attempt to try to secure the dominant mating position.

His success left her angry and disappointed, of course, just as he would have been had he lost the contest. That did not prevent them from consummating the confrontation with a flourish. Once defeated, a partner could not attempt to regain dominance either during or after coitus.

She would have to wait until next time. Respirating deeply in the aftermath, he decided he would be more than pleased to allow her a rematch.

It had been thus among his kind for as long as any could remember. Judged by the standards of the mating rituals traditionally evoked by other species, it appeared harsh, even brutal at times. Despite the protection afforded by elaborate rules and guidelines, injuries were not uncommon. But it had ensured that only the fittest AAnn propagated. It was also excellent exercise, ultimately relaxing (wounds sustained notwithstanding), and was not, he mused as he rinsed himself in the afterbath, wholly unexciting.

Later, they joined another couple in the sandarium, burrowing into the imported, sterilized, and properly heated sand up to their necks. After the physical exertion of contesting and mating, followed by the tepid washing, the enfolding warmed sand felt indescribably luxurious against his scales. He knew the other pair only casually, having encountered them separately within the administration complex. As his partner for the encounter clearly knew them better, he let her make the opening gestures and carry most of the conversation. She tended to ignore him now, as was only proper for a nye after contesting. After all, they had mated but were not bound.

He was preparing to leave to return to work, pulling and pushing himself as slowly as possible out of the deep sand in order to enjoy the last lingering piquant caress of the particles as they slid off his scales, when the messenger arrived. That in itself was unusual. What was so important that it could not wait for the bathers to dress and access the communicators that were an integral part of every nye's attire?

The anxious messenger scanned the figures occupying the sand bath. "Administrator Second Takuuna VBXLLW?"

Takuuna identified himself. "Administrator Second Takuuna urgency?" He was aware that from within the bath, his still-immersed bathing companions were watching him intently.

The messenger fluttered a hasty gesture of second-degree affirmation. "You are directed to report immediately to the office of the respected Keiiichu RGQQ."

From the storage alcove where he had carefully placed it, Takuuna was removing and slipping back into his work attire. "For what purposse?"

A swift downward hand swipe signifying ignorance. "I wass told to deliver the order. Nothing more."

Of course there wasn't. He was only a messenger, Takuuna thought understandingly. Young as he was, he probably still had at least a dozen subjunctives attached to his name. As the messenger left, the administrator saw that his communicator was indeed alight. It could not be too serious an emergency or the device would have interrupted his break with an alarm. That, at least, was encouraging.

It did not make him wonder less, or render him less nervous. What did Skokosas's primary administrator Keiiichu want with him? He had never dealt with Keiiichu personally, having encountered the senior official only on a few formal occasions. Keiiichu stood several levels above him in the administrative hierarchy. Aware that his bathing companions were still watching him, he turned and nodded knowingly.

"It sseemss that the venerable Keiiichu wisshess my advice. I am ssorry that I musst take my leave of you sso ssoon."

One of the other bathers hissed understandingly. "We

have sspent time enough here, I think. Work awaitss all of uss."

"Truly." Takuuna's challenger dragged herself out of the sand, her supple tail whipping lazily back and forth behind her as she emerged. Golden grains spilled in small sandfalls from her back and flanks.

He would have stayed to watch, but the last thing he wanted to do was keep someone as important as Keliichu waiting. Waiting for what? As he strode purposefully through the corridors of the complex, his sandals slapping on the smooth floor, Takuuna's worries deepened. The pleasures of a few timeparts ago were waning rapidly. Had he done something wrong? Had he done something right? What was so important that it could not be conveyed via communicator and required a tooth-to-tooth meeting?

A sudden thought so alarmed him that his pointed tongue shot out reflexively between his front teeth. Fortunately, there was no one around to witness the lapse. The human! This had something to do with that execrable excuse for a sentient that he had providentially knocked over a cliff, sending it to its doom. As was proper, his report on the incident had been filed immediately. By now he thought it had long since been reviewed and accepted. Had something unforeseen cropped up to compromise his carefully crafted tale of alien deception and desperate self-defense? As he walked, he mentally reviewed what he had scribed. He could find no fault with it. His failure to do so only rendered him that much more uneasy.

Dodging irritably around a couple of slowly hopping, visiting Vssey, he entered an appropriate lift and soon found himself at the entry to Keliichu's workplace. As befitted someone of such high status, it was located just below ground level, with a narrow horizontal port offering a view of carefully maintained external landscaping.

It was as close as one stationed on Jast could get to a homey panorama. Trying not to let his unease show, he flashed his presence.

Keliichu was waiting for him. The primary administrator's expression, posture, and tail position gave no indication of what the respected sandering was thinking. He appeared preoccupied, barely acknowledging Takuuna's entrance and elaborate salute as the newcomer sheathed his claws, turned his head to the right, and exposed his jugular. Nor did Keliichu come around the work desk to lightly grab Takuuna's throat in a polite gesture of greeting. Takuuna did not miss the gesture because it was not expected. This was not a personal encounter. Determined to stay calm, forcing himself to still the rapid side-to-side twitching of his tail, he waited silently.

Keliichu turned to him. Not on him, but to him, Takuuna noted with relief. An AAnn could read more into a body movement or gesture than even the most perceptive human, and there was nothing in the way the primary administrator held his hands or his head, his shoulders or his tail, to suggest enmity.

Keliichu wasted no time. "You have heard about the deathss at Morotuuver?"

Takuuna gestured swift acknowledgement. "Who had not? The horrifying incident was the talk of the AAnn community on Jast. "A terrible tragedy. Sso many good nye dead in the accident."

The senior administrator executed a brutally sharp gesture of disagreement muted by third-degree consideration. "It wass not an accident."

His visitor was taken aback. This was not the conversation he had expected to have. "But all the reportss indicated that—"

Keliichu did not let him finish. Noted for his patience, the primary administrator was exhibiting all the signs of one for whom time had become shortened. It occurred suddenly to Takuuna that even someone as senior as his host could come under pressure from above. That in turn suggested the involvement of authority beyond the merely local, perhaps stretching all the way back to Pregglin itself.

What had happened? And how, by all the heat of all the sands of home, did it involve him?

"It wass an act of ssabotage," the administrator informed him moodily.

Takuuna's head was spinning as he tried to keep up. "Ssabotage? But by whom, and to what purposse?"

The administrator's head came up and he met his visitor's eyes squarely. Another time, another place, it might have been interpreted as a personal challenge to combat. But not here, not in this office, not during a prescribed meeting between superior and subordinate.

"You, of all nye, sshould know that, Takuuna."

His thoughts raced. Why would anyone suppose that he would be familiar with . . . ? He began to smile inwardly. There was a childhood legend about guiding stars that favored certain newly born. He was beginning to believe that his was shining brightly. He could foresee the diminishment of a subjunctive already. Having arrived full of ignorance and worry, he strove to adjust his posture to reflect inner confidence. It was something he was beginning to feel.

"Truly," he responded ingenuously. "Why wass the event reported as an accident?"

"To keep both AAnn and localss from leaping to unefficacious conclussionss. To maintain the public calm. While our possition here on Jasst is ssecure, it iss not ever-lassting. Whether that will eventually come to pass awaitss further decisions by the Vssey. And as you know, what a nye can decide in a *tssing*, it takes at leasst three Vssey a month to work out. Sso we remain, and quietly pursue our interesstss, and try not to give offensse to our dithering hosstss. But there are evidently ssome Vssey who can reach decissionss more sswiftly than the resst of their ssluggissh brethren. Thesse unknown hosstile elementss have decided to take action againsst uss." To relieve his resstlessness, he reached down with a clawed finger and traced abstract patterns in the disc of colored sand that reposed on his desk for that purpose.

"Forensssicss found tracess of oxygen-ssenssitized explossive in the wreckage of the dining area at Morotuuver. Additional ressearch revealed that a complete identity package for a Vssey worker at the facility had gone missing ssome months earlier. Sso the attack wass well planned." His expression was grim. "Thiss initial hint of rebellion againsst our pressence here musst be sstamped out immediately! Our friendss among the Vssey have promissed uss full cooperation. Such violence dissgusstss them equally. Or appearss to," he added, his tone softening.

"What hass this revelation to do with me?" Takuuna thought he knew, but needed to hear it from the adminisstrator himself. Keliichu didn't hesitate.

"It wass you who propossed that the unexpected appearance on Vssey of a sseemingly unconnected, apolitical human wass ssuggesstive of ssomething more than it appeared to be. When you returned from traveling with it to the backcountry and declared that you had been forced to kill it, I musst confess that I wass among thosse disinclined to take your sstory of deception and sself-defensse ssseriously." With the inner will that had always sustained him, Takuuna kept his expression unchanged.

"Then along comess thiss terrible incident at Morotuuver. It sseemss that I, among otherss, may have been wrong in our initial assumptionss, and that your ssusspicionss of human involvement in esscalating Vsseyan animossity to our pressence on thiss world may in fact have been correct."

Takuuna reacted with a becoming modesty that posistively oozed. "I wass only doing my besst, respected Keliichu, relying on my insstinctss and training to analyze all that I wass observing."

Keliichu hissed softly. He had no time for such unctuousness, but was willing to tolerate it. His personal feelings toward this Takuuna were irrelevant to the situation at hand.

"It hass been decided that a specialized invesstigative unit sshould be created, whosse sstaff will be drawn from ssome of the ssharper mindss within the Authority. A unit whosse purpose will be to root out and identify ssources of Vsseyan resstlessness that are ssufficiently disscontented to resspond to our pressence on Jasst with violent demonsstrationss. By decission as well as review of record, it hass been decided that you are pressently the mosst qualified nye to command and direct ssuch a unit."

Takuuna stood stunned. What a wonderment of sandfalls the morning had brought! First the delicious encounter with the dynamic female Geelin. And now this. Anticipating condemnation over the outcome of his encounter with the intruding softskin, perhaps even a formal questioning by an interrogation panel, he instead found himself promoted! Any last vestiges of doubt he felt over terminating the visitor vanished beneath the import of the primary administrator's words.

"Doess thiss appointment include the formal divesstiture of a perssonal subjunctive?" Had a human in such a situation made the inquiry, it would have sounded pushy. For an AAnn not to do so would have been unnatural.

Hence, Keliichu was expecting it. "No. The appointment doess not carry that kind of hierarchical weight.

However," the senior administrator added in response to Takuuna's obvious dissapointment, "the ssuccessful ressolution of the ssituation we are facing and that you are being assked to deal with would almosst certainly produce ssuch a ressult."

Coming as it did from an official as high up in the local chain of command as Keliichu, the response boosted Takuuna's spirits even more than they had been already.

"Resst assured, venerated primary adminisstrator, that I will undertake to excisse thiss ssocial cancer with the utmosst vigor of which I am capable."

"I am ssure you will." Keliichu's tone was dry and polite. He did not know Takuuna well enough to dislike him. Such things, anyway, were not important. "Your mandate and directionss will be waiting for you in your office. Upon commencing your work, if you find that you require additional ressourcess, do not hessitate to bypass normal channelss to request them. Thiss iss a priority assignment."

After offering a heartfelt "truly" and taking his leave, Takuna departed the chief administrator's sector. He had to force himself to walk and not bound down the corridor of the complex. A special designation! Everyone would be watching him. Naturally, too, everyone would be hoping for him to fail. But this was an exceptional circumstance. He would be operating for the safety and welfare of all nye. The cooperation he could expect from those who would normally be his competitors would be atypical, and could not be refused. He was in a unique and enviable position. In fact, in examining his new circumstances from every possible angle, he could find only one potential complication.

To the best of his knowledge, there *were* no violently subversive groups operating among the Vssey.

Certainly the human had never vouchsafed any interest

in such. That had not stopped Takuuna from killing him. Just as the likely absence of any widespread organized opposition to the AAnn presence on Jast was not going to stop Takuuna from carrying out his newly assigned duties. In the absence of a reason to kill the softskin, Takuuna had managed to do so, anyway, neatly manufacturing a rationale after the fact. With the native authorities having promised to cooperate in any investigation, there was nothing to hold him back. Striding purposefully and proudly down the corridor, he hissed a happy threnody as he contemplated the first spate of anticipated arrests.

6

He remembered what rain was, but the remembering of it did nothing to sate his burning thirst or restore any more of his missing memory. Clearly, it rained in this land. There were too many growing things for it to be otherwise. He could not put a name to any of the growths around him, but many were very green, and he knew that meant the presence of moisture. So he kept walking and stumbling in the direction of the distant green line he had espied when he began to leave the great canyon behind.

The flying snake was light on his shoulders. Apparently she was accustomed to resting there, because she repeatedly touched down and settled herself without hesitation. That was interesting, he reflected. In addition to giving the creature a name, he also somehow knew it was female. What else did he know that awaited only a chance glance, a quick flash of insight, for him to remember?

If he did not find water soon, he knew, whatever he did or did not know would not matter. As days passed, the green line came closer, faded, darkened anew. He was near enough now to make out individual bits of foliage, strong and sturdy. Some of the growths were notably larger than himself. They obviously required a good deal of water, more than occasional rain could supply. So, where was it? He couldn't see it, couldn't smell it. Neither, if she had any heightened senses in that regard, could Pip.

The nearer he drew to the oddly squarish green growths, the steeper and more treacherous the route he had chosen became, until he found himself walking along a ledge running above a narrow gulch. The gully wasn't deep or wide, and he welcomed the shade it provided from the heat of the day.

He was growing delirious. He knew that was the case because for the better part of the morning he had been hearing the sound of running water. But there was no running water. The surface underfoot was solid rock, the bottom of the ravine dry and sandy, and no life-giving waterfalls cascaded from either rim. Already deprived of memory, his traitorous mind was playing further tricks on him.

An airborne Pip was gliding along parallel to him, occasionally crisscrossing the bottom of the gulch. Periodically she would climb up from the bottom of the ravine to flutter in front of his face before dipping downward once more. He did not find the behavior odd because he could not recall anything of her normal behavior and therefore had no history with which to compare it.

Then he misstepped, his right foot bent sideways, he overcorrected to keep from spraining the ankle, and down he went. Faithless as it was, he still tried to protect his head as he tumbled over and over. At least, he thought as he fell helplessly, the sand at the bottom of the canyon looked soft. It was, but not in the way he had expected.

Faced with the fact that the large gangly object accelerating toward them was not going to halt, the pack of somnolent creek browsers, who spanned the watercourse from bank to bank and whose natural camouflage consisted of adjoining flat backs that looked just like a sandy surface, inflated the myriad of tiny airsacs concealed beneath their skin and rose into the air of the gully. Still tumbling uncontrollably downslope, arms and legs flailing in a feeble attempt to halt his plunge, he caught a quick, wild glimpse of the free-flowing creek the ascension of the rapidly rising browsers had exposed. Then he splashed noisily into it. He lay there in the shallow water, stunned by dual sensations of wet and cold that were as welcome as they were unexpected.

He was not delusional. The sound of running water had been real. The stream had been there all the time. It had simply been hidden beneath the bodies of dozens of sand-backed browsing things.

Lying in the little creek, the placid current applying the gentlest of pressure against his limbs and body, he began to drink. It was effortless. He simply opened his mouth and let the water flow in. Almost immediately, he began to choke.

Drowning here and now, in this dry, desiccated place, would be more than ironic, he decided as he forced himself to sit up. He did not try to crawl out of the stream. Instead, he let it flow around him, quietly ecstatic in the grip of its moist caress, and brought water methodically to his lips by forming a cup with his hands. The fresh spring-water soothed his bruised, abraded exterior as effectively as it did his insides. Nearby, Pip lay flattened and fully extended on the sandy shore, pleated wings folded against her sides, and sipped delicately from an eddy.

When he had drank as much as he dared and an ache was threatening to develop beneath his ribs, he struggled to the bank beside her and lay there among the coiled green and vermilion grass-like growths, watching the stream that had saved his life. The cautious creek browsers were returning one by one. As they resumed their immobile feeding positions spanning the watercourse, they once again blanketed it from sight above and below his location. But the several meters of creek running in front of him remained open to air and sky. Their caution was well considered, as he found himself beginning to wonder if any of the grassy coils or creek browsers might be edible. Sating his thirst only served to magnify the weakness he felt from hunger.

If he wanted to take chances with his digestive system, there was plenty to choose from. The profusion of mostly waist-high growths and ground cover attracted by the permanent water were in shades of deep, dark green to pale pink. Finger-length fruits hung from one growth. Plump and pale blue, they were as tempting to the mind as to the eye. But though he studied them for what felt like an hour, not so much as a wandering arthropod availed itself of this seemingly vulnerable and extensive food supply. The lack of attention suggested that, attractive as they were, the blue fruits might be something other than edible. Even in the absence of memory, he retained caution. Tempted as he was, he forced himself to keep looking.

In addition to the gently sloping, sandy banks of the stream, the water itself was swarming with life. Translucent fronds like the tentacles of coelenterates thrust upward from the bottom. As he rose and stumbled downstream, scattering browsing sandbacks like tawny bedsheets, he encountered deeper pools where such growths reached lengths of several meters or more. Though they were nearly transparent, he was able to make them out because they undulated with the current. When they did so, they would catch the light and bounce it upward. Small balls of dark green carpeted the sides of the deepest pools, quivering like anxious rodents in the racing water.

Out of strength at last, he sank exhausted to his knees. Pip rose from his shoulders as he slumped, circling around to flutter in front of his face. Feebly, he waved her off. There was nothing she could do. Potentially toxic or not, he realized that he was going to have to try to eat something before he lost even the energy to chew.

In front of him, a host of small creatures were rising and falling from the depths of the pool. Inflating diverse arrangements of small airsacs on their backs, they would shoot upward from below, break the surface of the water, and continue upward toward the rim of the gulch, only to disappear over the edge. Meanwhile, others would vent air from their lifting bladders and drop into the water. There they would descend to feed on the underwater forest and the tiny swimming things that dwelled within it. It was an arrangement as practical as it was novel, since each small diver would retain enough air in its sacs to enable it to breathe underwater.

As he was debating whether to try plucking and munching on some of the long, translucent streamers, the green globules, or one of the lazy swimmers, a pair of new arrivals caught his attention. About a meter long, they had slim bodies that flattened to sharp edges at both sides, as if their bodies had been squeezed from opposite directions. In color they were silvery, with black stripes running the length of their flattened forms. Triple lifting sacs ran from just behind the integrated head down to the broad, flattened terminus. Large eyes with prominent golden pupils were set securely in hard-shelled foreheads that tapered to narrow, pointed snouts. From the snouts, tongues a third the length of the entire creature flicked repeatedly in and out, reminding him of similar oral appendages in hummingbirds. Hummingbirds—something else remembered, he realized with a jolt of satisfaction.

But the tongues of these new arrivals were not designed for delicately sipping flower nectar. The last several centimeters of each appendage was tipped with lethal-looking, backward-facing barbs.

By venting air from the lifting bladder on either side,

the creatures were able to move fairly quickly back and forth. Anterior nozzles pushed them forward. As they hovered, they scanned the water below. He blinked. He *had* to try to eat something, and soon.

An explosive puff of air interrupted his reverie. Venting the contents of all three longitudinal lifting bladders simultaneously, the slightly smaller of the two tongue-masters plunged nose-downward into the water. Its companion followed within seconds. Leaning forward and peering into the depths of the crystal-clear pool, he saw them combine to attack a school of slow-drifting, dual-finned, bluish-purple spheres. Though the spheres scattered rapidly, they were unable to avoid the attack from above. The shape of the lancet-like diving carnivore was as hydrodynamic as it was aerodynamic.

Helpless victims squirming on the end of barbed tongues, the two divers made a leisurely ascent to the surface. There they floated while drawing their still-living prey into their gaping, narrow jaws. As an increasingly shaky Flinx watched, they slowly reinflated their lifting bladders.

Three more of the lithe, lethal flesh-eaters arrived, dropping down over the rim of the chasm. Like nearly every other aerial animal he had encountered on Jast, having no wings to beat they made no sound as they descended. He expected them to repeat the predatory dives of their predecessors. They did not.

Instead, venting air from their propulsive nozzles, they drifted curiously in his direction.

He was having difficulty sitting. Drained of fuel and pushed to their limit, his muscles struggled to hold him in an upright position. It would be so easy, so simple, his addled mind insisted, for him simply to lie down. Have a good rest, and then try again to find some food. Dimly, he saw Pip interpose herself between his prone form and the barb-tongued fliers. But she was weak and tired, too. She could not stay airborne forever. At her intervention the fliers backed off. But they did not leave. Two more joined the first five, then another quartet.

He felt something sharp probe the bare skin of his right leg, where he had torn his pants during the plunge into Saudaunn Chasm. Glancing back and down, he saw a barbed tongue ripping away a small piece of flesh. Pip was there in an instant, but she did not have the strength to spit. As the audacious flier retracted the barbed appendage back into its mouth and backed off, others began to close in from the opposite side. Flying protective circles around her inert master, Pip held them back. She could not do so forever.

Rest, his mind told him. What was a little meat between visitor and locals? He contemplated crawling into the water to escape. But that wouldn't protect him from these carnivores, who were as adept at spearing prey underwater as they were above. No, rest and sleep were the simplest options. They would allow him to ignore the new pain in the back of his thigh as well as the two new ones that were beginning to trouble his back.

Faintly, he heard a voice. It was not human. That was hardly surprising, since he was in all likelihood the only human on Jast. He did not think of it as an exception, however, any more than he particularly thought of himself as human. He was just himself. And, anyway, the important thing was that he could understand the speaking.

It was very sibilant.

There was more than one voice. They began to shout. Large shapes moved to and fro around him, dimly perceived. The multiple pains went away. He felt strong hands lifting him, turning him over. A slight weight landed on his chest. The flying snake chose not to intervene with the newcomers who were handling her master.

Or perhaps, exhausted, she could not. He struggled to focus on the face that was peering down at him. For a brief moment, lucidity returned and he could see clearly. The face was bright of eye, shiny of scale, and sharp of tooth.

"It livess," the voice that belonged to the face murmured in surprise. "I think it iss a human."

What's a human? he wondered. Then he passed out.

Voices, echoing. Warmth against his back. Something caressing his chin. Nothing known.

Try opening your eyes, idiot. Idiot. He knew what that was. He tried. Light replaced darkness.

Alert, vertical pupils stared back out of a scaled, iridescent green face. Hissing with delight at the sight of her master once more revived, Pip took to the air and spun circles around the ceiling. It was an interesting ceiling, he decided. Lying flat on his back, he had an excellent view of it.

It was fulsomely decorated with hovering clouds of cotton candy. Predominantly pink and rouge, pale carmine and umber highlighted with gold and yellow, the intricate sworls and sweeps of gossamer material hung from the ceiling as if spun by a million tiny spiders giddy with delusions of grandeur. Seemingly weightless, the ethereal puffs of pastel-hued lightweight material formed clouds and star maps populated by all manner of imaginary creatures sprung full-blown from fevered imagination.

Except they were not imaginary. The spun-glass artwork dazzling his newly roused consciousness replicated real animals and plants. That he first thought them mythological was not his fault. They dwelled on worlds neither he nor his kind had ever visited. And the imaginations, as well as the skills, that had reproduced them on the ceiling of the chamber in which he lay recuperating were anything but fevered. By nature and by choice, their creators were in fact calm, considered, and contemplative. Their contemporaries also thought them mad, but he knew nothing of that particular sociological divergence yet.

He managed to sit up. He was in a large, circular room with a gently domed ceiling to which the wonderful art-work clung. The walls were composed of some trans-parent brickwork that enabled him to see the Jastian landscape beyond. There were a lot of plants outside, too politely spaced to be anything other than gardened. Be-neath him and supporting him was perfectly clean, brushed flat, sterilized sand, the fine particles heated from beneath to a temperature that bordered on blistering. Their sub-ject matter alien, a couple of slender sculptures rendered in what might have been black marble, or black metal, thrust upward from the sand. Rising, he started to brush it from his pants—only to discover that his pants, and his shirt, had been replaced by a loose white robe that had been embellished with swirling patterns of tinted ferric oxide. He did not recognize the patterns. Nor did he have to brush sand from the garment when he stood. It had been treated and shed any clinging sand like water. Twist-ing to peer behind and down at himself, he did wonder why the rear of the robe featured a slit running from waist to hem.

Its purpose became self-evident when a lean, scaled fig-ure dressed in a similar though more intricately scribed robe entered through one of the chamber's two doors. A similarly tailored and hemmed slit in the rear of the new-comer's garment allowed a svelte, whip-like tail to emerge and move freely. Intricate inlays of silver and gold thread were embedded in the scales of its head, beautifying it on top and sides.

"Ssst-ssta, you are awake. Good."

His visitor was an AAnn, he knew with a sudden start.

There was no telling, no predicting, when a fragment of his fractured memory would unexpectedly fall into place. One more piece of knowledge to dump back into the still largely empty hopper of his mind.

The visitor briefly turned her head sideways in a reflexive gesture of greeting before meeting his gaze. "You were seriously dehydrated, even for a human who iss esspecially ssensitive to ssuch thingss. The organss that commprisse your digestive ssysstem were empty. Though we of the Tier of Ssaiinn know very little about humanss, it wass not difficult to ressearch ssuch detailss. As a conssequence, and after much consideration of the necessary nutrientss, you have been provided with intravenouss nourisshment." The scaly, stiff face and snout could not manage a smile, but he effortlessly perceived the reptiloid's attitude. It was full of compassion and concern. Something about that did not seem right, but he lacked both the inclination and the memory to examine it further.

"Thank you," he murmured through still-dry lips. "For saving me."

"*Chisst ssalee na*," his visitor responded. "We could do no less, even for a human. Unlike the Ssaiinn, there are many otherss who would have left you for the prekalez to feed on. You were fortunate to be found by memberss of the Tier." She looked him up and down. "Your height required the making of a cusstom garment. I hope you find it ssuitable. We have ssaved the attire in which you were found, but I fear it iss in a deplorable condition."

Cool and durable, the robe rested in caressing folds against his body. They had washed and cleaned *him*, too, he noted. *That* must have provided food for comment among those who carried out the sanitizing.

"It's fine," he told her, feeling a fold of the material. Spiraling down from the ceiling, Pip settled familiarly on his shoulders. "I'm very comfortable."

"With many thingss, it would appear. In the dayss of delirium while you lay recuperating here in the north contemplation room, you sshouted out your unconscious disstress in tonguess we variouslly identified as terranglo, ssymbossspeech, and sseveral unknown languagess as well as our own. Whoever you are, it iss evident that you are well educated."

Approaching him, she reached swiftly toward his neck. Noting that her claws remained sheathed, he held his ground while she grabbed his throat. Almost automatically, he clutched at hers.

Now where did I learn how to do that? he found himself wondering.

"I am Chraluuc," she told him. "It hass been given over to me to watch over you."

Or just watch me? he mused. "I am Flinx," he told her without thinking. "You flourish no subjunctives?" He seemed to know a great deal about these creatures, he reflected.

She dipped her head slightly. "We of the Tier do not desscribe our sstatuss or family possitioning by meanss of ssuch antiquated frivolitiess. We believe that there are better wayss of judging an individual." Her attentive, reptilian gaze rose again to meet his. " 'Flinx' will work very well among uss. Unlike many human namingss, it iss not difficult to pronounce." From the depths of her robe she withdrew a small, tapered flask. Like the ceiling and his robe, it too was lavishly decorated with embroidered swirls and ornamenting motifs.

Taking the flask, he sniffed of it hesitantly. His caution was misplaced, he decided promptly. If these people had meant to do him ill, they could simply have left him where he had passed out next to the creek that had been rife with expectant predators. The bouquet emanating from the bottle was piquant and inviting. Raising it to his lips, he started to sip.

Hissing the AAnn version of laughter, Chraluc rushed to grab his wrist. "No, no. Tuyy iss not for drinking." Stepping back, she mimicked turning the bottle sideways against herself and urged him to do likewise. Imitating her example, he inhaled the resultant fragrance as a few drops of the liquid emerged from the stylish container to spread against his skin. Clearly, while he knew a great deal about his saviors, there was much he didn't know.

He had nearly taken a hearty swallow from a perfume applicator.

He had the grace not to ask whether it was being offered as a gift or a perceived necessity. With his mammalian odor suitably masked by the bottle's contents, she led him through the rear doorway and out of the glass-walled chamber.

They emerged into an open courtyard flush with local flora and fauna. In a trio of cages, what appeared to be long, colored tubes rose and fell according to the amount of air contained in their lifting sacs. Peering closer, he was able to make out tiny eyes. What at first glance looked like paper-thin, membranous wings were in fact ears. As they passed the gauzy cages, the delicate captives within began to sing. Their dulcet trills lingered in his ears as he followed close on the heels of his long-striding guide.

Grouped around the central courtyard were several clusters of whitewashed buildings. None rose higher than two stories above the surrounding desert terrain. Occasionally they would encounter other AAnn similarly clad in free-flowing robes such as the one he now wore. While their expressions as they glanced in his direction were usually neutral, their emotions often were not. Reaching out with his talent, he sensed curiosity, anger, hunger, contempt, repressed fury, and a host of other sentiments directed his way. The overriding feeling he received was one of guarded curiosity.

That was hardly surprising, he thought. No one was less curious about himself than he.

While his own background remained a dark, shadowy, shifting place lost in the deep recesses of his mind, more and more data about his reptiloid hosts came rushing unbidden to the fore. These were enemies, he felt. Yet their reactions to him were confusing. Instead of leaving him to die, they had rescued him. Instead of subjecting him to starvation, he had been given nourishment, fluids, and even freshening scent. In place of harsh interrogation he had been offered a kind of formal welcome not unlike what would have been offered to any visitor of their own kind.

Plainly, these were not the AAnn of his reviving memories. If not that, then what were they?

He tried to draw some conclusions not only from how he had thus far been treated, but from his surroundings. These were AAnn: he knew there should be weapons in evidence, if only as a sign of tradition. Yet he saw nothing of the kind. Chraluuc certainly was not armed, and unless their artfully adorned robes masked concealed arsenals, neither were any of the nye she and he encountered as they crossed the courtyard. He saw not so much as a ceremonial knife.

It could be his devastated memory playing tricks, he knew. Perhaps the AAnn were not, after all, the hostile weapons carriers he seemed to be recalling. But no matter how hard he tried to rationalize it away, that much of what he was remembering struck him as conclusive and irrefutable. It was puzzling. No less puzzling than their treatment of him.

Were there different kinds of AAnn? From what he

could recall, knowledge of them was fairly extensive but by no means absolute. They were aggressive competitors for power and influence everywhere throughout the Orion Arm. They hated the thranx, disliked humans, and held many other sentient species in casual contempt—none of which fit with how he was being treated.

Unless it was all a ploy of some kind, he decided. But to what end? To get information from him? If that was their ultimate aim, they were going to be gravely disappointed. It was hard to imagine any enterprise more futile than trying to pump an amnesiac for information. Meanwhile, he would observe and learn, and try to remember more and more while building up his strength.

"The Ssemilionn has been made aware that you are awake and well, and that your knowledge of a proper language iss ssatisssfactory." Chraluuc directed him to a doorway. He had to duck slightly to clear the lintel. Even it was decorated, garlanded with floating simulacra of Jastian flowers and plants.

As she entered, she moved quickly to stand to one side and with her back to him: standard AAnn posturing to show that she remained personally vulnerable and therefore intended him no harm. He found himself in another room. This one had opaque walls but large windows. The far wall was sharply curved and offered a fine view through a single, sweeping, gold-tinted transparency of the boulder-strewn ridge beyond. He squinted. The boulders, some of them quite large, appeared to have been deliberately repositioned according to a planned but unnatural schematic. The room's domed ceiling was dominated by a similarly golden-hued translucency.

The floor of the front half of the room where he was standing was tiled. The other half that backed up against the curving window was paved with smooth sand, ocher daubed with yellow in swirling patterns. Seated on high, backless cushions on this half were three elderly AAnn: two males and one female. With the exception of one male, time had robbed their scales of youthful luster. The younger one peered back at him out of artificial eyes. The female sported a tail that was half prosthetic, as if the original had been damaged in a fight or lost in an accident.

Their naked emotions washed over him. In large part it was the same mix he had encountered while crossing the courtyard, but tempered. The antagonism was not as sharp, the curiosity more pronounced.

Introductions were made. He filed the names for future reference and was pleased that he could recall them. His memory facilities were not permanently damaged, then. Only drained.

"You are a human," the older male Naalakot declared. Flinx saw no especial reason to dispute this, having more or less reached the same conclusion himself. "What iss a human doing out here, alone, on the unpopulated reaches of the Ssmuldaar Plateau?"

"It's not unpopulated," Flinx countered immediately. "You're here."

Hisses of amusement emerged from the mouths of the Elder's companions while Chraluuc discreetly clamped her snout shut with one hand. Unoffended, Naalakot responded with a gesture of polite concession as his synthetic eyes focused more closely on the visitor.

"Your point iss granted, but fails to enlighten. What happened to you? Ceerani the physician reported that when found you were near death."

"I was—I am . . . ," Flinx struggled to remember. "I was just looking around."

" 'Jusst looking around,' " repeated the elderly female Xeerelu. "That iss not ussually a fatal passion. Nor doess it explain what happened to you, and why you were found in such a dire sstate."

"I was . . ." On his shoulders, Pip peered anxiously at her master as he fought with himself. "I—I don't know what happened to me. I don't *remember*. All I recall is passing out and then waking up to see"—he indicated the patiently watching Chraluuc—"her coming toward me."

The triumvirate of the Ssemilionn exchanged gestures of agreement. "Sso you inssisst you were 'jusst looking around.' How doess that relate to you individually? Where are you come from? What iss it that you do when you are not 'looking around'?"

They were interested, he felt, not only out of natural AAnn caution, but because they were genuinely curious about him as a person. If he was interpreting their emotions correctly, that was reassuring. He hoped his response, the only response he could give, would not change that.

"I don't know. I don't know much of anything. Little things keep coming back to me, unexpected and unasked-for bits of information. But very little about myself. I don't"—he was surprised to find that his eyes were filling with moisture—"I don't remember who I am, much less where I come from or how I ended up the way you found me, where you found me."

"Interessting." The second male, Viinpou, gestured with a claw. "Obsserve the creature'ss generation of ssoothing eye fluid in ressponsse to the obviouss emotional disstress it iss pressently feeling."

Xeerelu chastened him with a sharp gesture Flinx did not recognize. "Be less analytical, Viinpou. The ssoftsskin iss plainly ssuffering."

"Memory loss," hissed the male softly. "That iss not helpful."

"Believe me," Flinx told him as he wiped angrily at his

moist eyes, "nobody wishes the situation was otherwise more than I do." Reaching up with one hand, he absently stroked Pip behind her head.

Naalakot had continued to watch him closely. Now the senior AAnn pressed his fingertips against one another, claws extended so that the points met. It was an AAnn gesture, Flinx knew, that could mean many different things.

"The quesstion before uss, ssoftsskin, iss not even sso much who you are, where you have come from, or what the nature of your true purposse in being in thiss place iss—but what are we of the Tier to do with you?"

Standing before them in golden-hued surroundings that bordered on the serene but nonetheless remained fraught with uncertainty, an uneasy Flinx felt he could share their concern. After all, he was not at all sure what to do with him, either.

7

There were six individuals in the elite strike force that was evenly divided between AAnn and Vssey. They turned quietly and with caution into the dark backstreet. Though shadowed by the high mounded structures it cut through, it was wide enough to allow access to small vehicles and personal transporters. While their Vsseyan counterparts made use of the latter, the AAnn members of the strike force disdained them. The more machinery one employed, the bigger the target it made and the more it reduced a soldier's maneuverability. So while the Vsseyan police formed a short column of transporters down the center of the secondary avenue, the heavily armed AAnn clung to the fronts of shops and apartment structures, keeping to the shadows and to whatever cover was available while advancing in fits and starts.

With their eyes mounted on stalks, the Vsseyan officers were able to look in almost every direction at once. This allowed them to sustain their stately progression down the middle of the street in comparative confidence. Meanwhile, the AAnn went from shop front to alcove, covering one another with long weapons clutched securely in clawed hands. While the Vssey were far from technologically illiterate, it was the AAnn who brought with them the latest in military search-and-discover gear. Among other things, each soldier was equipped with instrumentation that could detect and identify, at a distance, the great majority of potentially explosive compounds. It would also warn them in advance of the presence in their vicinity of advanced weaponry.

It was a bit of technoverkill, but after Morotuuver, the always suspicious, ever-vigilant AAnn were in no mood to take chances. One bomb, one unpleasant incident, was enough. With the concurrence of the Vsseyan government, the hitherto unsuspected violent opposition to their kindly presence on Jast was to be snuffed out forthwith.

The soldiers relaxed only slightly when, after their equipment detected the presence of potentially volatile compounds, they smashed their way into a closed shop with opaqued windows only to find themselves in the midst of a group of startled Vssey who were busily engaged in trying out new combinations of body stain to be used in personal adornment. It took the three accompanying Vsseyan police a good part of the morning to calm the consequent panic.

Miffed, the patrolling officers and soldiers resumed their rounds only slightly chastened. Better, the subofficer in charge of the three AAnn felt, to inconvenience a thousand of the miserable lumpish locals than for one more innocent AAnn to suffer so much as a broken tail-tip at the hands (or rather, tentacles) of the as-yet-unidentified dissenting faction. Peering over the ridge of his neuronic rifle, he longed for one of the nameless ones to make itself known so that he could personally put a charge into its trunk-like body and watch while it slowly asphyxiated, its neural system paralyzed, its organs fibrillating uncontrollably.

Even with the Vsseyan police making use of their silent individual transports, the patrol was progressing at a speed that for an AAnn bordered on the terminal. Time and again the subofficer had to hiss a loud command to one of his two subordinates to slow down, back off, and wait for the others. Sympathizing with their impatience to get on with it, he did not admonish them. He felt exactly the same.

Gurra, who was striding point, abruptly paused and beckoned for his companions to hurry and join him. The subofficer gratefully lengthened his stride while the trio of Vssey used tentacle tips to nudge the accelerators of their transports. Ever wary, the other members of the patrol coalesced around the trooper.

"Ssee here, honored ssubofficer." Gurra was pointing to a spot on an old stone foundation that supported a more modern structure.

Subofficer Jyiivad and the others looked down. There was no question but that several of the large underpinning stones had recently been moved. Perhaps, Jyiivad thought, moved and replaced. His own gear was confirming what had initially attracted Gurra.

There were dangerous composites behind the stones. Not volatile chemical compounds such as they had encountered earlier at the unlucky group ornamentation session, but seriously explosive materials, concentrated and ready to be detonated. He turned to Nuwaabaw, the senior of the three Vssey.

"What building iss thiss, only whosse back we can ssee from here?"

The Vssey consulted his own instrumentation. The hearing frill that encircled his upper body rippled with realization. "We are directly behin' the Aulauwohly City Offices for offworl' Export Control!" Almost reflexively, he began to back his transporter away from the unmistakably shifted stones.

Such a department would have AAnn on its staff and work closely with those portions of the Vsseyan government and public that favored increased contact with the

Empire, Jyiivad realized. An obvious target. As such, in the wake of the Morotuuver incident, it would have extra security stationed inside and out front—additional targets. There would be commendations for the discovery Gurra had just made.

Now it was decision time. Should he broadcast a recommendation to evacuate the building—or try to remove the explosive material? Further probing by his sensors suggested that the concealed explosive materials were presently stable. They would have to be, he knew, if whoever had planted them anticipated having to leave them in place for a while. Since they had not yet gone off, that was manifestly the case. It was a plan that was about to be foiled.

The first step was to utilize one of the many bits of specialized gear they carried with them. While the Vssey backed off slightly and stood guard, the suboffer and his companions proceeded to carefully shift the concealing stones to expose the package of explosives. Once this was revealed, they then carefully scanned from a safe distance the area surrounding the sizable package. Readouts continued to indicate that the material, while potentially powerful, was presently inert. Scans showed the presence of nothing resembling a detonator; not even a receiver that could be used to apply a remote signal. Only then did Suboffer Jyiivad direct his subordinates to move in and remove the half-dozen individual packages from their hiding place.

He studied the recovered material with interest. It was of Vsseyan manufacture, cobbled together from chemicals that could be obtained from any one of numerous sources. Ultimately effective, certainly, but also decidedly unsophisticated. He had expected nothing else. After all, the malcontents they were dealing with were only Vssey. That he and his team had located and removed the material before it could be primed for detonation was as much a matter of good luck as skill. That would not matter to the commission headed by the laudable Takuuna VBXLLW, who would be most pleased by the squad's accomplishment and would cite them accordingly.

As he was slipping one package of explosives into a neatly labeled forensics pouch, he noticed Trooper Isooket leaning back to stare skyward, up between the buildings that enclosed the street on both sides. The suboficer prepared to ask the trooper what he was looking at, but he did not have enough time.

Pursed by a single tashwesh, the flock of bourebeil spilled between buildings and into the street below, venting air from their lifting bladders as rapidly as they dared. There were thirty of them, perhaps more. Their bulbous, blue-and-red-speckled bodies resembled pop-eyed balloons that had broken free from some psychedelic party. Each sported a pair of equally florid lifting sacs from their rounded backs.

The tashwesh was an intimidating predator. A glossy blue-black, with double pairs of gliding wings, it harassed the rear of the flock, its four piercing spines protruding from above and below the tooth-lined, circular mouth. Instead of attacking, it almost appeared to be herding the panicky bourebeil into the street. From the ribbed platform of his individual police transport, a companion remarked that the tashwesh might be going for a multiple kill. By forcing the flock into a limited space, it greatly increased its opportunities to do so.

As he swatted away a descending bourebeil, Jyiivad was only irritated by the distraction. Every sensor in the patrol identified both multiple bourebeil and singular tashwesh as wholly organic. None detected so much as a molecular-level transmitter, far less anything more suspicious. The incident was a perfectly natural, if distracting, occurrence.

Hemmed in by buildings on either side, pavement below, and the marauding tashwesh overhead, the swirling, densely packed flock of bourebeil set up a desperate mass keening. Jyivad and his subordinates found themselves wincing. The high-pitched, piercing wail scraped at his ears. One of the Vsseyan police assured him it would end as soon as the unusually patient tashwesh selected its prey from the massed flock and struck. Jyivad would have been interested to know that he was hearing only a small portion, the AAnn-audible portion, of the massed boure-beil wailing. Much of the noise the flock was generating consisted of subsonic vibrations too low for him and his companions to hear.

These vibrations happened to affect the explosive material the patrol had just recovered only because said material had been modified specifically to react to them.

From a safe, innocent distance, Qyl-Elussab watched the smoke rise from the ruins of the collapsed, hollowed-out building that had formerly housed the Aulauwohly City Offices for Export Control. The damage had been even greater than one could reasonably have expected. The unavoidable loss of the tashwesh that had for over a year been lovingly trained to herd and panic bourebeil was to be regretted, but could not have been avoided. A winged, if unknowing martyr to the cause of Jastian independence from Imperial AAnn interference, Qyl-Elussab felt.

The specifics of the destruction could be learned later, by skimming the media. Pivoting, Qyl-Elussab hopped down the pedestrian passage of the main avenue, moving against the flow of stunned, curious onlookers who were hurriedly hopping in the opposite direction, toward the rising column of smoke. The yowl of municipal rescue units could be heard approaching from above. They might be in time to save some of those traitors who had worked in the export agency to further dilute the purity of the Vssey. They would be fortunate to find even fragments of the patrol whose progress Qyl-Elussab had spent the morning tracking from a distance.

Their transporters inclining slightly forward because of the unaccustomed speed at which they were traveling, a police patrol was coming straight down the avenue. Qyl-Elussab studiously ignored their approach. One by one, they whizzed past. Their tentacles writhing in agitation, none of the police turned so much as a wandering eye-stalk in the lone Vssey's direction.

Public transport conveyed the contented insurgent to the far side of the city. From its next-to-last stop, it was a modest hop to the simple, subsurface living chamber where productive days were spent crafting the next assault on the reprehensible AAnn interlopers. It was a dark, dank place, unlike the well-lit homes and workplaces of many of Qyl-Elussab's former friends. Former, because they either consented to the AAnn presence on Jast, or remained assiduously neutral. In the matter of alien ascendancy there was no neutrality, Qyl-Elussab felt. This was known with the surety that had become the lone Vsseyan renegade's motivation in all things.

Fortunately, the vital work would soon have allies. Takuuna and his fellow AAnn would have been stunned to learn that thus far, Qyl-Elussab had planned and carried out the attacks in both Morotuuver and Aulauwohly with the help of nothing more than the insistent multiple voices that induced constant headaches within that meter-wide, dome-shaped upper body/head. Painful voices that had plagued Qyl-Elussab for years now, until the cerebral pounding had driven the former officer to finally take action against the only cause remaining when all other possibilities had been discarded: the pushy, increasingly obtrusive AAnn.

The furtive, unnamed organization of cunning insurgents that had succeeded in unsettling both the AAnn Imperial Authority as well as the Jastian planetary government had an aggregate roster of one.

That would change soon, Qyl-Elussab knew as he stroked the concealed switch that allowed access to the sub-basement. Dozens of others were already on the way to join with their spiritual and moral leader. Allies who would not question what was being done would offer no objection to the violence that was being planned. Followers who would act and not question.

In response to the pressure of several tentacles, light came on in the sub-basement. Hopping slowly down the ramp, Qyl-Elussab approached his budding associates. They were budding in every sense of the word: all seven of them. Germinated from Qyl-Elussab's own body, in a few months the maturing sprouts would develop into adolescents capable of taking their first independent hops. Already, their eyes had emerged from their upper bodies, and short but rapidly lengthening tentacles probed inquisitively at their silent surroundings. The parent smiled fondly on these developing offspring.

What had been done in budding them was highly illegal. To reproduce, one first had to apply to the local branch of the Ministry for Procreation. Uncontrolled reproduction could not be allowed because it would lead to feuding, war, and eventually, serious overpopulation. From time immemorial there had always been food pressures on the species. War, disease, and famine had kept the Vsseyan population in check until the development of civilization and its benefits. That was when social controls had been put in place to replace the natural ones that had been superseded by technology.

In order to reproduce legally, a Vssey first had to find two friends or relations to form the traditional circle of single support. All would cooperate in the raising of the single young, to the latter's benefit. Although still physiologically possible, multiple budding was strictly outlawed. As for individual parenting, that was a relic of ancient times, a sign of barbarism. Qyl-Elussab, however, was not one to be intimidated by something as impersonal as social convention or Jastian history. Having done what had already been done, the possibility of being branded with a social stigma was hardly a concern. Nor were there any others who could be trusted to keep silent about the sole defender of Jastian integrity's murderous activities. As a proud and expectant Qyl-Elussab bent toward the swiftly maturing young, his eyes roving fondly over their rapidly spreading domes, the now ever-present voices that echoed through the dissenter's head voiced their approval.

In every sense of the word, planning for the future allies of the illustrious insurgency had been carefully conceived.

The unexpected news from Aulauwohly City left Takuuna much conflicted. On the one claw, he had been looking forward to some time to ease into his new position: rounding up suspects (easy to do with the slow-moving Vssey), questioning, striding importantly through the offices of AAnn officials across the planet. With the attacks on the base compound outside Morotuuver and the export offices in Aulauwohly, he now had a real insurgency to deal with instead of an imaginary one. With the latter, he would have been able to take his time, relax, and enjoy the perks and approbation that came with his new status. Ordered to root out those behind a real uprising, he would be expected to produce results. And swiftly, before any more nye perished.

Working with the Vsseyan authorities only increased

his frustration. It was impossible to obtain rapid decisions or move anywhere nearly fast enough. Every request for assistance, information, personnel had to wend its sorry way through the typical Vsseyan bureaucracy. That meant no less than three officials had to give their approval to anything that came their way. It was a system of mass consensus that had worked very well for the modern Vssey, resulting in a generally peaceful and civilized society. Not that it was devoid of malcontents. They just generally chose to express their disapproval with petitions and debate, not with bombs. That was not the Vsseyan way.

Obviously, certain unknown elements had arisen that disagreed with that tradition.

But who were they? Where were they? The sophistication of the two attacks suggested a large, well-organized group of malcontents. It ought not to be too difficult to track them down. Yet all the efforts of his newly formed unit had thus far turned up nothing. The excuse that everyone was still learning their job would carry no weight with his superiors. They wanted results, and fast. They wanted identified individuals they could execute. Takuuna knew that if he failed to find some of them within a tightly proscribed period of time, he would be replaced. And, most likely, demoted.

Such worries and anxiety dogged him as he lashed out with his tail, striking at Geelin's flanks. Leaping and spinning sideways, she avoided the blow, landed, and lashed out with her right foot. Claws retracted, the hit still stung as it caught him across his bare chest. The scales there took a scraping but did not bruise or bleed, as would have been the case had she so struck a softskin.

Staggering backwards as she followed the tail swipe with a charge, he tried to recover by balancing adroitly on his tail and kicking out with both feet. Anticipating the traditional defensive maneuver, she slid beneath the double kick, her body slamming into his tail and bringing him down almost on top of her. Then she was behind him, hissing into his left ear, her teeth clamped on the back of his neck, arms and legs locked around his. He struggled halfheartedly in the robust grip.

"You are disstracted today, companionye. Ssince your heart iss not in thiss mating, I pressume nothing elsse iss, either!" Wrapped around him, the tip of her tail wagged back and forth in front of his face. She was taunting him. In concert with the mild insult, it was clear she was doing her best to stimulate him to action.

He did his best, bracing himself against her while snapping his body up and over. It broke her hold, but sloppily. They both ended up kicking and tail-thrashing on the sand. Grit flew. While this enhanced the mood, it was still inadequate to draw him out of his preoccupied funk.

She finally slid out of reach, staring at him across the sand and breathing hard. "If you will not sshare mating with me, try wordss. I am fond of you, Takuuna-nay, but not to the point of coddling. Thiss moodiness iss not like you."

Rolling over, he settled into a reluctant defensive position. "It iss my tassking. It troubless me like itching under my sscaless."

"We are all troubled by our tasskingss, Takuuna-nay." She added a second-degree gesture of sympathy.

"I am charged," he told her, "with uncovering the Vsseyan perpetratorss of the recent atrocitiess againsst our people here. Though I work hard and drive thosse under me relentlessly, we have found nothing."

"Patience rewardss the perceptive," she responded as she edged toward him across the sand. He was wary of another assault, but she was genuinely trying to show empathy.

"The Administisstration will not hear of it. They want ressults, not aphorissms, no matter how true the lineage."

Geelin's tail lashed out at him, but not so swiftly that he failed to detect the movement and duck. Morose but alert for such moves, he rolled across the arena away from her. "Then arresst your ssusspectss," she hissed tightly as she rose into a striking crouch.

"What ssusspectss?" he lamented. "I told you: we have found nothing to implicate sso much as a damned ssprout among the nativess."

"If you need ssusspectss, and do not have any ssusspectss, then you will have to invent ssome ssusspectss," she suggested slyly.

"Invent . . . ?" Double eyelids blinked.

"Why not?" She moved toward him, and he edged to his right to keep out of her reach. "Do you have any sspecial love for the sslugss who are our hosstss?"

"No, it iss not that."

"Well, then." Rising to her full height, she assumed a tense, muscular stance, challenging him yet again. "There musst at leasst be ssome you predominantly disslike. Ssurely there are ssome Vssey who are vissible in their dissent? Who have expressed disspleasure with our pressence here?"

"Many," he admitted as, reinvigorated by her suggestion, he launched himself beneath her, reached up, grabbed her tail with both hands, and twisted hard. She was slammed against the ground. In an instant he was behind her. "Truly, ssuccess hatchess from the egg of invention." He bestrode her furiously. She clawed up and back, but was unable to do anything more than scrape his ribs. Her continued efforts only served to inspire him further.

What she was suggesting without realizing it, he understood as he rode her, was that he employ the same stratagem he had used in explaining the death of the softskin. If he could not yet identify the actual source of the organized opposition to the Imperial presence on Jast, Takuuna did not doubt that he could invent one. There were a number of nonviolent, legal philosophical Vsseyan groups who were quite vocal in their dislike of the AAnn visitors. These could be questioned, their motives impugned, their actions scrutinized. Eventually, under "appropriate" questioning, a few of them might crack. After all, there was nothing imaginary about the devastating bombings that had taken place. Why, one of them might even have a line on the identity of the actual saboteurs. He was surprised he had not thought of it himself.

That the female fighting beneath him had was not only a tribute to her shrewdness but also to her palpable ongoing interest in him. He was already fond of Geelin CCRQPLL. It was apparent that her physical talents were matched by a commendable cunning. As they continued their traditional struggle, he found himself grateful.

When this was over, he decided, when he had uprooted and destroyed the Vsseyan radicals, he would make a ceremonial offer to formalize their mating. He hoped she would respond with suitable ritual vehemence. Of all the females he had had occasion to skirmish and mate with during his sojourn on Jast, Geelin was clearly superior to the rest, while overtly sympathetic to him personally and professionally as well.

That did not mean, of course, that he trusted her for one moment.

8

Lwo-Dvuum was completely at a loss. So upset was the prisoner that the tips of the tentacles that lined the protruding, disc-like upper third of the educator's body had withdrawn in upon themselves. The flexible eyestalks were also partly retracted. But the teacher's aural frill remained fully erect, intent on catching the slightest reference to ongoing events.

They had come for Lwo-Dvuum in the middle of the night, rousing the groggy educator from the quiet sleeping cabinet that stood between beloved stacks of antique literary texts and the more modern electronic readout that was used for daily tasking. There had been no need to restrain the prisoner. A Vssey subject to arrest could not hop from the law. All that was needed was to keep a detainee away from other means of transport.

Objections to the unwarranted intrusion poured forth as fast as the bewildered educator was able to compose them.

"What is the meaning of this?" Lwo-Dvuum demanded to know of his captors. "Where are you taking me? I warn you, I am a highly respecte' mentor. I will be lodging complaints against this incident at the highest levels!"

"Then you'll enjoy where we're taking you," one of the apprehending police informed the outraged captive.

Enclosing the detainee in the center of an official police

circle, they forced Lwo-Dvuum to hop outside the building in tandem with them, leading the educator out of the stylish residence for unbudding professionals and toward the waiting transport. Lwo-Dvuum noted with dismay that it was unmarked. Once inside, increasing altitude prevented any chance of escape as the humming police transport rose above the surrounding structures. A fall of more than thirty body lengths would kill even one of the physically resilient Vssey.

Expecting to be flown to a local police post, or at worst to the central restraining facility for the socially ambivalent, Lwo-Dvuum's unease only increased when the transport instead began to descend in the direction of the main AAnn administration center. Within that diplomatic compound, even a highly respected Vssey such as an educator would have little recourse to universal rights. There would be no circle of compassionate judges to confront and challenge over a prisoner's fate. There would be only the AAnn; they of the nimble feet, snappish temperament, and sharp claws.

Knowing that much, Lwo-Dvuum was prepared to make his peace with the Great Circle—if only someone would deign to inform the mystified prisoner as to what charges were being laid. The educator asked as much of the nearest armed officer.

"That's for our friends the AAnn to explain." The guard's tone was sufficiently brusque to cause the sensitive Lwo-Dvuum to flinch. What had an honest, hardworking mentor done to deserve such opprobrium? If the officer was correct, he would find out only from the authorized agents of Jast's scaly guests.

By the setting light, the prisoner thought apprehensively, at least one representative of the people should be present, if only for appearance's sake.

The transport touched down, and its passengers disembarked. The last thing Lwo-Dvuum expected to see as the escort ushered its bemused prisoner away from the landing area was a familiar figure. The educator called out.

The response was immediate. Though they were marched into the shadowed rear of the looming structure by separate, silent squads, they were close enough to converse.

Bno-Cassaul was clearly distraught to see a close friend and another member of their special circle caught in the same dispiriting circumstances. Prudently, the restrained programmer made no allusion to any of their absent companions. There was no sign, for example, of Mua-Briiv, Tvr-Vheequa, or any of the other members of the speculative group.

Of course, Lwo-Dvuum reflected somberly, that did not mean they were not already being held inside, or were on the verge of being disturbed in their sleep.

The presence of the two friends and their respective Vsseyan escorts drew hardly a glance from passing AAnn. When they did, it was invariably one of scarcely concealed contempt. Lwo-Dvuum reflected that the members of the circle were more attuned to this general derision than the majority of their kind. Though continually expanding their presence and their interests on Jast, it was plain to anyone who took the time to still their tentacles and look that the AAnn cared next to nothing for the Vssey themselves. That was one of the central points of the circle's main thesis that they hoped to convey to the mass of Vssey. Now it looked like they might not ever get the chance.

Be calm, Lwo-Dvuum mantraed. The reason for the nocturnal seizure remained unknown. When surrounded by fire, the wise Vssey stands its ground and does not hop off in panic. One could only hope that Bno-Cassaul shared the same wisdom.

Any similar Vsseyan institution would have been crisscrossed with moving walkways to speed travel. In the absence of such, both prisoners and escorts were required to engage in some extensive hopping. They did not tire—the Vssey were durable travelers—but it did take them a fair amount of time to reach their destination. Outside the doorway, the two prisoners were turned over to AAnn guards. Lwo-Dvuum's unease increased as the last of their fellow Vssey headed back the way they had come, hopping in unison back down the high-ceilinged corridor.

Their modest restraints were removed. As Lwo-Dvuum stretched his liberated footpads, one of the two AAnn guards hissed at them in a crude approximation of the local Vsseyan dialect. Unbound, the two mystified locals hopped forward as ordered.

They found themselves in a windowless chamber lit only by dimly luminescent walls. There was no décor, only a single table and two chairs. The furniture was designed to accommodate the builders of the complex. No chairs were provided for the prisoners, since the Vssey did not sit. Where standing straight for long periods of time was discomfiting to more flexible species such as the AAnn, the Vssey found the reverse to be true.

Inclining sideways, Bno-Cassaul whispered of anxiety made worse by the fact that there were not even enough of them present to form a comforting circle. At least three were needed, and there were only the two of them.

"Why are we here, my frien'? When the police picke' us up, I coul' envision several possibilities. None of them involve' the AAnn. What coul' they want of us?"

Lwo-Dvuum was under no illusions. "I don't think it is to partake of our respective expertise in teaching an' programming. Beyon' that, I cannot guess." Movement at the other side of the room drew his attention. "By my last tentacle, I believe we are about to fin' out."

A door silently appeared in the otherwise blank wall at

the back of the room. Two AAnn stepped through, whereupon the door shut tightly behind them. Not even glancing in the direction of the two detainees, they proceeded to occupy the two chairs behind the table. One removed a pair of small electronic instruments from a pouch slung at its waist. While the other waited patiently, these were activated. Both mute Vssey eyed the devices. Lwo-Dvuum decided they were not directly threatening. If their hosts intended to do them physical harm, some sort of restraints would surely have been put in place, with guards in attendance. The educator relaxed, but only a little. The AAnn might be bad-tempered, but they were a civilized species. To get what they wanted, surely they would not resort to something so inconceivably primitive as physical abuse.

Mental maltreatment—now *that* was something else.

The larger of the two toothy aliens spoke curtly, without any attempt at formality or greeting. His Vsseya, Lwo-Dvuum noted, was excellent, the mark of an experienced bureaucrat who had spent some time on Jast.

"*Fssadd*—you are the educator Lwo-Dvuum, and you the programmer composser Bno-Cassaul."

Since the identifying was not posed as a question, neither Vssey saw reason or need to respond.

Their silence constituted sufficient acquiescence for the AAnn. "I am Takuuna VBXLLW, head of a sspecial unit of Vissitor Ssecurity." He did not have to denote which visitors or whose security he was working for.

"What has that to do with us?" Bno-Cassaul pleaded his case with a fluttering of forward-facing appendages. If the AAnn recognized the meaning behind the gesturing, he did not respond.

"While it iss well known that not every ssection of your populace lookss favorably upon the Imperial pressence on Jasst, heretofore ssuch dissapproval hass taken the form of petitioning, argument within the general media, and occassional philosophical and ssatirical broadssides. It hass been brought to my attention that both of you have for ssome time participated in jusst such a circle of dissputation right here in Sskokossas."

"There iss nothing illegal about any of that which you allude to." By responding boldly, Bno-Cassaul hoped to put their inquisitors on the defensive. "We an' the other members of our discussion circle have done nothing wrong."

Distracted by something significant buried within the AAnn's accusation, Lwo-Dvuum hardly heard the programmer's response. "What di' you mean by 'heretofore'?" Alert, vertical pupils turned to eye the educator. "I think you know perfectly well what I meant."

It was Bno-Cassaul's turn to look curiously at the educator. Lwo-Dvuum paid no attention. "I do not. Nor does my frien'. Nor, I believe I can say with some confidence, woul' any other member of our circle. If you woul' consent to explain what you mean, perhaps we can she' some light on the situation."

Extending one arm, Takuuna dragged the point of a claw across the smooth tabletop. The subsequent subdued screeching induced brief but excruciating pain in the hearing receptors of the two Vssey. Perhaps it was intentional, perhaps not. Lwo-Dvuum did not care, as his aural frill snapped almost flat against his upper body in a futile attempt to shut out the piercing squeal. The timbre of it did not seem to affect the AAnn.

When the official finally lifted his finger from the hard surface, both Vssey were swaying weakly.

Takuuna affected ignorance. "Oh, I am sso sorry. Did you find that uncomfortable?" Still recovering from the excruciating aural assault, neither of the sensitive Vssey responded. The AAnn leaned slightly toward them. "Did it perhaps sserve to clarify your memory?"

Lwo-Dvuum swallowed air. "T-truly," the educator whispered, utilizing the favored AAnn preamble, "we have no idea what you are referring to, or what you could possibly want from us. That is why I sought clarification. I did not mean to offen'."

"We don't like you," a stiffening Bno-Cassaul declared forthrightly. The programmer ignored Lwo-Dvuum's frantic gestures and rambled on. "We don't like having you on our worl'. While doing business here and persisting with cultural exchanges, you seek to infiltrate an' undermine our institutions an' our culture. We will conduct formalities with you, but we will never be part of your Empire."

Exchanging a glance, inquisitor and recorder exchanged hissing laughter. Neither appeared to take offense at the challenge. "I sseek new information, not what hass been known for ssome time." Penetrating eyes met Bno-Cassaul's. "Fortunately, there are a great many Vssey who think and feel differently from you. There are thosse who quite like uss. There are even thosse who cannot wait for Jasst to be formally brought within the Empire. Ssuch ssentimentss are to be encouraged." He sat back in the chair, his tail switching methodically back and forth behind it.

"While we do not encourage dissenting opinion, we are perfectly willing to tolerate it. After all," Takuna added magnanimously, "ssuch open debatess are fully protected by your lawss."

For how much longer? a still-recovering Lwo-Dvuum could not keep from wondering.

"But, kssassk, when opinion turnss to violence, and to murder, then our outlook changess rather sseverely. Your government iss of the ssame mind."

Lwo-Dvuum was completely at a loss. At such a moment one wished for the flexibility to convey true inner feelings by flexing one's face. Since the Vssey did not possess faces of the commonly accepted kind, this means of expression was denied to them. All the two Vssey could do was ripple their dozens of short tentacles passionately.

"What violence? What murder? Our circle philosophizes and discusses, nothing more."

The recorder leaned sideways to whisper something in the AAnn tongue. Takuuna listened gravely, gesturing from time to time, while the mystified Vssey could only wait.

Finally, the administrator straightened in his chair. "It may be that you are telling the truth." As he spoke, one extended claw hovered above the tabletop, drawing lazy circles above the unyielding surface. Lwo-Dvuum and Bno-Cassaul tracked its movement with a kind of stolid, horrified fascination, as if watching an old-type fuse burn shorter and shorter. They would have sweated, had their systems been equipped for it.

"It may be that you are telling the truth," Takuuna observed quietly. "If not, then what I am about to ssay will already be known to you. It will not matter. The end will be the ssame.

"Sseveral of your time periodss ago, a violent explossion claimed the livess of many innocent nye at a military and sservices ssupport base located outsside the city of Morotuuver. A ssingle time period passt, a building in the city of Aulauwohly that houssed, among other agenciess, the one ressponsible for much of Imperial-Jasstian trade was desstroyed."

Bno-Cassaul's eyestalks retracted slightly. "I am familiar with both incidents. The first was cause' by a ba' electrical circuit flashing volatile materials kept in storage, the secon' by faulty maintenance of the building's climate control system."

Takuuna gestured knowingly. "After consultation with your government, thosse are the explanationss that were released to the media." The administrator's eyes glittered in the diffuse light. "The reality iss ssomewhat different."

Bno-Cassaul's tentacles rippled uncertainly. "What possible reason coul' justify prevarication in such a matter?"

The AAnn official was clearly controlling himself with an effort. "I think you both know very well, tssissk." It was immensely frustrating, Takuuna thought, to have to deal with sentients who had no expressions whatsoever and whose posture was virtually impossible to interpret. He would suck the truth out of them in spite of that. But whether they were still insufficiently intimidated or truly ignorant had yet to be determined. What he wanted to do was walk up to the more defiant of the pair and begin ripping its tentacles off, one by one. He restrained himself. Time enough later to engage in time-honored ritual.

For the sake of the official record that would be viewed by his superiors, among others, he proceeded to elucidate.

"It hass been determined, with only the sslightesst probability of erroneousness, that both incidentss were the ressult of deliberate hosstilitiess on the part of as yet unknown perpetratorss. You are both known to be active memberss of a circle that iss vociferoussly opposed to the Imperial pressence on Jasst. Do you wissh now to deny thiss?"

Lwo-Dvuum did not even glance in the direction of the silent AAnn operating the formal recording device. Much as the educator would have preferred to reply in the negative, there was not much point in denying what the AAnn obviously already knew.

"As my frien' has already state', we don't like you. To be fair, there are many Vssey who fin' your presence here not only acceptable but welcome. It happens that the members of our particular circle do not." A dozen tentacles gestured in unison in an attempt to encompass all of their immediate surroundings. "I fail to see how that justifies an arrest that borders on near abduction, or this style of questioning, or your attempts to intimidate us."

With difficulty, Takuuna continued to restrain himself. "Leaving aside for the moment the matter of the damage to relationss between your government and mine, the casualtiess among my kind from both incidentss total in the hundredss. Among my people, that justtifiess a reaction far sstronger than anything you have thuss far experienced, either individually or collectively. I ssuggesst that you take a moment to reflect on the fact that I and my kind have thuss far sshown considerable resstraint." It was the closest to an outright threat the administrator had issued since the uninformative pair of Vssey had been brought before him.

It did not appear to rattle the two detainees any more than they already were. Either they were dedicated fanatics, as Takuuna half hoped, or else they were secure in their ignorance.

"Furthermore," he continued when no response was forthcoming from the pair, "it iss ssusspected that the wider organization to which your circle iss believed to belong wass receiving advice and possibly material assisstance of an as yet unknown nature from a recently deceassed vissiting human sspy."

This last accusation was a wild shot in the dark. Ever suspicious, he had always wondered about the real reason behind the dead human's presence on Jast. By throwing it into the interrogation he might perhaps, like the prowling sand skimmer of Old, sink his claws into something as tasty as it was unexpected.

The allegation certainly took the prisoners aback, but not for the reason the watchful Takuuna hoped.

What, a now doubly bewildered Lwo-Dvuum wondered dazedly, was a human? Rotating one eye leftward, the perplexed educator saw that poor Bno-Cassaul was equally baffled. Straining his memory, he vaguely recalled an image and description of a tall bipedal creature not unlike the AAnn, only devoid of scales and with a pulpy physical texture completely alien to his own kind as well. In concert with another, more appropriately hard-skinned species called the thranx, these humans dominated the vast interstellar political entity known as the Commonwealth that was permanently at odds with the Empire of the AAnn.

He had never seen a human, of course. Only a very few had ever visited Jast, and he had never encountered one. There were only the few isolated mentions in the official media. And now this relentless AAnn official was claiming that he and Bno-Cassaul and the other members of their circle had not only had concourse with such a creature, but had actively engaged in antisocial activities with its aid. It would all have been hysterically amusing—under different circumstances. A glance was enough to show that the AAnn administrator was not laughing in the manner of his kind, or in any other manner. He was quite serious.

At such times, Lwo-Dvuum reflected, it must be interesting to be gender differentiated, if only to be able to view an identical situation through a different mental prism. Being essentially sexless, the Vssey could only ponder such possibilities from a purely philosophical point of view.

Irregardless of gender, the characteristically impatient AAnn was visibly awaiting a response.

"We know nothing of this human of whom you speak, or of any representative of its kind. To the best of my personal knowledge, neither I nor any member of our circle has ever encountere' such a creature. I am compelle' to re-iterate that the objections we have raise' to the Imperial presence on our worl' have taken the form of civil dis-course only." Tentacles fluttered in a steady, rippling mo-tion, creating a continuous cilia-like wave around the upper portion of the speaker's body. "I am an educator. Bno-Cassaul is a programmer. Even if we wishe' to carry out the kinds of actions to which you refer, neither we nor any of the members of our circle have the requisite tech-nical expertise to do so."

"Ssay you," Takuuna shot back. "Next I ssuppose you are going to tell me that newss of the atrocitiess that have been perpetrated againsst my kind did not fill you with glee?"

Lwo-Dvuum was forced to consider his own personal reactions to what the AAnn had so far told him. There was more going on here than what met the eyes. If he and Bno-Cassaul could figure out what was really behind this ill-mannered interrogation, they might be able to turn it to their advantage. But they would have to be careful, a consideration the educator was afraid his friend had not yet taken to account. From what he knew of AAnn ges-tures, expressions, and postures, Lwo-Dvuum could sense that this Takuuna official was simultaneously angry and nervous: a volatile combination. If they could keep him calm, the two bemused Vssey might well acquire bits and pieces of worthwhile knowledge.

Properly finessed, interrogation could be a two-way street. The AAnn were not the only sentients on Jast who could claim shrewdness as a racial attribute.

If the prickly administrator was to be believed, while Lwo-Dvuum and the members of his circle had spent long timeparts debating the best way to give the unwelcome visitors a jolt, some unknown Vssey had already gone ahead and done so. Rather more serious a jolt, too, than anything Lwo-Dvuum would have proposed, but one whose efficacy could hardly be denied. *Could* the hostile acts have been perpetrated by members of their circle, unbeknownst to the others? The educator doubted it. They knew one another too well. And none of them, Lwo-Dvuum was convinced, possessed the necessary murderous streak. While the Vssey could fight, and had done so frequently in the past, today they much preferred peace and harmony.

With, if the AAnn official was to be believed, at least a few notable exceptions.

"You have not replied to my quesstion," Takuuna hissed at the pensive educator.

"If I did feel as you suggest about what you say truly happened, would I admit to it?"

The AAnn made a gesture of third-degree gratification to the recorder. "An honesst ansswer at lasst. Your wordss also tell me that you are not sstupid. But that iss to be expected, given your professionss." A clawed hand made small circles on the table, not scraping this time, stroking sand that wasn't there. "Let uss ssay for the moment that I accept your protesstationss of ignorance and innocence. Will you act as civilized as you profess to be? Will you help uss to find and identify the cowardly assasssinss hiding among your own kind?"

Lwo-Dvuum did not hesitate. "It would be the polite thing to do." Bno-Cassaul looked at him sharply. The educator ignored his companion.

Takuuna hissed an appreciative reply. "I appreciate the cleverness of your ressponsse, but it doess not ansswer my quesstion. Will you, or will you not?"

"We will," Lwo-Dvuum assured him.

The administrator rose. The insignia on his lightweight jacket shimmered in the dim light. "Then thiss interview iss at an end. I will take you at your word, educator. You will be provided with a ssufficiency of background material to enable you to assisst, inssofar as you are able, in the ongoing ssearch for the unknown malefactorss. Your own actionss will of coursse be ssimultaneoussly monitored. If it iss felt at any time that you have consented to assisst in the hopess of secretly providing information about the ssearch to the very oness we seek, I assure you that you will ssuffer a fate as ultimately final as it will be exquissite in the detailss of itss execution." The recorder shut down his instrumentation and stood as Takuuna prepared to exit the room. Halfway to the door, the administrator paused to look back.

"You truly have had no contact with the human, or with any of hiss kind?"

While both eyes remained focused on the AAnn, Lwo-Dvuum tilted forward the domed upper third of a much relieved body. "Not to my knowledge. My friends and I know so little of the species to which you refer that I am almost too uninforme' to reply knowledgeably on the matter."

Takuuna's only response was to emit a long, slow hiss as his tongue flicked out absently between the long upper canines at the front end of his jaws. Lwo-Dvuum could not be certain, but it struck him that the negative reply on this particular subject struck the AAnn as particularly disappointing. The educator could not help that. Throughout the course of the interview, only truth had been told. Except for the part about helping the AAnn locate and identify the insurgents. That had been a bald-faced lie. But it had bought time. It was something that had to be explained to a certain quietly fuming programmer as soon as the two of them were released outside the AAnn administrative complex.

"What di' you mean, teacher, when you sai' we woul' help these trespassers an' thieves find those among us who have decide' to resist the Imperial presence on our worl' with more than just words?"

Lwo-Dvuum's eyestalks twisted around to allow a cautious glance directly behind them as they hopped steadily away from the heavily fortified complex. "What woul' you have ha' me sai'? 'No?' Do you value your manipulative appendages? While I am not entirely sure I approve of the actions of our unknown brethren, even if I ha' an inkling as to their identity I woul' no more relay it to these AAnn than I woul' unsanctify my parent." He paused while they hopped onto one of the ubiquitous moving sidewalks that sped Vssey around the interiors of their cities.

"Do you think the AAnn believe' you?" Bno-Cassaul wondered aloud.

"What does it matter? We are out of that awful place."

"They will begin monitoring us." The programmer glanced around uneasily. "They may be doing so already."

"Let them." Lwo-Dvuum settled comfortably into an open support slot and let his lower body relax against it. "It is clear they have been 'monitoring' our circle anyway."

"Yes, that's true," the programmer had to admit. "They will seek results."

"An' we will happily provide them with information that is as believable as it is innocuous. We will seem to aid them without actually doing so. There is little else we can do about it. Despite what the official seeme' to believe, we have no idea what individuals or what circle carried out the attacks to which the male referre'."

"No," Bno-Cassaul declared, "but I wish I di'. I woul' seek to graft a budding from anyone so brave."

Lwo-Dvuum looked thoughtful. "They must be very clever, whoever they are, to have overcome the stringent AAnn security measures on not one but two different occasions. We coul' learn much from such individuals." The educator eyed the upper bodies of the many Vssey passing them in the opposite direction. "Perhaps someday we will. Perhaps someday the honor of meeting these brave representatives of our people will fall to us."

"How do we know there are several?" Bno-Cassaul averred after a moment's thought. "Might there not be only one militant, acting alone?"

Lwo-Dvuum's hearing frill rippled in quiet amusement at the programmer's credulity. "Don't be a bent budding. How could a single dissident accomplish all that the AAnn relate'? No, I am convince' the destruction is the work of no less than a circle of four or five. That woul' be the minimum necessary to deceive an' circumvent those as clever as the AAnn. Has not our own circle recognize' their abilities, their persistence, and the long, difficult hopway we must travel to ri' ourselves of them?"

Several of Bno-Cassaul's tentacles gestured assent. "I suppose that is so." Programmer eyed educator curiously. "What do you make of the AAnn's obsession with this human creature? Do you think it has a basis in fact, or was he using it to surprise and to test us?"

"I'm not sure," Lwo-Dvuum confessed. "Why he would think we might have been in contact with, much less been receiving advice or material aid from such an exotic creature, I cannot imagine."

"Do you think there really might be a human on Jast, perhaps even in the vicinity of Skokosas, and that is why the official felt the nee' to pose the query?"

"I don't know." The moving hopway turned a corner. Ahead lay a local transport terminus. Lwo-Dvuum would have preferred access to his ouvomum, but it could only accommodate one passenger in any case. Besides which, Bno-Cassaul was a confirmed user of modern transportation. The educator would resign himself to speed. "But given the AAnn's obvious concern about the possibility, I think it woul' behoove our circle to initiate a few discreet inquiries an' fin' out.

"Any species that can give the toothy ones the jitters is one whose acquaintance I would like to make."

"Assuming the human person actually exists," Bno-Cassaul was quick to point out, "an' is still on Jast."

"Even if it is not," Lwo-Dvuum replied, the soft words emerging slowly from the flattened mouth that split the front part of his upper body, "I believe that the AAnn's reaction to even the possibility means it is a subject worth the circle's time."

With that, Bno-Cassaul was in complete agreement. As they boarded the next transport for shifting to the neighborhood where both lived, the programmer was determined to run a search on a personal scanner the instant personal privacy was restored. Unlike the educator, Bno-Cassaul knew nothing at all about humans. He accepted their existence because Lwo-Dvuum did. Were they anything like the AAnn? Potential allies or not, that was a disquieting thought.

He hoped they would be at least a little bit different. Because hope was about all the circle of dissenters had in their arsenal. In all likelihood, dislodging the persistent AAnn from Jast was going to require something considerably stronger.

9

A thoroughly frustrated Flinx felt as if he were living in two worlds. The most prominent, the one he knew for certain he was living in, was ordered and stately, populated by busy bipeds who looked nothing like him but with whom he for some reason shared language, some common references, and a growing empathetic bond whose depth was a continual surprise to him. This world was also home to the small flying creature whose name was Pip, the minidrag being one of the few certainties he could cling to. That, and his ability to know, most of the time, what those around him were feeling. While unable to make up for his poor manners, his strange accent, his lack of claws, decent teeth, or tail, he was still able to insinuate himself with those around him through the use of that veiled talent.

The other world he inhabited was one of fog and shadows, of memories that were nothing but ghosts and spirits. Occasionally there were glimpses of that alternate reality. Memories of an old woman coddling him one moment and swearing at him the next. Strange shapes that seemed to speak to him but were more like the small arthropods that skittered across the sands outside the Tier's compound. Wise voices speaking in a language other than that of his smooth-scaled rescuers. Angry voices utilizing the same tongue. Endless searching of he knew not

137

what, and by means he could not identify. And always questions, questions, questions.

None of which Chraluuc or any of her apologetic brethren could answer.

Since the collective opinion among the members of the Tier held that he was still recovering from his ordeal, and since his mental state was still self-evidently precarious, he was largely left to himself. He took to wandering the grounds of the compound, inquiring as to the purpose of this building or the function of that decoration. Only rarely were his queries ignored, his requests to observe denied. Though never entirely able to vanquish their suspicions of the human who had tumbled into their midst, the more time he spent among them, the more the members of the Tier came to believe that the tall softskin represented a different kind of human. Of his empathy there could be no doubt. In some ways, and with the passage of time, he was becoming more like them than his own kind. To the members of the Tier this slow metamorphosis was at once gratifying, puzzling, and exhilarating.

Flinx did not regard it so because he was not aware of it. He was simply trying to fit in. It was the least he could do, the polite thing to do, to thank those who had saved his life. Though accounted a human by everyone he met, he did not feel particularly human. He did not feel especially anything, except alive. At first, that had been enough. But as the days passed and he ate and talked and slept among the Tier, life without memory or meaning was beginning to pale.

Since she spent more time with him than any of her colleagues, Chraluuc was more sensitive to his moods than any others of her kind. One early morning she happened to find him out alone, walking one of the several meticulously maintained paths of contemplation the Tier had established in the vicinity of the compound.

She greeted him with the familiar head turn and closed claws. He responded absently. The gesture, like so much AAnn body language, had become second nature to him. On his shoulder, the ever-present flying snake dozed contentedly.

"Truly, honored friend, you have made of morossness a fine art." Hissing softly, she added a fourth-degree gesture implying irony.

He responded with a second-degree arm flex signifying appreciation of both sentiments contained in her salutation. "I can't help it, Chraluuc. How would you feel if you found yourself lost among strangers, not knowing anything about yourself, who you were or where you came from?"

Feeling, not for the first time, oddly drawn to the softskin, she did her best to offer what encouragement and support she could. It made no sense: the softskins were allies of the thranx, traditional enemies of the Empire. But there was something different about this one, something that reached out beyond his pitiful mental stasis to touch those near to him. Her reaction to him was not an isolated one. Others of the Tier had felt it as well.

"Ignorance of the latter doess not invalidate the reality. You *are* ssomeone and you *did* come from ssomewhere. It iss only a matter of time, one hopess, before memory returnss."

He knew what she was doing and was grateful for it, but he was less sanguine. Many days of research using the Tier's facilities had filled him in on what it meant to be human, on the nature of humankind's presence in the galaxy, and on numerous other factors, but had told him nothing about himself. Perusing the vast information at hand, he felt at times as if worlds of revelation lay hidden just behind the next statement, the most recent diagram— only to have the immanency of disclosure break up and scatter like a flock of edgy, whorled souluvu. It was all very well and good to acquire, or reacquire, the details of life on this planet or that (insofar as the AAnn had obtained such knowledge about the Commonwealth), but what he wanted, what he needed, were details of the history and development of the world that was himself.

While he had read that AAnn and humankind were enemies, or at least existed in a state of perpetual wariness regarding one another, he felt no animosity toward them. Had they not saved his life? Admittedly, based on what he read, the members of the Tier appeared to differ in significant respects from the greater population of their fellows. But they were still AAnn.

What was it that made the Tier so different? With a start, he realized that he had been so focused on learning about himself that he had neglected to find out anything much about his rescuers beyond the fact that they had taken him in and kept him alive. Nor had any of them, including Chraluuc, volunteered such information. At best, it was an oversight on his part; at worst, impolitic. At least he could blame it on his condition.

Was their apparent reticence an indication that they had something to hide? There was one way to find out.

"I've been here for some time now, Chraluuc."

With weave of hands and sweep of tail she executed a second-degree gesture of agreement underscored by encouragement. "And doing better every day, Flinx."

He paused before a bunch of vonowolp bushes. Tall enough to just see over the crest of the cluster, he watched as an arc of tiny tenelbs, their oversized electric blue eyes dazzling in the sunshine, munched their way through the vonowolp's bright pink fruit. Using the tiny spine that protruded from its forehead, a tenelb would advance, puncture a fruit, and then skitter back out of the way until the vonowolp ceased firing tiny but potentially lethal jet-black seeds. Only when the plant had exhausted its defense would the tenelb move forward to feed.

"Better?" He glanced sideways at her, round pupils meeting slitted ones. "I still have no idea who I am, or where I'm from, or what I'm doing on this world that is the natural home of neither my kind nor yours." Restlessly, he chewed his lower lip while Pip looked up anxiously from her perch on his shoulders. "I am nothing. I have nothing. Except this pet—though why she stays with me, I can't imagine." His voice tightened. "I wouldn't stay with me."

Among the AAnn, such self-pitying would barely have attracted casual concern, if not outright contempt. But Flinx was a softskin, she reminded herself, and so had to be judged by different standards.

"All this time I've spent among you," he continued, "and I still don't understand your Tier."

She hesitated slightly, even though there was no real reason to do so. "Then it iss time that wass rectified. Come with me."

She led him away from the main buildings. While Flinx had been allowed to wander freely about the area, there were several structures he had seen only in passing, though he had observed other AAnn entering and leaving them on a regular basis. In accordance with AAnn preferences, their interiors were largely belowground. He had never entered any of them. Now they walked toward what appeared to be a series of camouflaged, squat domes that had been pushed into the sand and rocks. Their polarized, opaqued surfaces resembled the exposed upper curves of the eggs of some gigantic primeval beast. The camouflage effect, he saw, was unintentional, the result of abundant local plant life growing above and in some cases over the tops of the domes.

They entered a typical AAnn entryway, his sandaled

feet slap-slapping against the smooth artificial surface underfoot. As was customary with such passageways, it spiraled downward and to the right. Moments later they emerged into a hallway lit from overhead by a scattering of small skylight domes. He caught his breath. Each of the domes was fashioned of what appeared to be multiple floating layers of stained crystal. Invisible to anyone walking on the surface, from within the passageway they formed a scintillating kaleidoscope of shifting colors and scenes. As human and AAnn strolled down the subterranean passage, he felt as if they were walking through a tunnel of constantly metamorphosing gemstones.

"This is beautiful." He indicated the jewel-like skylights.

"Where did they come from?"

As she pointed out highlights with the tip of her tail, she hissed a fusion of satisfaction and amusement. "From the workshop of Teemylk QQPRKLS—over there."

Peering in the indicated direction, Flinx saw only a closed door. "So the Tier has an artist in residence?" On his shoulder, Pip was gazing mesmerized at the spectacularly vibrant ceiling.

This time her hissing was all laughter. "An artisst? Flinx, that iss what the Tier iss all about. Have you not noticed the profussion of artwork that decoratess our communal eating area, our living quarterss, the ssandarium, even the walkwayss?"

"Well, of course I *noticed* them. I just didn't think anything of it. Remember—until my memory returns, I have nothing to compare to this place."

She signaled mild understanding. "Take my word for it: you will not find sso much fine contemporary and forward-thinking artwork anywhere elsse on Jasst—and in few placess on Blasusarr itself. You ssee, we of the Tier are dedicated to the artss."

He nodded attentively. "You and your friends must have received many honors."

She stopped so abruptly, it startled him, and Pip had to flutter her wings to hold her perch. "Honorss? Truly, you know or remember little of my kind. We of the Tier are pariahss, Flinx. Why do you think we live like thiss, out here in the middle of nowhere on a nowhere world? While occassional art is appreciated in the Imperial corridorss, thosse who wissh to do nothing else for their life-work are regarded as foolss and worsse. We are all of uss here outcasstss within the traditional sstructure of the Empire." She gestured around them. "We have congregated here sso that we can work in peace, away from the inssultss and whisspered sslurss that would afflict uss elsswhere."

Outcasts, he thought silently. While he was of a different species from the members of the Tier, mentally and emotionally they had much in common. No wonder he felt so at ease in this place.

It struck him then, and with considerable force, that he felt as if he had always been an outcast, though without access to his mislaid memories he could not say exactly why he should feel that was so. But the certainty, and the related emotions that came rushing through him at the realization, were undeniable.

"And you?" He stared into bright yellow eyes.

"I am a botanical reanimator." She gestured back the way they had come. "Much of the ornamental foliage and many of the decorative growthss you have admired within the complex were found by me, or brought to me, in a near-lifeless condition. I aessthetically resstore them sso that they regrow in sshapess and formss that are pleassing to the eye." She resumed walking. "You have sseen exampless of Teemylk'ss work above you. Follow now and I will sshow you more."

As was typical with AAnn construction, the underground portion of the artists' complex was far more extensive than any portion viewed from above would lead a casual observer to believe. Some of the workshops were large enough to include works in progress that ranged over several levels. It was all fascinating and new to Flinx, who had never seen anything like it. Or, he was obliged to remind himself, maybe he had, and the remembrances of such wonderful creations were lost in the dark, inaccessible depths of his memory.

In one studio, an elderly AAnn was crafting an entire community in miniature. Every element of the creation was beautifully designed and executed, from the tiny buildings to the diminutive landscape to the individual plants, animals, and wee AAnn who populated the setting. The two visitors watched in silence, admiring the solitary creator who ignored them as she went about her work of molding, manipulating, and coaxing the minuscule representation of reality into moving, talking, animate life.

"This is Wiilat'ss work. Sshe iss quite famouss on more than two dozen worldss within the Empire." Chraluc leaned over the railing that separated visitors from the artist.

"What happens to all this?" Flinx's gesture took in the large room that was lit from overhead by several triangular skylights while Pip eyed the small moving figures with interest. "When it's finished, I mean. Does the artist disassemble it and then start a new one?"

"You are half correct. When Wiilat hass completed the ssimulacrum, sshe will indeed begin a new one. But thiss one"—she gestured with both hand and tail—"will be sold, closed down intact, and sshipped to an off-world cusstomer."

"I don't understand." He watched closely as the elderly

nye, utilizing the intricate and difficult-to-master mechanisms of formata construction, wove to life another tiny citizen of the self-contained, artist-imagined community.

"If everyone here is an outcast, and your work is looked down upon, then who buys it?"

Knowing eyes glanced up at him. "There are always collectorss for good work, no matter how notoriouss the origin. While hierarchical AAnn ssociety at large may frown upon the actual methodology of creation, ssociety in private iss ever ready to welcome the new, the exciting, and the fasshionable. How iss it among humankind?"

"I seem to remember it being similar, though in the society of the Commonwealth I believe that all artists are respected, no matter how controversial their art."

"Then you are fortunate in that resspect." They left the elderly Wiilat hard at work playing God, a role to which AAnn no less than human or thranx artists aspired.

For the rest of the afternoon, Flinx was subject to sensory overload. There was the young, energetic AAnn who through a combination of art and inorganic chemistry forced flowers of clear and colored quartz to replicate in odorless silicate bouquets that were dazzling to the eye. In a narrow but high studio, one-eyed Kaabu the Wild, as he was known to his fellow members of the Tier, created astonishing three-dimensional constructs of tactile paint. Madly flinging colors into the air and controlling the resultant eruptions with a singsong of musical commands, he induced the heavily magnetized paint to adhere in stunning combinations one could not only view, but walk around, behind, and beneath. His control of the medium was humbling to Flinx, who could not begin to fathom how the artist not only manipulated the media, but did so in a way that resulted in an unmistakable artistic vision instead of simply a multihued blob of hovering color.

Siivagg was a sand-sculptor. Utilizing special protective

command gloves, she whirled color particles about with the ease and touch of a lover caressing their partner. Contained within sculpted blasts of air, the combinations of tinted sand were in constant motion, so that the work of art was never static. In the chamber next to hers a bentbacked AAnn called Cuurajaa liquefied and transformed stone into curious combinations of abstract shapes that spun and writhed in, around, and among one another like live things. Continuing down the corridor, they encountered the drifting contributions of Doonim the Idler. These whimsical aerogel shapes were imbued with music that could be heard only when the shapes were punctured with a claw, whereupon each emitted its own individual ephemeral opus as it sank to the floor, there to eventually evaporate in a last puff of pianissimo. Doonim's compositions were as evanescent as they were enchanting. While the tonalities were alien to Flinx's ear, the skill with which they had been compiled could not be denied.

Eventually, both guide and guest found themselves sated by the surfeit of available stimulation. Despite the splendor he had imbibed, Flinx was almost relieved when they returned to the sere, rambling surface and headed back down a winding path toward the main complex.

"And you all live out here in the wilderness, by yourselves?"

Absently lashing out with her tail at a floating, wandering fvuorene and sending it crashing to the rocky ground, Chraluuc considered Flinx's question. Though he felt drawn to these people, he remained aware of the gulf that would always lie between them. Such casual violence as his guide had just demonstrated in killing the inoffensive fvuorene was as alien to him as the scales that covered her body or the vertical pupils that he frequently caught studying him with intense curiosity. Though these our-sider AAnn were the only company he had, he could not bring himself to emulate many of their habits.

"We prefer to live thiss way. It allowss uss to concentrate on our work without the disstractions operating openly in nye ssociety would imposse. We ssell enough to maintain the complex. That iss all any true artisst sshould want." Those penetrating eyes turned on him once more. "What about you, Flinx? I watched you watching. Have you yourssself any artisstic talentss or leaningss?"

He was taken aback by the question. Though surrounded by arr, he had not thought to draw anything in the way of a personal connection.

Draw. Experimentally, he moved the fingers of his right hand in a certain way. Was this something he had done? New memories took form in his mind; of the need to pass long hours alone on a ship. Why alone? Didn't everyone travel through space-plus in tandem with others? Or was he, as he was coming more and more to feel, an exception in more ways than one?

"Can you find me a surface to write on, and instruments to do so?"

She gestured second-degree accord and bounded forward, forcing him to run to keep up.

To their mutual delight, they soon discovered that much of what he could not remember in words he could evoke by means of sketches that were not only simultaneously facile and complex, but equally noteworthy for their aesthetic content.

Interesting, he mused as he drew, wielding with effortless dexterity the tapering electronic stylus designed for the slightly slimmer AAnn hand. I must have had some training in the arts. Was he, in fact, a professional artist? Unlike much of what he swiftly rendered, that notion did not feel right.

Disregarding for the moment her own work, which she had been compelled to neglect since being assigned to watch over the softskin, Chraluuc looked on in fascination as Flinx sketched one alien image after another. His first likeness was of an old softskin woman, a hideous sort of thing to Chraluuc but one that brought a torrent of childhood memories rushing back to her charge. Subsequent to that emotional flood, he found himself drawing like mad.

Starships appeared on the single sheet of rewritable material she had provided to him. Each time he prepared to expunge an illustration, she made sure it was first transmitted and saved to an appropriate file for later study. One particular image of a starship of small and unusual shape he kept referring to as his own.

She was patient with him. "Only the famouss, the important, and the very wealthy have sstarsshipss of their own, and you are neither of thosse thingss."

"I know, I know." He stared transfixed at his own creation. "But I can't escape this overriding feeling of possession and familiarity whenever I look at it." Holding up the flexible sheet, he manipulated it by hand so that the sketch automatically took on minimal three-dimensional properties. "This just feels like it's mine."

"Tssasst," she teased him roughly in the manner of the AAnn, "if it iss yourss, then where iss it?"

"I don't know," he was forced to confess. "Yet."

Intermittent hisses of amusement emerged from between sharp teeth. "Better to focuss your attemptss to remember on what iss likely and reasonable. Ample time later for dreaming."

She was doubtless right, he knew as he resumed drawing.

With a dedication that any of the AAnn artists in residence would have appreciated, over the following days

Flinx produced dozens of intricate renderings of scenes from many worlds. Every one of them was alien to the captivated Chraluuc. Many did not include depictions of softskins. Either they were less commonly found in many parts of the vast and hostile Commonwealth than the members of the Tier had been led to believe, or else her perpetually bemused charge was more widely traveled than anyone, including himself, had imagined. Or else he was simply conjuring the fantastical visions up out of whole cloth, because while he could produce images of such places, he could not put names to them.

"Ssurely," she told him one morning as he was putting the finishing touches on yet another depiction of a planetary surface rife with impossibly lush vegetation, "you cannot have vissited sso many different worldss. If nothing elsse, you are too young. I think what you do have iss a mosst vivid and entertaining imagination."

"I know," he murmured as he deftly manipulated the stylus. "Yet everything feels so real when I draw it."

"Comfortable delussionss often are," she assured him.

"But of one thing there can be no doubt: as an illusstrator, you have talent."

He shrugged modestly as he drew. "I'm just playing here, using these quick sketches to try to help me remember things."

"Truly, I realize thiss, and I ssympathize with your frusstration." She leaned close to peer over his shoulder at his latest creation. She was able to do so only because the exceedingly defensive flying snake was presently elsewhere, relaxing on a nearby shelf that was brushed with sunlight from the room's single skylight. So used to the human had she become that she no longer had to remember to constrict her nostrils to shut out the powerful mammalian muskiness that emanated from his pliable body. "It musst be exassperating to be able to create picturess of sso many different thingss and not be able to identify them."

He nodded, a reflexive cranial gesture she had come to know well through the time she had spent in his company. "It's getting better, though." He showed her his latest work. It was a sketch of a planet whose encircling rings boasted two extensive gapss. "This is Moth, where I grew up."

Curious, she mused as she studied the expert rendering. He did not refer to the unusual world as *home*: only as the place where he *grew up*. She had yet to hear him so identify of any of the worlds he had drawn. "A very attractive world," she ventured politely. "Do you think you could locate it on a star chart?"

"I hadn't thought of doing that," he replied with a start. His excitement was palpable. "We'll have to try it." With her left hand she gestured simple fourth-degree concurrence. "An eassy thing to arrange." She turned thoughtful. "What I have sseen you do during thesse past many six dayss hass ssuggesssted to me ssomething elsse that I am afraid will not be sso eassy to arrange."

Stylus activated and poised over the receptive sheet, he looked back at her. The proximity to his face of the powerful jaws and sharp teeth of the intelligent carnivore did not unsettle him. By now he was quite used to it. "You have something else in mind for me?"

"Perhapss." She was deliberately evasive. "It iss a— ssurprisse." The pleasure to be found in unexpected revelation was something else human and AAnn shared. "I would not tell you, in any casse, becausse if it doess not come to pass, it will provide no causse for dissappointment."

"You'll have to tell me eventually." He returned to his current drawing of a graceful structure on a world that was bathed in warm sunshine. A beautiful woman had been sketched in standing in front of the human-scaled building. She seemed to be looking directly out at the viewer. "You know how much I enjoy pestering you, Chraluuc."

She started to take a slash at him with her tail, only to catch herself in mid-swipe. While he might have misinterpreted the meaning of the leathery slap, that would not have invalidated the sincerity of the gesture.

"I—I have to leave. My own work wails for attention." She turned and backed away from him.

"Why?" he started to ask her. "What's the rush to . . . ?"

But she was already gone, out the door as fast as she could gracilely manage, the bewildering emotions swirling within her a disturbing muddle of growing friendship, misplaced affection, maternalistic instinct, and duty. It was fortunate, she reflected as she hurried down the corridor, that the softskin was unable to accurately interpret any of the associated signs, or her circumstances would have been twelve times worse.

The farther she got from the small apartment that had been allotted to him, the more her inner confusion eased. She knew who she was, and nothing could or would change that. Being an outcast did not render her any less what she was. Truly.

But despite her strong sense of self-assurance, recollection of the disturbing moment continued to perturb her for the rest of the day.

To say that the Ssemilionn of the Ssaiinn was astonished by her request was akin to her suggesting that the three Elders abandon their commitments to their respective disciplines and volunteer their services to the Imperial defense forces. One and all, they regarded her as if she had suddenly turned into one of the foolish, fluttery umorows that was constantly battering itself silly against the skylights of the Tier's buildings in repetitious vain attempts to burrow through and lay its eggs on the other side of the implacably impenetrable material.

"You are sseriouss in thiss propossal!" Xeerelu's half-prosthetic tail whipped back and forth in agitation.

Chraluuc stood her ground. "I think it would be a good thing. It would reflect well on the Tier of Ssaiinn."

"Truly, it would certainly reflect." Synthetic eyes whirred imperceptibly as Naalakot clicked his claws together to illustrate his unease. "The quesstion iss, what would that conssequent reflection reveal?"

"What do we care?" In the presence of the Ssemiliionn, Chraluuc was respectful, but not intimidated. Like any AAnn, she could be convinced, or persuaded, or even killed, but rarely intimidated. "We are already looked upon as different from otherss of our kind, and treated as outssiderss." She eyed each of them in turn. "Ssince it iss already expected that we will do the sstartling and unprecedented, sshould we not do our besst to confirm the ssuspicionss of our fellow nye?"

Vinpou continued to brood, though he was not as vissibly unsettled as his two companions. "Not necessarily. We musst sstill rely on the goodwill of the Imperial Authority to maintain our pressence here. Thiss is not an Imperial world, and we could be ordered off it at any time."

"Truly!" Chraluuc enthusiastically agreed. "Therefore we are obligated to rely on the goodwill not of the Imperial Authority but of the Vssey themsselves."

"You are being dissingenuouss," Xeerelu replied accussingly.

"Iss that not also a recognized art form among our kind?" Unable to smile, Chraluuc was reduced to communicating her reaction through gestures. "Sseriously, venerated Elders, if my ssuggesstion iss implemented, asside from the aessthetic asspectss, could it not have potential benefitss none of uss can forssee? And given the inability to forssee, sshould we not try thiss new thing?" Not only was she challenging them individually, she was challenging what they stood for. "Iss that not ultimately what art iss about?"

Viinpou was not so easily convinced. "What you proposse ssmackss more of politicss and ssociology than art."

"Do not people sspeak of 'the art of politicss'?"

The elderly female turned to her fellow Ssemiil. "Thiss weed-wisher iss too clever by half."

"I concur," hissed Naalakot, "but that doess not invalidate her argument. I can, however vaguely, tasste a glimmer of the possible benefitss to which sshe alludess. I believe it may be ssomething worth nibbling on."

Chraluuc slowed her breathing and stilled her tail as the Ssemilionn of the Ssaiinn continued to debate her radical proposal. If they turned it down, that would be the end of it. There was nothing more she could do, no higher court to which she could file an appeal. Not within the Tier.

After what felt like hours, the Elders ceased their animated wrangling.

"We think we undersstand the potential benefits," Xeerelu hissed softly at her. "We also, even though it conveniently appearss to have esscaped you, ssee the potential harm that taking such an unprecedented action could incur." Sharp eyes glanced at her expectant colleagues, and she continued—reluctantly, it seemed to Chraluuc.

"After consssidered debate, we have decided to proceed as you requesst. This will occasion much disscussion among the memberss of the Tier. That iss as it should be, and iss to be encouraged, we do not the three of uss foresee any objectionss—and there will be ssome— that cannot be overcome. When would you wissh to perform the necessary activitiess?"

"As ssoon as the Ssemiionn deemss it propitiouss," she replied promptly. Now that they had agreed to her proposal, the actual date on which it should be implemented was a matter of indifference to her.

"A day will be chossen." A still plainly reluctant Viinpou pulled his pale yellow vest tighter around him. The etchings on his scaly shoulders shimmered with intricate inlays of powdered metal.

Xeerelu continued. "I musst ssay, truly, that a part of me iss looking forward with great curiossity not only to the ceremony itsself but to itss unpredictable conssequencess. To the besst of my knowledge, thiss will be the firsst time in the hisstory of the modern Imperial era that ssuch a thing hass been tried." She gazed back at the female nye who had boldly flung the outrageous proposition in their faces, challenging not only them but the philosophy of the Tier itself.

"What of the one who iss to play the central figure in thiss drama? How do you think he will react?"

"Truly." Now even Viinpou was beginning to find himself caught up in the anticipation. "When the time comess, it may be that he will refusse to participate. What then?"

"He will not refusse." Chraluuc was completely confident. Well, almost completely confident, she told herself. "If nothing else, he will accept becausse it would be impolite to refusse, and he iss nothing if not polite." Her tail smacked the floor behind her. "If he hessitatess, I will thrassh him until he agress."

The junior male's pupils dilated strongly. "That iss very perssonal of you. May I ssay, mosst oddly sso."

She glared at the Ssemiil. "Like any artisst, I am interessted in doing whatever iss necessary to get ressults."

Naalakot spoke solemnly. "A sstrange ssort of art, thiss." Both clawed hands clove the air in a first-degree gesture of satisfaction mixed with third-degree anticipation. "I find that I am alsso looking forward to it. If nothing elsse, it will provide an interessting diverssion for the entire Ssaiinn." He leaned forward slightly. Though devoid of external ears to point in the petitioning female's direction, the Elder still listened intently. "What hass been the reaction thuss far of the ssoftsskin to your extraordinary propossal?"

For the first time since she had entered the room to confront the Ssemilionn, Chraluuc appeared tentative. "I cannot ssay. You ssee, I have not sspoken of it to him yet."

10

W hen, unable to put discussing it off any longer once
the Ssemilionn had chosen a date, she finally did confront
the subject of so much fervent deliberation, Flinx's reaction was decidedly ambivalent.

"I'm flattered, I guess." As he spoke in the small living
compartment that had been set aside for him, he was
playing with his pet. While he held his right arm straight
out in front of him, the flying snake was winding around
it in multiple coils. Only when her head reached his wrist
did she unfurl and exercise her wings, opening them to
their fullest extent and slowly moving them back and
forth. Since she was upside down, the striking pink and
pale blue membranous flaps hung from his arm like the
folds of some exotic, translucent robe.

"You musst undersstand." Standing by the entranceway, Chraluuc kept her tail in check. There was no need to
take a traditional swing at the softskin since he had not yet
turned down the proposal. "Inssofar as anyone knowss,
nothing like thiss hass ever been done before, either within
the borderss of the Empire or without, irresspective of the
nature of the proffering Tier itself. It may not even be
legal. But the Ssemilionn has agreed to it. All that iss necessary in order to proceed iss, obviousssly, your conssent."

"I don't know." As he lowered his arm, the minidrag
folded her wings flat against her body but remained

coiled around his limb. "What would be my responsibilities? What would be expected of me?"

"Very little," she replied encouragingly. "That you would do nothing to bring yourself or the Tier into dissgrace. That you would continue to practice a chosen art. That you would resspect your fellow memberss and their work."

"Some of them don't like me." He did not tell her that he could sense whenever animosity was being directed his way even when the perpetrator was being outwardly polite. Just as he could sense now that her feelings toward him were truly warm and friendly. "How would they resspond to something like this?"

"As any member of the Tier would to another. With courtessy and kindness."

Flinx wasn't so sure. During his stay there had been more than one instance where an AAnn had approached him with hand politely affixed to throat and head turned sideways, but whose true emotions he had perceived as bordering on the bloodthirsty. Still, since no one had tried to kill him the first week he had been at the complex, there was every reason to hope they would not try to do so now. Or try to do so following the singular procedure Chraluuc had described to him.

But he was still unsure. "You really want to initiate me into your Tier?"

Possible tail-thrashing forgotten, she began to pace in the AAnn manner: taking a step to the left, then to the right, then left again, essentially pacing in place. An on-looking human could have been forgiven for thinking that the slender reptiloid was practicing a new dance step.

"As I ssaid, it hass never been done before. As far as thosse who have done the relevant ressearch have been able to determine, you would be the firsst ssoftssk—the firsst human to be formally inducted into an AAnn family unit. Becausse in order for you to become one of the Ssai-inn, you musst alsso become a member of a family."

The more he thought about it, the more Flinx had to admit that the proposal held a peculiar appeal. As Pip slithered off his outstretched arm and onto the room's single, simple table, Flinx reflected on his lack of any kind of family: a lack that would persist at least until more of his memory returned. And if it never did? Wasn't an AAnn family—wide-ranging, belligerent, and frequently indifferent as it could be—better than no family at all?

"What AAnn extended family would adopt *me*?" he speculated aloud.

"Mine," she informed him without hesitation. "It hass all been worked out. The necessary recordss have already been transsferred to the deep-sspace communicationss ssysstem in Sskokossass for relay to the appropriate recordss-keeping department on Blausarr. Family adoption is common and cassual among my kind. Yourss sshould not even be noticed."

Because so many of you are busy fighting and killing, he reflected silently. Still, that was not enough to put him off the idea. The more he pondered on it, the more intriguing, if not necessarily conventionally attractive, it became.

"You will become a member of my family as well as the Tier of Ssaiinn," she told him. "Who better than to do ssuch a thing than an association of radical outcasst artis-sanss?"

It would be good to belong to a family of some kind, he mused. Even if it wasn't of his own species.

"All right—I agree. But with one caveat: for one thing, I'm not participating in any mating brawls," he told her firmly. "I'd be at a real disadvantage without a tail, not to mention claws, and I don't particularly like rolling around in hot sand."

"It would not be necessary for you to . . ." She broke off, gaped at him a moment, and then broke out in a stream of amused hisses like a toy steam engine. "Your ssuitably dry ssensse of humor is appropriate to your new sstatuss. Thiss unprecedented affair will go well, I think." Turning suddenly somber, her words were punctuated by an appropriate half-gesture.

"What will your own family think of thiss, when at lasst you are returned to them?"

"That won't be a problem." Reaching down, he stroked the back of Pip's neck, between her head and the place where her body bulged slightly and the muscles that moved her wings began. "Right now and for the foreseeable future, this is all the family I have, right here, and she's not objecting."

Chraluuc swallowed respectfully. "Ssurely, truly, there musst be otherss, ssomewhere. You musst have a female and male parent."

Her words sparked more remembrance. "There is an old woman who raised me, but she's not my true parent. My real mother was . . . my father was . . ."

Rudely, questions came flooding back. Dozens of questions, to which he could summon up only a few answers. She took an alarmed step toward him. "Are you unwell, Flinx?"

He mustered a smile. "No more so than usual, Chraluuc. *Jsstass-ca vss-ibb-tssak.* The sand on which I walk shifts, but is solid underneath."

Relieved, she gestured understandingly. "Then I will report your conssent to the Ssaiinn. The ceremony will take place in three dayss."

He was newly alarmed. "Ceremony? You mean, there's more to this than just entering the necessary information into a file?"

She made a second-degree gesture of acknowledgment

leavened with mild irony. "Did you think ssomething sso exceptional would enssue sso ssimply? There iss more to it than that, Flinx. It would be the ssame were the Tier inducting another AAnn." Turning, she approached and put a hand on his left arm, the claws digging in only enough to reinforce her words. "Do not worry. There iss no risk involved, and it will not take long. But it musst be done." Claws capable of ripping out his throat moved up from his arm to scratch him lightly under his chin. Had it been covered in scales instead of skin, he would not even have felt it. "Tradition."

Soon to become mine as well, he realized. Reaching out with his own hand, he drew his fingertips politely down the side of her exposed, muscular neck. Greatly to his inner embarrassment, he could not escape the feeling that he was stroking the sleeve of an especially well-tanned leather jacket.

It was early morning when Chraluuc escorted him to the convocation hall. Normally decorated lushly in adamantine chromatoswirls by the mated team of Yiicadu and Joorukij, the large circular chamber was bare now except for the diluted sunlight that poured through the domed skylight. It was noon, when the sun was at its highest, and therefore considered among the AAnn the most propitious time of day for the carrying out of ancient ritual. Even in the most modern setting and circumstances, the rapacious reptiloids were as devoted to the maintenance of custom as any primitive species with a long history of unbroken tradition.

Not all were present. As he was led by Chraluuc into the center of the spacious chamber, Flinx tried to give names to those who were absent. Significantly, the participation was not along lines of partiality. Some of those who waited in the chamber were fond, or at least tolerant, of his presence among them. Others he suspected of actively disapproving, or forthrightly disliking, him. But several of the latter were present nonetheless, proud of their ability to set personal preferences aside for the sake of the Tier.

At Chralauc's urging he had left Pip behind, asleep in their room. He felt naked without the flying snake snugged around his shoulders and neck. This was not surprising, since he was naked. He felt no shame and believed that he never had suffered from a nudity phobia, but he did feel more vulnerable. In a room abounding with exposed claws and sharp teeth, he was virtually defenseless. Not that the unpretentious attire he normally wore would have afforded much protection anyway against a concerted attack from so many directions. If he was going to go through with this, he had realized from the time Chralauc had first proposed it, he had to trust the members of the Tier. He had to trust her.

Nudging and hissing to one another, the assembled artisans eyed him with undisguised curiosity. Until he had fallen into their midst, few of them had ever set eyes on one of the notorious softskins. Certainly none had ever seen one unclothed. Swirling around him, Flinx could sense feelings that traveled the gamut from jaded indifference to outright revulsion at the sight of him. Approving or not, everyone held their emotions in check.

Though there were many present he had barely spoken to, there were none he did not recognize. He had lived long enough in the Tier to know everyone by sight. For their part, they all knew him. He was impossible to miss.

The Ssemilionn of the Ssaiinn approached. As the triumvirate of Elders drew near, they turned their backs on him. Chralauc moved back to take her proper place in the circle. Words were hissed. Flinx felt multiple tail-tips patting his body. The sensation was not unpleasant, but he tensed nonetheless. The age of their owners notwithstanding, the same leathery tails that were caressing him reassuringly could just as easily knock him senseless.

They did not. Testimonies concluded, the members of the Ssairin also rejoined the circle. A moment of silence hung as heavy in the air as a blast from muted trumpets.

Then something hit him. Hard.

Looking down, he saw that he had been struck by a blob of iridescent color. It clung to his waist, twisting and coiling like a line of live neon freed from its tubing. Something else smacked into the back of his head. Reaching up, he drew back fingers stained with moaning ocher. The sound fit the color. Turning slightly, he sought a friendly face in the circle. His gaze immediately settled on Chraluc's. With one hand she gestured first-degree reassurance. With the other she flung something bright and green at him, too swiftly and accurately for him to duck. Striking his left arm, its roots quickly wrapped themselves around his elbow, securing a firm perch. That was when it hit him.

He was being assaulted by art. Every member of the Tier present was assailing him with some variant of their particular forte. The intent was not to injure, or to wound. The clinging iridescence, the moaning tint, the grasping carefully nurtured plant: all were intended to combine to form a single unified composition at the center of which was—himself. He was becoming not an art form, but an art formed.

Clenching his teeth, arms held loosely at his sides, he tried to shield his more vulnerable parts as best he could without flinching. Otherwise, he stood and took it. Though it seemed as if the induction took hours, in reality it lasted much less than that.

Then there came a moment when he opened his eyes to see that no one was hurling anything in his direction. Battered and not a little bruised, he struggled to make sense of the alien emotions that filled the room. Most smacked of approval—and not a few of admiration. Though whether this was for his display of stoicism in the face of the artistic assault or the aesthetic results, he could not say.

His sight was blurred by the sparkling lights that danced before his eyes—part of the redoubtable Naakuca's luminescent work. Through the twinkling he could see a figure approaching—Chraluuc. A mix of respect and satisfaction radiated from her.

"Almosst finisshed," she hissed softly. Her pointed tongue flicked out to touch his chin. "Come with me."

Taking his hand, she led him toward one side of the chamber. The assembled members of the Tier stepped aside to make way for them. Confronted by an ordinary mirror, Flinx found himself gazing at a figure that was barely recognizable. It was himself, transformed.

A Naakucan torus hovered around his head. Flowers bloomed from his elbows and knees (Chraluuc's work, he knew, and that of the Tier's several other botanical artisans). Colored lights formed patterns around arms and legs that were splattered with sculpted paint that shifted and heaved like sentient sculpture. Tinted sand spiraled around hips and torso, held in place close to his body by shaped charges of static electricity. It itched, but he refrained from brushing it away. He was as beautiful as he was unrecognizable.

And it was all temporary, he knew. All rendered solely for the sake of his induction. He hoped.

"What next?" he mumbled to his escort. "Everyone takes pictures?"

A soft hiss of amusement issued from between powerful jaws. "All necessary recording hass already been done. All that iss needed now iss to complete the compossition that you have become."

He wanted to groan. "There's more?"

Reaching into a pouch, she withdrew a familiar stylus.

"The opuss iss not finisshed. You have to finissh it."

He was startled. "Me? What am I supposed to do?" Gazing into the mirror at the extravagant image of himself, he could not see where anything was lacking.

"It doess not matter. Sso long as it iss part and parcel of yourself. The artisst musst complete the art." She stepped back.

Turning back to his reflection, he gazed bemused at the kinetic wonderment he had become. What could he possibly do to enhance the dramatic resonance? What could he add to complete inspired perfection? It didn't matter, Chraluuc had said. What was important was that he do something. He was not sure he entirely believed her, but since he couldn't think of anything else to do anyway . . .

Reaching up with the activated stylus, he drew. When he was done, he turned to face the expectant multitude. If anyone had any objections, either aesthetic or personal, to the mustache and beard he had drawn on his face, they kept these to themselves.

He sensed approval. There was only one more thing to do to complete the ceremony. There remained the business of bestowing on this inducted oddity a proper name. The task fell to the female Elder Xeerelu. As she approached him, Flinx perceived her ambiguity. He contented himself with the belief that she now disliked him somewhat less than previously.

"We welcome you as a creative ssentient," she hissed simply, "as one of uss, to the Tier of Ssaiinn, Flinx LLVVRXX. May the footsstepss from your hunting be wet with blood, your accession swift, your family prossperouss, and your art dazzling to the mind and heart."

Something struck him hard on the back and he whirled around—only to see Hiikovuk, one of the younger artists, striking him respectfully with open palm, claws retracted.

Soon he was being warmly pummeled from all sides. Chraluuc joined in, battering him as enthusiastically as any of the others. Methodically, courteously, they beat the art off him, until he once more stood naked among them, flushed (a condition that they found attractive), and sweaty (a condition that even those who liked him most assuredly did not).

Responding to the physical fusillade of congratulations as best he could, he excused himself before he suffered any serious injury and hurried back to his room. Pip was waiting for him, airborne and anxious. Letting himself into the makeshift shower they had fashioned for him, he washed and scoured away the remnants of the ritual. Only when the last daub of motile paint, the last grain of electrostatically charged sand, had been scrubbed off did he allow himself to relax a little and reflect on the ordeal he had just undergone.

So I am one of them now, he reflected thoughtfully. As much as it was possible for a softskin to become AAnn. And not just AAnn, but an artist, respected for what he could create as much as for who he was. At that moment, in that place, he found that he did not miss others of his kind. Wasn't he supposed to? Landing in his lap as he sat on the edge of his bed of smoothed, heated sand, Pip recognized him as both tired and conflicted. Since there was nothing she could do about either, she curled up and promptly went to sleep.

I should do the same, he told himself. Though quite aware that something exceptional had just taken place, he did not feel any different. Whether he felt more AAnn or not he was not yet able to say for certain.

Not a bad life to look forward to, he decided as he lay down on the warm, sterilized sand. An artist among friends. He certainly could survive as such, at least until this or that memory returned that might dictate he should be and do otherwise.

If any such remembrance ever did return, he reminded himself.

Several weeks passed, during which time he occupied himself with coming to terms with his new status and in striving to improve what seemed to him a wholly inadequate ability to draw. It was mid-morning of a fine sunny day marred only by a few high clouds when Chraluc interrupted his work.

"I have ssomething to sshow you," she told him. Though her expression remained unchanged and her tone formal, he could sense the excitement within her. "It wass felt that it wass time."

"Time for what?" Setting aside the small landscape he had been working on, he rose to join her.

Yellow eyes glistened. "To introduce you to The Confection."

Pip riding his shoulder, he allowed himself to be led out of the room. "Sounds tasty," he quipped.

"It iss. But not in the way you are thinking. Remember that we of the Tier are defined by what we do."

So it was some kind of artwork, he decided as they ascended the access ramp and emerged into the hot sunshine of morning. That didn't rule out the possibility that food was involved. He had come to enjoy the daily menus that were prepared in the Tier's kitchen, though the meatheavy diet forced him to exercise regularly and to seek out wild fruits and nuts to supplement the almost exclusively carnivorous bill of fare.

They passed the floating obelisk of the air sculptor Givet and the dancing garden on which Chraluc herself had collaborated. The sprayed paving of the walkway they were taking dissolved into loose gravel mixed with sand. The Tier's complex receded behind them. If there was food to be had out here, it would have had to have been hauled out on somebody's leathery back, he reflected.

Unexpectedly, she turned off the main path onto an even narrower trail that led down into a steep-sided canyon whose entrance was hidden from above. Instead of sandstone banded taupe and umber, they found themselves in an isolated fragment of Karst terrain. Rain and running water had carved the dark gray stone into an array of shapes as fanciful as they were lethal. Every rock, every pillar and pinnacle, was sharp-edged and bladed. It was as if they were hiking through a forest of ancient weapons.

"Thiss iss a favorite place," she told him. "It hass been sso ever ssince the Tier ssettled on, and in, thiss part of Jasst."

Studying the lancet-like hoodoos and grimacing limestone goblins that now surrounded them, Flinx could understand why. Whereas humans favored shapes that were soft and rounded, the AAnn gravitated to the jagged and prickly.

The canyon narrowed until it was barely wide enough for a single individual to pass through without turning sideways. Abruptly, it dropped away. A ladder, that most functional and basic appliance common to nearly every bipedal species, bridged the gap between canyon's end and the floor of the slightly wider chasm beyond.

At the base of the ladder, the rift widened significantly. There appeared to be no other way in or out of the rocky cleft other than by air. But arriving by aircar, Flinx saw immediately, would remove all the romance from the place. The bottom of the chasm was covered in soft white sand that had drifted in from surrounding dunes and hollows. Somehow finding a footing in the shifting surface, red-crowned baloovots and upward-curling sendesuff bushes reached for the life-giving sunlight. Other than a mature keevut that scurried on multiple legs into a sheltering crack in the weathered limestone, the chasm was devoid of movement. He remarked on the dearth of wildlife in such a protected place.

Leading him across the sand, Chraluuc indicated the spiky crowns of the heavily eroded rocks. "Mosst Jasstian fauna avoid this place. Making a ssafe landing down here would tax the sskillss and luck of the mosst agile flier. One wrong turn, one missguess of the wind, and they would find themsselves plunging to earth with punctured air bladderss."

Tilting his head back slightly, Flinx was able to see the truth of her remark. For a lifting, bladder-supported Jasstian flier, achieving the safety and solitude of the inner chasm would be akin to trying to land in the center of a gigantic pincushion. Pip would have no trouble doing so, nor would most Terran birds, but a windblown keelmot or a douvum, for example, would be risking their continued survival by coming anywhere near the place. That explained the prevalence of uneaten ripe berries on the branches of the sendesuff.

Come to think of it, he mused, a single Terran hawk or eagle would be emperor of the skies here, able to maneuver effortlessly around and through the free-floating, air-bladder-supported local life-forms. For some reason—a newly recurring memory, perhaps—he had the feeling that the AAnn looked upon themselves as the hawks and the Vssey as the slow-moving, ungainly potential prey.

But not the members of the Tier, he reminded himself. They were different. They had set themselves apart.

Something new drew his attention, and he strained to see past a sheer-walled, gray-faced bend in the limestone ahead. "Is that music I'm hearing?"

She gestured second-degree concurrence. "Mussic, yess—and ssomething elsse. Ssomething more."

"Like what?" On his shoulder Pip was alert to, but not agitated by, the rising volume.

"You will ssee. And hear."

Rounding a second bend was like passing through a door. The intricate, convoluted wall of harmony that struck him as they turned the corner was harsh to his human ears, but not painfully so. He felt he had heard worse. In any event, any discomfort he might have felt was erased by the sight that met his eyes.

The chasm widened briefly before dropping off into a larger canyon beyond. Flocks of gaily colored flumeeji, their oblong airsacs fully inflated and their bulging eyes scanning the riverbed below, drifted past, heading northward. Cutting through the comparatively soft limestone deposit, the now-vanished stream that had cut the sandy chasm down which he and Chraluuc were walking had left in its wake a soaring limestone arch. Long-dead stalactites hung from the underside of the arch—and that wasn't all.

Stronger than glass, lighter than quartz, a host of crystalline structures that were as complex in execution as they were beautiful to look at grew from beneath the arch. Others sprang from opposite sides of the chasm or arch. Most, though not all, of the thrust upward from its bed. Most, though not all, of the motifs, were abstract in design. There were blades and barbs, spirals and spikes, globes within globes, and mad, sweeping runs of glassine color that resembled nothing so much as unkempt hair. The patterns and devices reflected not only AAnn tradition but AAnn moods. As a human, he could respond to the physical beauty of the art even without being able to appreciate the emotional overtones.

Wherever the sun struck the tinted, shimmering surfaces, colored light exploded in all directions. It was as if someone had taken a shipload of sapphires, warped them into a thousand new shapes, combined the results with a load of transparent glue, and flung them all in the direction of the chasm's end, hoping some of it would stick.

As for the complementary music, it sprang from a trio of instruments. Though the devices themselves were unfamiliar to him, Flinx recognized two of the three players as fellow artisans of the Tier. All three paused in their playing to look up at the newcomers while one waved a greeting with her tail. Its flower-like terminus resting on the ground before her, the apparatus she was holding was twice her height and equipped with numerous fingerholes and tabs.

"That iss a vourak." Chraluuc led him toward the players, all of whom were seated on rock or bare sand. "All of the instrumentss that are ussed in creating The Confection are wind insstrumentss. The interlace resspondss better to the vibrationss they generate than to the vibrato of sstringss or the thump of percussion."

"Interlace?" On his shoulder, Pip was alert and attentive. She liked music.

"Watch." Chraluuc stopped.

The trio of musicians resumed their playing. As the sonorous piping of the vourak and the other instruments rose in volume, so did particulate matter from the vast reservoir that had accumulated at the bottom of the chasm. While Flinx looked on in fascination, the twisting streams of levitated sand flowed through a single large mechanism that was set in place against the far wall of the narrow gorge. They emerged transformed from spouts on the top.

"Insside," Chraluuc explained, "the ssand iss ssubjected to heat and pressure that transsformss it into a ceramossilicate composssite. A range of trace mineralss are added to create different colorss. As you can ssee, at pressent the artisstss are working with purple."

Indeed, three thin streams of deep color twirled upward from as many issuing spouts. As Flinx watched, they danced and coiled in perfect time to the music that was being played by the artisans. Certain notes caused a bit of one dancing stream or another to impact on the already immensely elaborate creation that lined the arch, walls, and floor of the chasm's terminus. The nearest analogy he could think of to what he was seeing was a growing, evolving, three-dimensional stained-glass window. At the same time, it was being fashioned not by hand or pro-gram but by sound as the streams of intensely colored material were manipulated and put in place by the music being played by the highly focused trio.

"It's beautiful," he finally thought to murmur.

"The Confection iss a creation of the entire Tier, an ex-pression of all that we believe we can accomplissh. Every-one participatess in itss fabrication. At the same time, one working on it iss very relaxing. Thiss iss one thing that we do when we are not working within our own individual fieldss, with our own chossen media." She gestured in the direction of the alien fabulosity. "When it iss finisshed, we will find another ssuitable place, another natural frame, and make another. And another, and another, until all the land around the central complex iss itsself transsformed into a unified work of art. Truly, none of thosse of uss currently working on it will live long enough to see thiss come to fruition, but ssuch iss often the casse with great art that iss rendered on a large sscale and iss the product of mass collaboration."

"Wonderful, wonderful!" Flinx was unable to take his eyes off it. The amalgam of natural setting, the dancing jets of chromatically colored sand, the steady stream of alien music, and the sparkling, shimmering Confection itself were mesmerizing.

Taking one of his soft hands in her leathery, scaled one, she drew him forward. "And as a member of the Tier, it iss incumbent upon you, too, Flinx, to contribute to the creation of The Confection."

"Me?" He allowed himself to be led toward the slope where the three player/sculptors were sitting in front of a small building that was used as a temporary shelter. "I'm no musician, Chraluuc. I can't play any of the instruments of my kind, much less one of yours."

"Only a few memberss of the Tier have mussical training, Flinx. We are artisstss, not mussicianss. But for the ssake of The Confection, we have learned. We practice." She gestured third-degree reassurance; almost a contradiction in terms. "You, too, will have time to practice, and to learn—and to contribute. There iss no hurry." As she gazed up at The Confection, a dazzle of ambient color danced in her eyes.

Pausing in their playing and sculpting, the trio greeted the visitors and listened attentively as Chraluuc explained her purpose in bringing the softskin to witness their work. To Flinx's dismay, all three expressed enthusiasm at the possibility of his participation. Compelled to choose among the instruments whose sounds were linked to the sophisticated mechanisms that produced and applied the brightly colored sand to the ever-growing Confection, he settled on the yoult. It was the smallest and simplest of the three, though one would never know it by the sounds that emerged following his first attempts.

Following the inevitable good-natured hissing and tail-slapping, Chraluuc and the others proceeded to instruct him in the use of the sculpting instrument. Not that finger, he was told repeatedly. Use your thumb. Apply the base of the left palm, so. Compensatory movements were designed on the spot to offset the fact that he only had five fingers on each hand instead of the usual six. At least, he thought to himself as he struggled with the yoult's dynamic fingering, none of the instruments was played with the tail.

When, after hours of instruction and feeble attempts, he at last managed to generate a simple melodic line and raise a trickle of bright violet particles from the palette of ceramosilicate, his companions applauded his effort with approving hisses. When just before sunset he managed to sustain a tonality long enough to actually induce a handful of the material to fuse to the crest of a curving six-sided tower that protruded from the wall of the chasm, he felt a sense of accomplishment that surpassed any praise they could lavish upon him. The feeling lasted until all five returned to the main complex, hiking back in the dark along a trail lit by light generated by their own sandals.

More congratulations were to be had when others were informed of the new acolyte's first successful work on The Confection. He accepted them all with quiet good grace, as he had come to do whenever a compliment was directed his way. Choosing not to linger following the communal evening meal, he retired to his tiny room.

It was all so very strange, he reflected as he lay on the sleeping sand that conformed to the contours of his body even as it warmed him against the night air. He had by now recalled enough to know that the reptiloids were sworn enemies of both the thranx and humankind. Yet these had saved his life, taken him in, and made him one of them—albeit not without some objection and controversy. Thus far, no one had tried to eat him, though he had on occasion caught aimed in his direction one or two less than sociable emotions. He was confused. The kindness of the Tier did not square with his memories.

Of course, they were social outcasts among their own kind, devoted as they were to something besides the immutable Imperial AAnn expansion. What more natural than that they should accept even an obnoxious amnesiac softskin as one of their own? He thought about it, let it worry him entirely too much. They had even allowed him to participate in their most important project, the creation of The Confection that would eventually constitute the crowning achievement of their Tier. He had been accepted. He was one of them. Truly.

Except that he was not. No matter how accepted he felt, no matter how completely he blended into the ways and workings of the Tier of Ssaiinn, he would always be a softskin, an outsider among outsiders. Worse, deprived of so much of his memory, he could not even be himself.

Rolling over onto his side, he stared through the dim light that filtered into the room from a high window at the stexrex arrangement Chraluuc had fashioned for him. In the faint moonlight, the tiny blue-and-yellow blossoms expanded and contracted slowly, as if breathing. The sight soothed him. Something about plants and growing greenery always did. He didn't think the feeling was anything exceptional.

The stexrex did, but was unable to give form or voice to its opinion.

11

In the depths of the simple living quarters that had become much more than merely a place of dwelling, Qyl-Elussab perused the news floating in the air before one disenchanted eye and brooded. The other eye was twisted around to contemplate the camouflaged, hidden compartment that held sophisticated electronics and undemanding explosives. Despite all that had happened, no significant public debate had emerged regarding the extensive AAnn presence on Jast. Was everything for naught? Was the body of the Vsseyan public really that uninterested in the unhurried but measured takeover of their world by the scaled bipeds? Could no one else see the sinister future that loomed over them all?

Qyl-Elussab had done as much as any single Vssey possibly could to awaken his kind to the subtle threat in their midst. From the lack of any significant reaction so far, it was evident that was not enough. A third passionate provocation was therefore in order. To distinguish itself, to rise above its predecessors, it should be considerably more destructive than those that had preceded it. A provocation on a wide scale was called for. To carry it out would require much careful planning, lest innocent (or more than the acceptable number of innocent) Vssey perish along with the AAnn interlopers.

Still, it could be done. There were several possibilities.

Qyl-Elussab was becoming more proficient at taunting the AAnn, as well as at killing them. Confidence brightened the dim confines of the dwelling area.

Give any Vssey a new vocation and they would inevitably get better with practice.

If not for the presence among the searching party of the two Imperial troopers and Takuna himself, the raid would have taken on the aspects of a comedy performed by the famous AAnn farceur Louhkouk VBLL. Dismounted from their individual transports, the squad of Vsseyan police hopped through the shattered doorway with all the urgency of a tired cub emerging reluctantly from its bed of sand. The only true indication of their resolve was the agitated writhing of their tentacles.

After allowing the Vsseyan authorities to enter first, just in case anyone within actually happened to harbor a hostile notion and was hefting the means to propitiate it, Takuna and the pair of troopers pushed their way in past the hopping, bounding police. They found themselves confronting a cluster of a dozen or so startled locals. While several of the Vsseyan police moved to check for weapons, others rushed to the computation equipment that flashed from the back wall. An electronic "freeze" had already been clamped on the entire building to prevent anyone within from erasing archived material of potential significance.

The officer in charge of the Vsseyan contingent beckoned for Takuna to come forward. The impatient administrator found himself confronting a quavering local of slightly less than average size. Both eyestalks had retracted as far as they could, giving the native's eyes the appearance of resting directly on the cap-like upper portion of its olive-gray body. The hearing frill hardly rippled, while the mouth slit was emitting so many bubbles of nervousness that Takuuna had a hard time seeing through them. Irritably, he reached out and brushed them aside, popping a goodly number in the process. It was a sorry breach of civility, but he was in no mood for coddling.

"This individual is identified as the nominal leader of this circle." The Vsseyan officer lowered the several small but effective weapons he clutched in his tentacles.

"Yes, I am Moulapuu." In response to the officer's non-threatening tone, the eyestalks extended themselves timidly.

"I am today's designate' principal here."

"Today'ss?" As always, Takuuna found himself struggling to understand the mushy argot that passed for a language among the locals.

Tentacles gesticulated, and the obnoxious flow of bubbles from the Vssey's mouth mercifully diminished. "Tomorrow, another will be chosen, and after that, another. We rotate our leadership."

Takuuna nodded, and spoke as if he knew something important the Vssey did not. "A truly excellent way to sshield your membership. Everyone takess a turn at giving orderss, sso that if anyone is killed, any other can handle the dutiess of leader. An admirable ssysstem for a terrorisst cell."

"Terrorist cell?" the Vssey squeaked. Both eyes turned to the officer of police. "What is the visitor talking about?"

As the officer replied methodically, tentacles gestured. "You an' your associates are suspecte' of having ties to the unknown organization that has recently carrie' out acts of sabotage against our good Imperial friends."

"Sabotage? Us?" Tentacles starred to ripple with amusement, but the motion ceased when the speaker saw that the intruders, AAnn and Vssey alike, were deadly serious. "What woul' ever give you such an idea? What coul' we have done to inspire such a nonsensical conception?" Behind them, the other members of the group had been herded into a tight knot by the Vsseyan police. The two AAnn troopers were already examining the impressive bank of electronics that dominated the back wall of the room.

Removing his tablet, Takuuna called up the relevant information. "Downsstream monitoring of thiss ssector by elementss of your own government hass revealed frequent and ssysstematic cycling of material relating to demolition, desstruction, and general warfare." Reversing the tablet, the administrator held the damning screen out for the circle leader to see. Eyestalks strained for the best view.

When no response was forthcoming, a hopeful Takuuna prompted. "Well, *pyssin*, are you going to tell me that you and your friendss do not recognize any of the viewed material that hass recently been recorded as passing through thiss location?"

His words moved the bewildered Vssey to reply, "No. Of course I recognize it."

"You are witness." Takuuna glanced over at the Vsseyan officer. "Thiss one confessess to making usse of the specified material."

"Certainly I do." The Vssey was torn between confussion and amusement. Tentacles fluttered at those who had been encircled. "We constitute the circle of Beirranus Enlightenment—Fourth through Twelfth Dynasties."

Takuuna blinked both sets of eyelids. "Explain yoursself," he hissed.

Hearing frill undulating serenely now, the speaker proceeded to do just that. "We are a research society whose particular interest lies in re-creating the great battles of the eight fractured ruling families of southern Jast. It is an extensive and ongoing project. Our objective is to imagine and reconstruct the many possible outcomes base' on known historical factors as viewe' through the prism of contemporary knowledge."

The Vsseyan officer could not repress the twitching of dozens of tentacles as the last of the weapons they held slowly pointed toward the floor. "Historians! This is a conclave of historians." As word spread around the room, even the AAnn troopers were hard-pressed to conceal their amusement.

Takuuna was not pleased. This was not the overwhelming breakthrough he had hoped to make. Aware that everyone, and in particular the two now-hesitant troopers, was watching him, he fought to fit the preconceived notions with which he had organized and mounted the raid into the inconvenient reality that had presented itself.

"Truly, it seeemss that you are even more clever and cunning than I had thought possible. It iss a very clever cover you have concocted here, but it will not ssave you from further interrogation. Perhapss then other truthss will emerge." He turned sharply to the Vsseyan officer in charge. "Bring them in. All of them. We will find out how much truth there iss in thiss one'ss claimss and how much may lie sshrewdly concealed beneath artful wordss."

Weapons drawn, the two troopers advanced to comply with the administrator's orders. The cluster of Vsseyan police were less immediately reactive. Holding their weapons at ease, not hopping to obey, they looked to their superior for further instructions—and clarification.

The leader of the circle of anxious researchers hopped forward until he was within tentacle-touching length of the officer. "Your pleasure, respecte' one! We are nothing more than what we are." Flexible limbs indicated the speaker's assembled colleagues. "We conduct our research in private because it is frowne' upon by those of the establishment who would brook no questioning of the history of this part of our worl'! Hence the nee' to pursue our work in this private place. We are peaceful citizens who know nothing of the terrible events of which you speak. All of us here have our own friends to return to. Some of us have buddings to nurture. Nothing will come of questioning us about matters on which we are blissfully ignorant, and will only result in deprivation and distress for all concerne'." Seeing the officer hesitate, the speaker continued.

"All of us are well known. We have recorde' places of dwelling where we can be found at all times, and positions of responsibility that are easily monitore'." Tentacles indicated the wall of electronics. "If you must, confiscate an' examine everything that we have utilize' in our work, but please, let us go. We will voluntarily accept monitoring devices." A chorus of agreement rose from the others. "You will quickly see that we pose no harm to anyone or anything, except perhaps orthodox historical theory."

The plea was as wily as it was impassioned, a frustrated Takuuna realized. Monitoring devices could be tricked. He wasn't so easy. "We will investtigate everything at the proper time. Bring them along."

Next to him, the Vsseyan officer was plainly hesitating. Unlike the rest of the squad, the officer was not intimidated by the AAnn administrator or his well-armed escort. "I must tell you that, after hearing what I have hear' and seeing what I have seen, I am no longer convince' such a step is necessary." Limbs gestured at the nervous assembled. "These citizens are either the finest actors I have ever encountere' in my professional career, or else they are nothing more than what they claim to be: students and investigators of an alternate history. I am incline' to accept their offer to wear monitors until they can be cleare' unreservedly or charge' without hesitation."

Takuuna whirled on the officer, shoving his face toward

the staring eyes. "I have disspenssation to do whatever I deem iss necessary from the uppermosst level of your government, and I ssay all of thesse dissemblerss here need to be brought in for formal questtioning!"

The officer's eyestalks did not flinch, and the Vssey held its ground in the face of the AAnn's anger. While retaining its distinctive wispishness, the native's voice grew tight.

"While I do not dispute your status, respecte' administrator, I must remin' *you* that I am in comman' of this local force, an' until an' unlesss I receive a directive to the contrary, they respon' to my orders an' not to that of guests. No matter how respecte'."

There was that word again. *Guests.* Takuuna hoped he would be stationed on Jast long enough to see the appellation removed. But Jast was not yet a part of the Empire. However grating for the AAnn assigned to the world of the Vssey, its nominal independence had to be respected. For a while longer, anyway.

He had worked among the Vssey long enough by now to be able to judge their moods. Eyeing the ordinary members of the constabulary, it was clear that their sympathy lay with their uneasy brethren rather than the task at hand. Though he well knew this clutch of panicky locals was far more likely to consist, as claimed, of revisionist historians instead of murderous conspirators, he was loath to concede the point. Nor did he relish the idea of appearing to concede a posture of control to the obdurate Vssey officer.

But Takuuna had not survived and prospered for as long as he had by showing the stubbornness of a moleq in heat. Ordering one of his troopers to put a gun to the official's upper body might regain the administrator the upper hand. It might also provoke a firefight between AAnn troopers and Vsseyan police. No matter who won, such a confrontation, it would not look good on his record. This time, then, it suited him to defer.

He executed an intricate gesture that, in AAnn circles, would have cast the gravest aspersions on the legitimacy of the officer's lineage. Unfamiliar as he was with the arm and tail movements of the scaled visitors, the subject of the appalling slander did not respond. But both of the AAnn troopers hissed a mixture of shock and amusement.

"Ssince you are determined to inssist on thiss matter, I sshall concede the point. If future eventss sshould determine that your assessment of the ssituation iss horribly wrong, I have no doubt that your own buddingss will be assigned to pull out your eyess and tentacless one at a time." While far from satisfied with the outcome of the raid, Takuuna took satisfaction in knowing that he would depart fully insulated from any adverse consequences that might ensue.

The Vsseyan officer tensed visibly, tentacles stiffening and hearing frill going motionless. "I accept the responsibility." Pivoting in place, the whole trunk-and-cap body inclined slightly in the direction of the still tightly bunched cluster of suspects. "As we have only a few monitoring devices with us, we will nee' identification and notification of places of residence from all of you so that those not properly equippe' can be fitte' at a future time an' date."

"'Future date.'" Takuuna inhaled stiffly through the nostrils set on the end of his short snout. "If you are wrong about any of thesse, you will never ssee them again."

As the officer's subordinates moved to fix several of the assembled with the tiny tracking devices, the senior Vssey's eyes swiveled to regard the AAnn administrator.

"You shoul' not concern yourself. It is my eyes that are pledge', not yours."

"Truly," agreed Takuuna. He was not entirely displeased. Any operation that perpetuated his authority was a useful one. Any circle of Vssey that could not be indicted for being filthy with dangerous malcontents was one that could be officially listed as inoffensive. Either assessment was of value.

Prove them guilty or prove them innocent, he could take the credit for being the one who had done so.

Days later, back at work in his expanded, much enlarged office within the Imperial Administration compound on the outskirts of Skokosas, Takuuna took time to savor some of the snacks that had been set out on his desk by his adjutant. The expensive treats had been imported all the way from Goavssay, an Imperial world noted for the excellence and sophistication of its food exports. As a secondary administrator he would never have been able to afford such luxuries. But as the head of the special detachment in charge of rooting out the perpetrators of the violent outrages against the Imperial presence on Jast, he had received a salary increase commensurate with his promotion in status. It was not quite the equal of an official divestiture of a personal hierarchical subjunctive, but as an intermediary rise in status it brought with it unquestionable advantages.

The snacks did their best to escape his attention, racing about on miniscule legs. Unable to escape the smooth, polished confines of the serving dish, they eventually resorted to trying to hide in its corners. Since the serving dish was perfectly round, this tactic was doomed to failure before it began. He relished them one after another, using his long tongue to ritually lick their sticky internal body fluids from his claws after each was crunched and consumed, until at last the dish stood silent and empty. Only then, his appetite sated, did he activate his personal communicator.

It took several moments for a response to form. That was to be expected. As the head of Imperial Administration on Jast, Keliichu was forever busy. He could not be expected to drop whatever he was doing simply to reply to a call from the head of a special unit, much less a secondary administrator. Eventually, however, the imposing figure of the elderly AAnn coalesced out of the air to the immediate right of Takuuna's desk.

And as usual, the gaunt, ax-like face wasted no time on pleasantries. "What newss of your progress, Unit Leader Takuuna?"

The administrator gestured second-degree satisfaction. "As the ressult of careful planning and preparation, a recent raid in the city of Wevepevv in the southern continent exposed a ssecret faction of native academiess whosse activities invite not only general ssuspicion but in all probability will necessitate a good deal of additional monitoring of their immediate circle. I have already put in the requesst for the necessary additional personnel."

Keliichu glanced briefly at something out of the range of his pickup. "It lately sstrikess not only myself but otherss that the ability on your part to expand your budget and sstaff iss not matched by a corressponding facility for actually capturing thesse malefactorss."

Takuuna was glad his tail was out of range of the pickup on his desk, so that the senior administrator could not observe its nervous twitching. "While it iss true that one musst proceed expeditiously in ssuch matters, proper care and prudence musst also be taken. Imagine the harm to our image among the population sshould we unjusstly accusse or imprisson any of the guiltless among them." He delivered this admonition with practiced skill, blithely ignoring the fact that that was precisely what he had nearly done in Wevepevv.

Keliichu gestured first-degree irritation, a dollop of digital punctuation so biting that it caused Takuuna to cringe. "I want ressultss, Unit Leader! Caution in a difficult ssituation iss to be commended. Incapability iss not. You are presently in command of extensive ressourcess, at considerable expense to the Imperial financess. Other ssectorss of our pressence on Jasst are doing without sso that you may do with." Keen eyes glared from the depths of the senior administrator's image.

"If you cannot be productive in the capacity to which you have been assigned, perhapss a more appropriate possting can be found. I await with eagerness your next report."

The communication's image dissipated in a flicker of discontent, leaving a troubled Takuuna alone in his silent, impressive new office. There was no mistaking Keliichu's warning. Either the special unit Takuuna commanded produced an actual radical or two, or he would quickly find himself back shuffling reports and dealing with the mundane problems of the everyday AAnn presence on Jasst. Not a likely position from which to obtain significant advancement. He hissed wearily. It appeared that he was going to actually have to *do* something. A difficult undertaking, he reflected, given the distinct possibility that there *was* no large-scale insurrection directed at the AAnn.

But *someone* was responsible for the two serious acts of violence that had been directed at the Imperial presence. About that, there was no dispute. All he had to do was find those responsible. It seemed such a simple, straightforward task. If only these so-called sentients, these somnambulistic Vssey, were more like the AAnn! Everything moved so slowly on Jast, everything had to be done by consensus. As far as he was concerned, the natives were barely a generation removed from the fixed-site creatures from which they had evolved.

He wracked his brain for a way to accelerate the process of search and discovery. His efforts as he plowed grimly through the endless reports that drifted above his desk spawned a substantial headache, but no insight.

The last thing he expected to find was a diversion.

It was not marked urgent, or pressing, or deserving of any more than passing attention. Had he not been so preoccupied, with half his mind trying to focus on his work while the other half sought a means of delaying Keliichu's wrath, he might have skipped over it entirely. But the division of mental labor slowed him down somewhat.

Hissing a sharp, startled command, he froze the specific report in place. It hovered before him, the information floating in the air. As he leaned toward it, it automatically drew back to remain in focus.

It made no sense. Ordinarily, he would have dismissed it out of hand, had he even bothered to read it. For one thing, it bore no particular relation to his specific mission. In that respect it was remarkable that it had even found its way into the endless file of suspect data that he was obliged to peruse. In fact, he would have ignored the body of the report save for the fact that it contained a pair of integrated images. That he recognized them immediately was not surprising. That they existed at all was mind-numbing.

The report had been filed by one of his unit's operatives who had actually been off duty at the time. Nevertheless, though engaged in a period of relaxation, the operative had remained mindful of the task to which she was normally assigned. Something she had encountered in the course of her traveling had piqued her interest. She evidently thought it might also pique that of the unit's commander. She was right.

Of the two images incorporated into the report, one had been taken from a distance while the other showed its subject in close-up. The first was a view of several figures dressed in idiosyncratic costumes strolling together among some admirable landscaping and simple, low buildings. All of the figures except one were AAnn. The close-up showed the questionable figure engaged in conversation with a shorter, female nye. Takuuna rotated the images carefully, examining them from all sides. There was no mistaking the identity of the non-nye.

His designated human spy was still alive.

That was crazy. Takuuna had killed the softskin himself, had seen him fall over the cliff face of Saudaunn Chasm and plunge to his death.

No, the administrator corrected himself cautiously. He had seen the softskin go over and, scrambling to look down into the canyon, had subsequently failed to catch sight of the human. He had *not* actually seen him plummet to his death. Clearly, something had caught and stopped him before he had taken the fatal plunge, because he looked none the worse for what should have been a fatal experience.

But if he had survived, and made his way to civilized surroundings, why had he not reported in, much less leveled some kind of accusation against the aggressive Takuuna? It made no sense. The administrator enlarged the accompanying words.

According to the information provided to the wandering but resourceful underling, the human had little memory of who he was, where he had come from, or what he was doing on Jast. Takuuna allowed himself to relax ever so slightly. If the softskin was suffering from loss of memory—as seemed to be the case—there was no guarantee it would never return to him. However, *if* it did, the softskin would be in a position to make things very uncomfortable for a certain rising secondary administrator. Furthermore, the human seemed to have been taken in, if not outright adopted, by the Tier of Ssaiinn.

What in the proscribed nomenclature of all the Twelve Deaths was the Tier of Ssaiinn? Some speedy research produced the required explanation. Takuuna almost laughed aloud as he read. A misbegotten lot of wacky creative types who had isolated themselves on a plateau in search of peace, quiet, and artistic enlightenment. That much, at least, *did* make sense. Who else among the AAnn would take in a softskin and care for it, instead of eating him outright?

Just to be sure, he checked the pair of visuals against the immigration record in the files. They were a perfect match. The one who had called himself Flinx had returned from the depths and the dead. But if the report was to be believed, the human remembered next to nothing of what had happened to him. Doubtless he did not recollect the sharp blow from Takuuna's tail that had contributed to his present mental state. Takuuna did not intend to give the death-defying softskin a chance to remember.

He would have preferred to ignore the situation. But he could not. Should the human's memory return, he might take the story of how he had come to strike his head with the walls of Saudaunn Chasm to Imperial Administration. While they would not have much sympathy for an itinerant softskin, they would have even less for one of their own suspected of treachery. And filing the kind of false report that he had turned in concerning the encounter would hurt even more. There was always the small but potentially sobering possibility that the unit commander's superiors would believe it.

That possibility could not be allowed to eventuate. The best way to ensure that Keliichu and the others did not have the opportunity to hear the softskin's story was to make certain it could never be told. Rising from his desk, he instructed it on how to deal with the rest of the day's queries and conversations, and what kind of excuses to make for his absence. As for himself, Takuuna VBXLLW was in such a hurry to take care of the unfinished business that he rushed off without even confirming his appointment for the evening's mating clash.

All was silent within the KK-drive ship *Teacher*. Automatics recycled the atmosphere and kept clean the water in the vacant relaxation chamber's decorative pond and waterfall. Artificial gravity prevented the normal shedding of the chamber's plants from flying off to clog the various ducts and intakes.

The relaxation chamber was the only place on the ship where there was any kind of movement or organic life. Unneeded elsewhere, the lights in the corridors and rooms, the shuttle bay and pilot's bridge, remained dark. But there were decorative plants in the chamber, and they needed light as well as air and moisture. Occasionally, unobserved, a few branches belonging to certain particularly exotic specimens twisted or coiled in silence, an occasional tentacle-like root went exploring. But for the most part, the lounge was as quiescent as the rest of the vessel.

When a certain predesignated period of time had passed, previously inactive circuits engaged. New programming was triggered. This notified the ship that its owner should by now have issued a command or two in person, and that he had not done so. Given this specified lack of communication, it was determined that certain consequences should ensue.

Dormant instruments became active. In the absence of command input, programming took over. One of these involved a certain level of concern. Already anxious about the emotional stability of its owner, the *Teacher* was now forced to contemplate the fact that it had not had any contact with him in too long a time.

Inquiries were broadcast. They were not answered. Signals were sought. They were not found. In its memory, the ship possessed, among other identifying features, the complete genome of one Philip Lynx as well as that of his pet Alaspinian minidrag. As an extensive long-range scan for such biological factors was not feasible, other tracing methods would have to be employed. One of these involved placing demands on other memories, organic as well as mechanical. The *Teacher* had been trained to carry out such inquiries in a clandestine manner.

Dropping orbit closer to the planetary surface beneath it, the ship began surreptitiously querying the storage facilities of both the resident and guest sentient species. There was more material to examine than even a very smart person could have scrutinized in many lifetimes. The *Teacher* was able to remote-view the information rather more rapidly than any organic intelligence, however. Millions, billions of bits of information were stealthily scanned, analyzed, and discarded. This lack of success did not frustrate the ship. Frustration was not a fault to which its programming was susceptive. It simply continued to search.

Flinx had landed on Jast. Therefore, though his physical condition could not at present be properly ascertained, it was most likely that Flinx was still on Jast. It was just a matter of finding him.

The search continued, unremarked upon by any by-standers—save perhaps in their own unique, unfathomable way, a certain small portion of the decorative flora that filled the ship's relaxation chamber with unusually perceptive greenery.

12

The twosome of troopers who were accompanying Takuna frequently argued among themselves. While it was flattering to be asked to accompany the head of the antiinsurgency unit, he had acquired a reputation for being easily aggravated, and for subsequently taking out his exasperation on those unfortunate enough to be in his vicinity. On the other hand, both knew that a successful mission could result in the granting of favors, or even promotion within the corps. As the latter was certainly not to be gained by patrolling office buildings or sifting through endless reports devoid of anything consequential, there was a certain amount of competition among the lower ranks for what were regarded as potentially plum assignments.

That did not keep them from squabbling among themselves or wondering what they were doing so far from the nearest AAnn outpost. Piloting the aircar across the plateau, they found themselves racing farther and farther away from Skokosas and any center of civilization—Vssey as well as AAnn.

While the troopers bickered quietly among themselves, Secondary Administrator Takuuna sat in the back of the aircar and brooded, only occasionally deigning to speak. Not that the troopers expected him to provide entertaining conversation, but it would at the very least have been nice to know where they were headed and what was going to be expected of them when they got there.

Finally, Yerelka could stand it no longer. Ignoring her confederate's cautioning gestures, she swiveled around in her codriver's chair and hissed politely but firmly in the direction of their supervisor and passenger.

"Mosst honored unit leader, while we at all times resspect the need for official secrecy, it sstrikes my companion and me (Trooper Craaxu tried to bury his head in the control console) that we cannot be expected to be very effective in carrying out a mission whosse purposse is forever kept from uss."

Outside, native vegetation sped past beneath and alongside the aircar. Takuuna sniffed, his tail switching once from left to right as a sign that he had heard. Craaxu held his breath.

"A not unreassonable request," Takuuna replied considerately. A relieved Craaxu inhaled. "We are going to make an arresst, of a dangerouss anti-Imperial activisst."

"One of the murdererss." Yerelka's impatience promptly gave way to excitement.

"Not precissely," Takuuna was quick to explain. "While not being directly ressponssible for the deathss of sso many of our fellow nye, it iss believed that thiss individual hass contributed to the general unresst that hass insspired other localss to carry out ssuch desspicable actss."

"Jusst as bad." Craaxu caressed instrumentation as the aircar's autopilot sought clarification of an indeterminate landmark. "One who perssuades another to pull a trigger iss jusst as guilty as if he had fired the weapon himsself."

Takuuna smiled inwardly. "I knew, of coursse, that you would both ssee it that way. There iss no other way to ssee it."

Yerelka continued to confront the administrator. "It iss

difficult to believe that anything could rousse thesse creatures to ssuch violent action. The one we sseek musst be a very active Vssey indeed."

Rising from his seat, the administrator moved forward to position himself behind and between the troopers. Beyond the transparent dome of the aircar, the countryside had become familiar. Recent unpleasant memories returned to him, unbidden and insistent.

"The individual we sseek iss not a Vssey, but a human."

"A ssoftsskin!" Craaxu looked back sharply, eyes wide, both eyelids retracted, nostrils flared. "There iss a ssoftsskin on Jasst, agitating the Vssey?"

Takuuna gestured third-degree confirmation. "Why sshould you find that ssurprissing?"

"It iss jusst," the trooper hesitated, unsure, "I did not know there were any repressentativess of the Commonwealth government on Jasst."

"We do not know that thiss individual directly repressentss his government. Only that he iss a troublemaker who hass been ssowing uncertainty and disscontent among the Vssey." The administrator hissed softly. "When we get him back to Ssokossass, we will find out who ssponssorss him."

"Truly," Trooper Yerelka had grown dark. "I had friendss in Morotuuver. Perhapss I might be permitted to offer my sservicess in aid of the official interrogation?"

"All thingss are possible," Takuuna replied paternally. He would have no trouble with these two, he saw. Whether he would with the eccentric talents among whom his quarry was sheltering, that still remained to be seen.

As the aircar banked gently to the northeast, he knew that the commendably eager trooper would not be given the opportunity to help in questioning the prisoner. Because the prisoner might decide, during interrogation or even before, to tell his side of a story involving a certain administrator, a canyon, and a near-fatal confrontation. That could not be allowed to happen.

As before, the softskin would "resist." And when he did so this time, Takuuna reflected grimly, no one would be left wondering as to the nature of his fate.

For an isolated experiment in living and working on a non-Imperial world, the compound that was home to the Tier of Ssaiinn proved to be greater in extent than he expected. As hints of more and more semi-subterranean structures manifested themselves beside the decelerating aircar, the administrator was impressed in spite of himself. He had come expecting to find a bunch of addled artisans scribbling abstract designs in the sand while scrabbling for food among the native fauna. What he found instead was a sophisticated, modern multiplex that, save for its alien surroundings, would not have been out of place on any developed Imperial world.

That was all to the good, truly. It meant he would be able to put his claws on the softskin Flinx all the more quickly.

Having called ahead to announce his coming, he was not surprised when the arriving aircar was met as it touched down at the designated arrival site. The female who greeted him was austerely clad in the favored style of her Tier. An additional bonus, Takuuna thought as he let his eyes rove over her from tail-tip to shimmering snout. If she was as talented as she was lissome, she would make a fine candidate for mating with a future noble like himself.

Throats were exposed, claws retracted as she acknowledged the arrivals. "I am Chraluuc. I will bring you to the Ssemilionn. They are curiouss as to your purposse in coming."

Takuuna fell into step beside her as the two troopers brought up the rear. Off toward the east, a large flock of moulops drifted steadily southward, their massed peeping a distant, high-pitched din. Looking like ballooning teeth, several more maneuverable gholomps ranged outside the flock, searching for stragglers. The active predators dared not dip into the flock itself. The moulops' effective defensive strategy consisted of surrounding an attacker with their bodies and slowly enveloping it with strands of mucus until the shrouded attacker, impossibly weighed down and unable to clean itself, fell harmlessly to earth. But stragglers outside the flock were easy prey. The gholomps dipped and rose, biding their time.

Takuuna made a gesture indicative of third-degree bemusement. "Why sshould they be curiouss? I communicated my intent more than an hour ago." He moved closer to the female. In response, she edged ostentatiously away, preserving the minimum formal distance between them. Oh well, *bissank*, he thought. Perhaps he had moved too soon. There was plenty of time before he needed to depart.

"Possibly they require clarification." She was polite, but reserved. A few well-placed tail slaps would loosen her up, the administrator decided.

"Clarification?" As they entered the nearest structure, he simultaneously hissed and gestured amusement. "I come seeking an illegal human renegade. I sshould think that sufficiently sstraightforward as to brook little in the way of confussion." Descending a gentle ramp, they turned into a wide, skylit corridor. As they walked, the two troopers murmured among themselves, admiring the spectacular swirls and colors of the elegant skylights.

"You will have to ask that of the Ssemiliomn. I am only a member of the Tier, not one of itss honored Elders."

"Truly yess. Your Tier." He studied her quite beautiful

face; the arch of eye, the shine of scale, the fine, white, sharp teeth that could equally well nibble playfully as shear through bone. "How do you find it, living out here in the emptiness of an alien world whose backwards inhabitantss are sometimess openly unfriendly to nye?"

"Being an artisst, I thrive in issolation." Her sandaled feet slap-slapped rhythmically on the decorated pavement underfoot. "We have no conflict with the Vssey, as few of them pass thiss way. What ssuppliess we need we bring in as required from Bouibouw, the nearesst town. The Vssey there, at leasst, are ussed to uss and give uss no trouble."

Takuuna hissed mild condescension. "At leasst they undersstand commerce." Changing tack, he asked abruptly, "The illicit ssoftsskin I sseek: have you sseen him?"

"Yess, I have sseen him. And talked with him."

Takuuna repressed his excitement. "I know that he sspeakss the civilized tongue remarkably well. What do you sspeak of?"

"Art, naturally," she replied. "Many things. As much as he can manage, ssince he came to uss devoid of memory."

The administrator kept his tone carefully neutral. "Devoid of memory, you ssay?"

"Truly. He wass found near here and near death. When he recovered, he wass without memory of himsself. It iss returning to him, but very sslowly."

"Remarkable. Hass he mentioned how he came to be in the sstate in which he wass found?"

"No." Her pink tongue flashed out to lick one eye before recoiling, snake-like, back into her mouth. "Of that he hass no remembrance."

Yet, Takuuna thought. This was even better than he had hoped. The human still had no memory of the administrator knocking him over the edge of Saudaunn Chasm. If all went well, the softskin might not even recognize Takuuna, in which event he was unlikely to offer any kind of resistance. Furthermore, in the absence of conclusive recollection, he would be hard-pressed to raise objections to the accusations Takuuna was now thinking of leveling against him. By employing sufficient effective sophistry, he might even be persuaded to think himself guilty! The only thing better would be for the softskin to actually admit to inspiring the acts of violence that had taken place against the AAnn. The more he thought about it, the more the administrator inclined toward taking the human back alive instead of simply shooting him while he was in the process of trying to "escape."

Takuuna could not have found things more to his liking had he programmed them himself.

They paused before a double door fashioned of sculpted sand that had been made permanent by the application of a glossy endurizer. To the touch, it felt like warm sand. But nothing less than a rifle would dent it. Following a brief verbal exchange between his sinuous escort and a wall communicator, they were admitted.

The Ssemiliionn of the Ssaiinn were an impressive tri-une. Doubtless he would have enjoyed conversing with them at length, if he'd had the time. But he was impatient to collect what he had come for and to return to Sko-kosas. Following a brief and courteous exchange of pleas-antries, he made the request. The response shocked him to his core. His request was perfunctory, forthright, and devoid of convolution.

The last thing he expected was for it to be denied.

In the silence that followed the downbeat declamation of the female member of the Ssaiinn, he struggled to col-lect his thoughts.

"Truly," he finally stammered in indignation, "you are ssaying that you *have* the ssofsskin but that you refusse to turn him over to my recognized authority?"

"Truly," murmured Naalakot with apparent regret.

Standing before the male Elder and his two companions, a quietly fuming Takuuna wondered at the genuineness of the sentiment.

Unable to think of anything else to say, the mystified administrator inquired icily, "May I assk why?"

Viinpou responded. "Firsstly, you have not shown any reasson why we sshould feel the need to do sso."

Takuuna felt as if the solid surface beneath his sandals had suddenly turned to pottage, and that he was sinking, sinking downward into a vat of suffocating incomprehension. What was going on here? Was this a dream, a nightmare? But the air in his lungs was pungent with room [ ]linked flagrantly, he felt the pressure

[ ]d to do sso'? I am not required to [ ]hingss—or anything elsse, for that [ ] Secondary Administrator Takuuna [ ]er of a special security unit of the [ ]n Jasst, and in that capacity I am not [ ]y actionss to you or to anyone elsse [ ]diate ssuperiorss! Are you really re-fussing to turn over to my cusstody an alien—a human, no less—who iss ssuspected of helping to foment anti-Imperial ssentiment on thiss world?"

"Truly," confirmed Xeerelu quietly.

Takuuna suppressed the fury he was feeling. "You ssaid 'firsstly.' Am I to infer that you have more than one 'reasson' for thiss blatant dissregard of authority?" While his voice stayed steady, his tail whipped back and forth in an uncontrollable display of anger.

"Yess." In the coda to a crescendo of surprises, it was his guide who stepped forward. "The Tier of Ssaiinn doess not matter-of-factly agree to the aresst of one of itss memberss without proof of wrongdoing."

"Proof of . . ." Takuuna gaped at her. Even the two

troopers looked disorientated. "Wait. 'One of iss memberss,' you ssaid?"

Chraluuc glanced briefly at the Ssemilionn. When Naalakot gestured imperceptibly, it was enough for her. "That iss right. The ssoftsskin iss a member of the Tier. He iss one of uss."

"But that iss, truly that iss inssane!" Takuna was beside himself. "The Tier iss of The Kind. Ssince when doess it admit hosstile alienss, and a human at that, into itss membership?"

Chraluuc walked around him to stand before and to one side of the silent, assembled Ssemilionn. "Ssince thiss particular one came among uss. Hiss kind may be hosstile to uss. That I do not know much of. I am, and all of uss of the Tier are, artissans, not politicianss. We do know that thiss one hass exhibited toward uss nothing in the way of the hosstility of which you sspeak, and that ssince coming among uss he hass comported himsself with the kind of decency and grace that would bring credit to any Tier or organization, regardless of sspeciess."

Takuna's hissing fell so low that it became difficult to understand his words. "I will ssay thiss only once. The human iss an enemy alien. If you choosse to sshelter him, there will be conssequencess. That you will ssuffer."

From behind Chraluuc, Naalakot spoke up. "We of the Tier are ussed to dealing with adverse 'conssequencess.' Unless you can produce hard evidence identifying thiss individual ssoftsskin as a real and present danger to uss and to our kind, he will remain here, under our protection."

Takuuna would have been excused for flying into a rage—but he did not. Uncontrolled fury was the province of the inept. So he contained, barely, his anger within him.

"You have given me your reasons for defying Imperial

authority. Now I want to hear what possible, conceivable rationale you could have for *wanting* to do sso."

Anticipating the question even before the administrator's arrival, Chraluuc had prepared a response. "The Tier of Ssaiinn iss about art, not about politicss. Above all elsse, we value individual creativity. Thiss ssoftsskin hass demonsstrated that he possessess that quality. He wass deemed desserving of becoming one of uss.

"He hass now dwelt among uss long enough for uss to determine that he posess no threat, either to uss or to anyone elsse. In that time he hass not left the confiness of the Tier or been in communication with anyone on the outsside. Therefore, truly, he cannot in any way be ressponssible for the atrocities againsst our kind that have taken place during hiss sojourn here."

Takuuna stared at her, all thoughts of possible mating forgotten. It took an effort for him to keep from lashing the furniture, much less this impertinent female. "Humanss are noted for their cleverness. Are you then sso ssure the one you harbor iss as harmless as you inssisst? You admit to your own ignorance. What do you, artisst, know of humanss?"

"What do you know of them, Adminisstrator?" she shot back. "Truly, we of the Tier know little of humanss. But we do know *this* one." She refused to back down, either verbally or physically. Nearby, the trio that comprised the Ssemilionn backed her up with stares and gestures.

Takuuna calmed himself. "There iss more to thiss than what you have ssaid. I ssensse that you sseek more here than defiance of authority." Behind him, the armed troopers shifted uneasily. Their heavy weapons rode awkwardly on their backs, ready to be drawn should the unit leader give the order. But shooting tentacular, headless Vssey or pale, soft-bodied humans was one thing. There was nothing appealing about the prospect of having to pull guns on their own kind.

Chraluuc gestured first-degree acknowledgment. "We of the Tier are artissts. As artissts, we seek to communicate through our work. We have come to view the human who fell to our care as a work in progress. He arrived here not knowing anything of himsself, hiss background, or much else. That includess any prejudice he previoussly may have held againsst our kind. He wass, in that ssensse, a blank sscroll. Ssince he hass been here, we have had the opportunity to write on that ssroll."

Takuuna gestured confusion. "I follow your wordss, but not your conclussion."

Grateful that the Ssemiionn continued to back her, Chraluuc continued. "In thiss human we ssee a chance to promote greater undersstanding between our resspective sspeciess. We believe that, given enough time, we can mold him into a usseful ambassador between human and AAnn. Nothing can sserve the Empire better than to esstablissh closser linkss with the humanss. The more that undersstanding growss between our two sspeciess, the greater the detriment to the thranx."

They *were* crazy, these hermetic, isolation-loving artists, Takuuna decided. "You cannot make friendss with the ssoftsskinss. They are ssteadfasstly allied to the thranx, and alwayss will be. Human and thranx are part and parcel of the ssame foe." He took a step passt her, toward the watchful Ssemiionn. "It may be that you are right, that the human hass done nothing wrong. But he *iss* under ssuspicion. He musst be taken to Sskokossass for proper interrogation."

"Under whosse ssupervission?" Chraluuc asked quietly.

Right then, he ought to have slipped out of his sandals and disemboweled her with a ritual double upward kick, Takuuna knew. The accusation was blatant. Behind him, he sensed the troopers stirring nervously. Even the heretofore phlegmatic Ssemilionn tensed. Instead, he did the unexpected. He calmly answered the question.

"As head of the unit charged with finding thosse ressponsible for the recent atrocitiess that have been committed againsst our people, it iss part of my job to identify and take into cusstody all thosse who fall under ssusspicion. The speciess to which he belongss iss by itself ssufficient to render the human ssusspect. I am ssorry you cannot ssee that, *vssassp*. But it doess not matter." He gestured second-degree reassurance coupled with an overt gesture of concession.

"Let me take him to Sskokossass. Nothing will happen to him without good and proven reasson. If he iss as innocent and ignorant of the affairss of which I sspeak, he will be returned to you in good order, at which time you may ressume your romantic, unrealisstic, and may I add, lunatic undertaking. It and itss outcome iss of no interesst to me. But I musst return with him in custody."

"No." All eyes turned to Naalakot. "The human iss one of uss. He will not go with you."

"No?" Takuuna made a sharp, short gesture. Reluctantly, the two troopers unlimbered their rifles. "You continue to inssisst on defying my authority?"

Despite her advanced age, Xeerelu advanced on him with surprising speed, stepping between him and the tautly muscled Chraluuc. "What authority, precissely, iss that, Administrsator? Becausse of the sspecial nature of the Tier's Imperial charter, you require a certification of second-degree emergency in order to be able to usse force here." She could not smile like a softskin, but her punctuating hiss accomplished the same thing. "We of the Tier of Ssaiinn are not nearly sso addled as you appear to think. Among other thingss, we are quite knowledgeable about the rightss that over the yearss we have sstudiously ssought to compile."

Takuuna hesitated. Everyone was watching him, including the edgy troopers. Since assuming the mantle of unit leader he always traveled prepared to deal with potential physical resistance. Resistance of the legal variety was another matter entirely. The Elder's words unsettled him, but he did not let it show.

"A moment, truly."

While everyone waited in silence, it took only a couple of minutes for him to check the truth of the Elder's statement. Gazing at the readout that appeared on his tablet, he was forced to still the trembling in his fingers. It was all there, just as the withered old recluse had insisted, in the official Imperial file relating to the Tier of Ssainn and its Imperial charter. Despite the mandate he had been given by the administrative authority on Jast, he could not initiate a forcible search of the Tier's premises without first securing the requisite certification of at least second-degree emergency. Furthermore, the necessary documentation could not be obtained secondhand. Because of its sensitive nature, he had to make the initial application in person.

Of course, he could go ahead, anyway, claiming the need to act on a developing emergency situation on the ground, and attempt to justify his actions later. But these were fellow AAnn he was dealing with, not dawdling natives. There would be many witnesses to dispute the veracity of his claim. Thinking fast, he mulled his options.

If they were so proud of this provocative human's presence among them, and ready to admit to it, that suggested no urgency on their part to hide him. Therefore, the soft-skin was likely to still be here, resting and relaxing among his fellow "artisans" for the foreseeable future. While the delay was frustrating, it was only that: a delay.

Continuing to repress his fury, he gestured as politely as he could manage to the Ssemilionn Elder. He deliberately ignored the acerbic female Elder. She did not seem especially distressed by the oversight.

"I, of course, have no intention of subverting Imperial law, desspite the urgency of thiss matter. I will therefore take my leave of you and not return unless I have with me the appropriate criteria for proceeding with thiss matter." He glared forcefully at each of the Elders. "Until then, I trusst that no attempt will be made to secretly move the ssoftsskin to another location."

"He iss one of uss," Naalakot declared yet again. "He will remain among uss."

"Deprived of hiss memoriess," Viinpou added, "where elsse would he go?"

While the response did not satisfy, it was sufficient to mollify Takuuna. With a last severe glance in Chraluuc's direction, he gathered up his abbreviated but heavily armed retinue and retired back the way he had come, disdaining her coolly courteous offer of an escort. As soon as the visitors had exited the building, Xeerelu turned to Chraluuc.

"Will the adminisstrator obtain the necessary order allowing him to remove the human from our cusstody, do you think?"

Chraluuc hissed softly and scratched at a loose scale on her neck. "I do not know. There iss ssomething more at work here, I think. Consssidering that Flinx iss but a ssingle human who iss only under ssusspicion and not openly accussed of direct participation in an actual act of violence, I thought the adminisstrator'ss interest in him bordered on obsession."

A somber Naalakot gestured concurrence. "I, too,

thought thiss bureaucrat'ss degree of interesst unhealthily intensse. We can only wonder as to itss causse. Perhaps the human himsself might enlighten uss?"

"If there iss anything there to sshed ssuch light," Chraluuc replied. "And if he can remember it." Tail whipping around behind her, she started for the doorway. "I will assk him, and sshare with you anything relevant that I learn."

"Besst to learn it quickly," Xeerelu advised her. One clawed hand gestured in the direction the departed administrator had taken. "I sussspect our sseething vissitor to process eventss as furioussly as hiss sspittle sstained hiss teeth."

"The name seems somehow familiar, but I'm damned if I can say in what context."

Sitting on the curving sweep of moglas, Flinx watched while Pip slithered in and out of its folds. The flying snake had made a game of trying to anticipate where new gaps would open and old ones would close within the animated sculpted bench. Alive with the internal synthetic life-forms that were a hallmark of its construction, the constantly shifting bench massaged Flinx's human backside as tenderly as it would that of an AAnn, with the exception that those extrusions designed to caress his tail continually sought in vain for an appendage that was not there. Flinx worried that Pip might get caught in one of the flowing textural folds, but she never did.

Chraluuc sat on a bench across from him. It was identical to his save that its primary warp tint was deep blue instead of a pale pink. "Try harder. Thiss administrator wantss you very badly."

The human shook his head dolefully. "I can't imagine why. Not only can I not imagine having anything to do with any kind of local resistance or rebellion, I wasn't even aware one was going on."

"It hass been kept as quiet as possible—or sso I am told." They both went silent for several minutes, distracted by the continuous movement of the benches on which they sat and the visually attractive artificial lifeforms that dwelled within the vitreous surfaces.

Looking up, Flinx shrugged. "Not much we can do about it, I suppose. If he comes back for me, I'll have to go with him. I don't want to cause the Tier any trouble."

"Truly." She made a third-degree gesture of accord. "You will have to go with him. We cannot defy proper documentation. I would jusst like to know the tailbasse of thiss individual'ss obsession with you. And it *iss* an obssession. The Ssemilionn agree with me." She leaned toward him, her sharp teeth gnashing gently close to his face. "Think, Flinx! If you are not a party to what he iss accussing you of, then why the firsst-degree interesst on hiss part?"

Fingers interlocked, Flinx repeatedly tapped his hands against his forehead. "I don't know, cherished Chraluuc. I just don't know." When he looked up again, she thought him as helpless as a cub. His gaze was as vacant as his memory. "I don't remember *anything...*"

Lwo-Dvuum was hopping toward the moving walkway that skimmed the exterior of the faculty lounge at the far end of the school. Work for the day having been concluded, it was time to relax and converse with colleagues. The questions that had been posed in today's several edification sessions by young, maturing Vssey whose frills had not yet changed color had been unusually draining, and the educator was looking forward to the customary late-day respite.

As a last hop placed Lwo-Dvuum on the walkway and a farther jump effected the necessary transfer to its faster adjunct, the communicator attached to the service strap that encircled the teacher's mid-trunk vibrated silently for attention. Bending forward brought it within reach of the tentacles that lined the educator's upper body. A simple curl of several proximate appendages lifted it close to the hearing frill that ran between upper dome and limbs.

"Lwo-Dvuum standing." Who would be calling at this time of the workday, the educator wondered?

"Svi-Ormoth talking. Is it quiet around you, mentor?"

Lwo-Dvuum tensed, his frill contracting reflexively. Svi-Ormoth was a member of one of the several subordinate sympathetic circles of objection that impacted on the larger philosophical circle comprised of the teacher, Bno-Cassaul, and numerous others. What made Lwo-Dvuum sensitive to the calling was that Svi-Ormoth occupied a particularly delicate position: the service specialist often did work within and for the resident AAnn Administration. It put the specialist in the unique position of being able to report from personal experience on the activities of the scaled ones. Doing so exposed Svi-Ormoth to considerable danger. It was a risk the specialist had been willing to take for some time now, for the benefit of all.

The educator checked the communicator's privacy signifier. It blushed a bright, reassuring orange. "Insofar as I can tell, it is quiet, yes. And I am in motion. You have news of mutual interest, praiseworthy frien'?"

"I have a story," the burbling replied. "It involves something your circle passed along to mine, among others. Concerning the unreasonable interrogation you and your companions suffered under the direction of a particular AAnn official name of Takuuna."

Lwo-Dvuum's eyes rotated atop their stalks. There was no one close by on the walkway, not even a preoccupied student. "Speak safely into the quiet, my frien'."

"There was talk and discussion here recently that I overhear'. Very lou' talk, even louder than the scaled ones usually deploy among themselves. Part of it reminde' me immediately of some things of which your circle spoke—of one thing in particular."

"Woul'! I recall this one thing?" Lwo-Dvuum lowered his voice and repressed any bubbling as a pair of student-educators passed him on the parallel walkway that ran in the other direction.

"I am certain of it. Your circle spoke of this AAnn accusing you of consorting with a representative of a species calle' human, to the detriment of the AAnn."

"Yes, I remember."

"That self-same AAnn administrator recently clomped through here raging alou' about the defiance of a group of his own kin' who were holding a human, an' refusing to surrender the creature to his custody."

Lwo-Dvuum's puzzlement must have shown in the twisting of many tentacles, but there were none close by to comment or question the display. "What does that matter to us? Of what use is it, practically or philosophically?"

"I wondere' much the same." Lwo-Dvuum could almost hear Svi-Ormoth bubbling merrily on the other end of the connection. "I almost set it aside. Then I found myself thinking: this AAnn official who arreste' you and the others of your circle seems to have become a law unto himself. Now, in addition to harassing innocent Vssey, he chooses to persecute an innocent representative of an entirely different species. In so doing, it develops that his action is opposed even by others of his own kin'."

"We don't know that this human creature is innocent."

"The AAnn who shelter him think so. I know: I managed to fin' and rea' the report. It must say that the creature who is the cause of so much upset does not look very threatening."

Lwo-Dvuum sucked in enough air to make the domed upper third of the squat body temporarily swell upward.

"That was very brave of you."

To the specialist's credit, no attempt was made to ride the compliment. "Don't you perceive the deeper possibilities, educator? If this incident can be publicize', we can show how the AAnn maltreat not only Vssey, but the innocents of other species as well. It does not matter whether the human is innocent of the charges this Takuuna has lai' against him or not. What does matter is that the population be made to see it that way. We can use the current state of commotion surrounding this human to expose the population to the true nature of the AAnn in a way that we cannot when their actions are solely directe' against us."

The last exit to the educators' lounge appeared around a corner. Lwo-Dvuum ignored it as the walkway continued to trundle on past. "Why shoul' the population respon' to the predicament of an unfamiliar alien?"

"Because," came the triumphant reply, "the human has lost its memory! It is an innocent in every sense of the wor'. If the scaled ones will accuse and harass a sentient with no memory, it suggests that no individual, no matter how guiltless, is safe from the indifferent vindictiveness of AAnn authority. At the least, any substantial public reaction shoul' make our own authorities think again about how much cooperation to exten' to these AAnn who are living and working here among us."

The more Lwo-Dvuum thought about it, the more efficacious the suggestion sounded. By directing support to an alien such as the human, no one could accuse the circle of attempting to shield one of its own. They could show that even other AAnn resented the activities of the Authority that had been put in charge of the investigation into the two incidents.

The human itself, of course, was incidental. Surely it could not object to the Vssey raising a defense on its behalf. Riding the walkway and plotting in silence, Lwo-Dvuum wondered if the human actually might be involved in some way with the two attacks that had been made against the AAnn presence. It seemed unlikely. Svi-Ormoth had said that the creature had lost its memory. That raised the intriguing question of why the interrogator Takuuna was so interested in it.

The more he pondered the state of affairs, the more Lwo-Dvuum saw possible benefits to the cause. The educator remembered wishing, some time ago, for something different with which to unsettle the AAnn. An incident. A diversion. An event. It was entirely possible that the resourceful Svi-Ormoth had found one.

Use the case of the human to aggravate the AAnn. It was an invigorating idea. What the human might think of it, the educator could not imagine. Perhaps, as events developed, Lwo-Dvuum might find the opportunity to meet the creature and learn what there was about it that so interested the detested AAnn official.

Meanwhile, the ever-expanding circle would use the case of the human to further their own interests. Without having met it, without even being familiar with its species, Lwo-Dvuum already considered the human an ally. Whether the human had any opinion on the matter was not important. Anything that unsettled the AAnn benefited the Vssey. With luck, the situation might even be used to sway the AAnn's greatest ally: the indecisiveness of Vsseyan public opinion.

Save the poor human. See how the AAnn truly treat sentients other than themselves, even one devoid of memory. Lwo-Dvuum was much pleased. The educator could see the leaders on the mass communications readings already.

As he made his way through the administrative compound, Takuuna wondered what Keliichu wanted that required the administrator's corporeal presence. He was very busy and wondered, sensibly, why information could not be exchanged via communicator. Passed into the chief administrator's inner sanctum, he did not have to wait long to find out.

Keliichu was upset. That much was readily apparent. Takuuna immediately slipped into defensive mode, his sandaled feet instinctively seeking firmer purchase on the smooth floor.

"I thought, truly, that the human sspy in whosse company you sspent time wass dead."

More than a little taken aback, Takuuna sought to gather his thoughts. "Truly, I thought the ssame, respected Adminisstrator. I ssaw him plunge over the edge of Ssaudaun Chasm. When I went to look over the sside, there wass no ssign of him."

"There iss now." At the terse wave of a hand, several images in succession materialized above the chief administrator's desk.

Takuuna recognized the human Flinx instantly. He also recognized at least one of the AAnn beside him: it was the attractive female from the Ssaiinn complex.

"Yess, I know. He dwellss among the missguided artissanss of the Tier of Ssaiinn, who live in issolation far out on the Smuldaar Plateau. I too wass only recently made aware of hiss unexpected and inexplicable ssurvival, and have only jusst returned from traveling there to bring him in for quesstioning. Unfortunately, the memberss of the Tier, operating under a ssysstem normal nye can only pity, refussed to let him return with me. Outrageouss, truly! Naturally, not wanting to provoke a confrontation with helpless artissanss, I wass compelled to return to Sskokosss to ssee to ssome necessary legalitiess. Thesse are now in hand. It wass my intention, truly, to return to the Tier'ss complex later thiss very day to bring the ssoftsskin in."

"No," hissed Keliichu.

Takuuna almost swallowed his tongue. "No,' honored Adminisstrator? You do not wissh me to recover the human sspy?"

Keliichu's tone was unrelenting. "Firsstly, Secondary Adminisstrator Takuuna, we do not know that the human iss in fact a sspy, or a persson of ssubverssive intent who hass been working with Vsseyan dissidentss."

"Honored one, I musst protesst! My perssonal experience clearly indicated that—"

"Calm yoursself, Takuuna. If the human hass indeed losst hiss memory, as our own people of thiss Tier inssisst, then it doess not matter what he wass—truly?"

"But he could recover thosse dangerouss memoriess at any time, resspected Keliichu," Takuuna protested earnestly.

"Perhapss. In any casse, the circumsstances ssurrounding the ssoftsskin have changed. Have you had occassion to recently view the latesst planetary media?"

Yet again Takuuna was confronted by a combination of request and accusation whose immediate significance escaped him. "Directing the special unit occupiess the great majority of my time, venerated Keliichu. I am afraid I have no time for perussing the ussual luguriouss native drivel."

Keliichu gestured third-degree understanding, oddly punctuated with second-degree irony. "Perhapss you sshould allocate it a little of your preciouss time." Another wave of his hand replaced the images of Flinx and AAnn artists with selections from the general Vsseyan media. Surprisingly, these in turn also contained images of the human, though Takuuna could not read the accompanying local script. He had never wasted any time learning it.

He did not have to strain for clarification because without pausing Keliichu proceeded to interpret it for him. "It sseemss that word of your previouss attempt to take the human into custody got out. There hass been a leak ssomewhere." As Takuuna stared to protest, the chief administrator waved him off. "How or where does not matter now. We have the reality of it to deal with. And the reality iss that at leasst an influential portion of the Vsseyan public now believess that the repressentativess of the Empire are only interested in perssecuting non-AAnn, irresspective of speciess. In consequence, they have taken up the causse of thiss human, legally admitted to Jasst, who iss obviousslly no danger to anyone ssince he hass no memory. It doess not help that certain of our own kind, however missguided they may be, have taken him in and placed him under their protection." Another curt hand wave, and the multiple images vanished.

Takuuna stood stunned. How had the Vssey found out about Flinx's presence among the Tier? More significantly, how had they learned of hiss, Takuuna's, attempt to take him into custody? A leak, indeed, as the chief administrator had suggested, and clearly somewhere within general administrative services itself. It would have to be found and dealt with.

Meanwhile, as Keliichu had so understatedly pointed out, there was the reality to deal with. Standing there before the senior administrator, Takuuna realized he simply should have shot the human when he'd had the chance.

"What if the human iss faking thiss loss of memory, essteemed Keliichu? He could be ussing it as a cover while he continuess to provide advice and assistance to the Vsseyan dissenterss."

"With what?" Keliichu was not convinced by the argument. "If the ssoftsskin had access to some kind of transsmitter, iss it not likely hiss hosstss, however otherwisse deluded they may be in their lifesstyle, would have found it by now? And if he wass faking the loss of memory, would they not alsso have disscerned that by thiss time? He hass apparently been living in closse quarterss with the Tier ever ssince your confrontation with him. And, anyway, fsstsst, as I have mentioned, eventss have overtaken hiss ssituation. You cannot take him into cusstody. Whatever he iss, whatever he may have done in the passt, iss of less importance than the bad publicity your attempt to arresst him hass engendered. We cannot rissk a recurrence right now. Perhapss in the future, when thiss fuss hass died down and the Vsseyan public hass losst interesst in the case."

But they couldn't wait, Takuuna knew. Because the longer they waited, the greater the chance that the human might recover his memories. Particularly one involving a confrontation on the rim of Saudaunn Chasm. Though Takuuna had no particular reason to think that his own superiors, Chief Administrator Keliichu, for example, would take the word of a human over that of a respected nye, there was no telling what the members of the mentally addled Tier might believe. It was not a possibility to be risked.

As he had informed Keliichu, he had finally obtained the necessary order of second-degree emergency. He was now legally empowered to remove the human from the confines of the Tier by force. Previous notions notwithstanding, he no longer had any intention of bringing him back to Skokosas for questioning. Things were becoming too complicated for such games. Once the human had perished "accidentally," Takuuna would make all the necessary apologies. There would be condemnation for his defiance of Keliichu's directive. He would be censured. But in the end, it was only the life of a single human. Surely there could be no great, lasting harm to his ambitions?

As if reading his thoughts, Keliichu told him, "Did you know, Honorable Administrator, that certain radical Vssey are even arguing in favor of requessting the Commonwealth to esstablissh a formal mission here, on Jasst? 'For the protection of itss citizenss,' or sso the principals ssay."

Takuuna swallowed. Events had indeed ballooned beyond imagining. "I had no idea, venerated Keliichu, that thingss had progressed sso far."

"A Commonwealth mission. To be followed, inevitably, by a consulate, and then an embassy, and that iss the end of our opportunity to quietly integrate Jasst into the Empire. All becausse of one lone wandering human. If he iss an agent of the hated Commonwealth, he could not have arranged eventss better to ssuit the purposess of hiss government." The chief administrator's hissing fell. "Damnable sslippery ssoftsskins are everywhere anymore. One cannot travel anywhere in the Army without encountering them. The stars stink of their presence." Takuuna indicated his understanding.

"Sso you ssee, Secondary Administrator Takuuna, why the besst thing for now iss ssimply to ignore the ssoftsskin. Gradually, thiss agitation among the Vssey will fade. Then we can determine how besst to proceed."

Takuuna gestured second-degree acknowledgment even as he knew that the human Flinx could not be ignored. He had to die—and soon. There was, of course, the chance that his reputed memory loss might be truly permanent. It was a chance the administrator felt he could not afford to take. Furthermore, from what he knew of the Commonwealth government, its bureaucracy moved no more swiftly than that of any non-AAnn regime. By the time anyone thought humans on distant Jast needed Commonwealth protection, there would no longer be any to protect.

It was all very risky, but a risk he was prepared to take.

"It sshall sslither as you ssay, honored Keliichu." He started to back out of the office. "In the absence of ssolid proof that the human is at leasst partially ressponssible for the incidentss in which our brethren died, he sshould be left alone."

"I am pleassed that you undersstand." Keliichu had already turned away from his visitor and back to the work at hand.

Takuuna left upper Administration fuming. This was all the fault of that obstinate Tier! He should have ignored them and simply taken the human when he'd had the chance. It would be just as easy to do so now. It was the aftermath that was going to be complicated. But he would manage. In departing the senior administrator's presence, he had managed to plant the notion in the mind of that wimpish worthy that it just might be permissible to deal with the human *if* real proof could be found that it was complicit in the deaths of so many AAnn. Evidence could be manufactured. It might not be conclusive, but that was not necessary. All that was required would be for Takuuna to produce data that called the human's purported innocence into question. This could, in turn, be laid before the Vssey and the Vsseyan media. It was not necessary to prove—only to create controversy.

The farther he got from Keiichu's office, the more confident Takuuna became. Already, a new scheme was forming in his mind. Cast suspicion on the human, discredit the Tier, raise enough questions and concerns about the entire matter, and accusation and blame would dissolve in a morass of misunderstanding and uncertainty. Meanwhile, if fortune favored him, his unit might at last crack the identity of the actual dissidents. Subjected to appropriate questioning, one or two of them might even be persuaded to identify the human as a source of counsel and assistance in their murderous activities. Since the human in question would already be dead, there would be no opportunity for potentially disconcerting rebuttal.

Although he did not know it, part of his plan was already coming to fruition—several days too soon.

*   *   *

Joofik WWLONDK was proud of his thoroughness. Like any responsible, ambitious, dedicated AAnn worker, he kept the results of his downtime work to himself.

It hadn't been all that difficult, really. All that was needed was a different approach. With everyone else in his section chewing the scales off their lips as they struggled to find leads to the well-organized bands of violence-prone Vsseyan dissidents, Joofik decided, in his free time, to utilize the considerable resources available at his disposal to try to find just one potential extremist. In the frantic, expensive search for large groups of radicals it would be easy to overlook a single fanatic.

And that was exactly what he had found: one.

The first thing he did was eliminate all the vocal dissident Vsseyan philosophical groups. To Joofik, they were too obvious, their profile too high. Given the dead-slow speed (at least compared with that of the average AAnn) at which the Vssey accomplished anything, and the need to arrive at a group consensus before doing anything at all, it seemed to Joofik that the more Vssey who were involved in an enterprise, the longer it would take to get going. Whatever could be surmised about whoever had twice attacked AAnn facilities, they had worked swiftly and with dispatch. That suggested fewer Vsseyan minds at work, not more. Following that line of reasoning to its ultimate conclusion, one Vssey could theoretically move faster than any faction.

Adopting the notion of the single saboteur as his research mantra, Joofik had set about the laborious task of collating forensics. Instead of trying to work his way up to identifying possible groups, he winnowed the available information down—down until it led him to a few dozen unlikely individual suspects. A month's work of monitoring the movements of these individual natives gradually reduced the number of possibles one by one, until he was left, at last, with only a single suspect.

As best as he could trace them, the movements of this penultimate entity on the days that both the AAnn complex at Morotuuver and the import-export service offices in Aulauwohly had been devastated by explosions were sufficient to damn the suspect creature. At the very least, an excited Joofik recognized, the indicated individual should be subjected to some serious questioning. If he was correct in his work and in his subsequent assumptions, he realized, the result could likely be swift promotion and accolade. Naturally, he told no one else. To have done so would have been imprudent, it would have been un-AAnn. All the glory and reward should deservedly be his.

In order to secure his triumph he needed to present his data to someone in a position to both verify and act on it, in addition to guaranteeing its discoverer the credit he was due. Joofik could have gone directly to Keiiichu, the senior administrator. But the senior administrator was responsible for far more than the hunt for the Vsseyan extremists. Below him were several secondary administrators. The most obvious of these to present with the information he had gathered was Takuna VBXLLW, the head of the special unit that had been created to track the perpetrators of the two atrocities. Transferring all the relevant information to his personal work tablet, he locked it down and made certain nothing remained within the Administration's system for the curious to uncover.

Though not the chief administrator, Takuna VBXLLW also seemed to be exceptionally busy of late. It took several days for the persistent Joofik to arrange a meeting. As Takuuna's work schedule was overfull, they agreed to meet not in an office but in a rejuvenation lounge at the end of the day.

When Joofik arrived at the designated meeting place, Takuuna was already there, sitting beneath a sandfall of powdered, recycled silica, a tired bureaucrat relaxing beneath the caress of glittering particles and the soothing sound of synthetic windrush tones reverberating in the background. Though large enough to hold a dozen or more AAnn, the lounge was empty save for the two of them—no doubt because it was well after duty hours. Except for the recently arrived minimal staff necessary to keep operations running smoothly during the Jastian night, the compound had been rapidly deserted by its weary diurnal occupants.

"Honorable Ssecondary Adminisstrator." Joofik gestured effusively as he began to remove his garments. Instead of a sandfall, he chose to sit beneath a hot air blower opposite the older nye.

Takuuna eyed the junior bureaucrat with tolerant disdain. He would have called the meeting off had he not felt the need for a time-part or two of augmented repose. Though his private apartment was comfortable enough, it was neither large enough nor sufficiently well equipped to support an extravagance as expensive as a silica sandfall. So he had magnanimously agreed to meet this unknown low-ranker at a timeplace that was convenient for him, thereby accomplishing two ends simultaneously. He hissed through the wisps of falling sand. The sooner he was rid of the subordinate, the sooner he could slip into a voluntary semi-comatose state beneath the sparkling veil.

"*Nsshasst*, what iss it that you have for me that cannot be forwarded via the ussual channelss, worker Jaalit?"

"Joofik," his anxious caller corrected him. Cloaked in the delightfully hot artificial breeze, the younger nye struggled to unlimber his tablet. "I have sspent much free time reaching the conclusions that I am about to present to you, honored Secondary Adminisstrator. I would not wissh them widely disseminated until proper accreditation had been prepared."

Takuuna replied with a gesture of third-degree tolerance. That, at least, was understandable, even if it was doubtful such precaution was required. "Get on with it," he urged his visitor irritably.

"Truly, honored ssir"—Joofik continued to fumble with his suddenly recalcitrant tablet—"I believe that I have for you that for which you have been ssearching for ssome time now, ssir."

Takuuna blinked away glittering particles and sat up a little straighter, so that the sandfall struck the back of his head and ran down his spine instead of cascading over his face and jaws. Despite the warmth of the silicates and the cocoon-like lounge, he felt a slight chill. "And for what have I been ssearching, youngling?"

"Why, in your capacity as head of the sspecial unit in charge of locating the native terroriststs, you have been looking for thosse ressponssible, of coursse." A vast hiss of pleasure escaped the junior bureaucrat's jaws. "And I have found it for you."

" 'It?' Not 'them'?" Lassitude, thoughts of lingering relaxation long forgotten, Takuuna was fully alert now. This might all be nonsense, of course—but if there was an inkling of useful information in it . . .

"That wass the key to my ssuccess." Joofik's neck swelled with pride. "To sseek one who might have been overlooked in the ssearch for many. It wass the correct approach to take. I am convinced of it."

"I ssee. And what iss it you have found that convincess you?"

"Thiss, ssarrick." Joofik finally succeeded in activating the compact device he had brought with him.

In the sere atmosphere of the lounge, images coalesced in the dry, sterile air between them. Takuuna swiftly scanned the charts and lists that Joofik had compiled. Records of movements, of personal histories. Lines that inexorably connected places, events, and individuals. All of it uniting around the figure of a single Vssey. There was a three-dimensional likeness that meant nothing to him: all Vssey looked the same. Unsettled more than he would have cared to admit by the charting's comprehensiveness, there was also an attached name his eyes skipped over: Vsseyan names were nothing but a barbaric oral diarrhea of vowels, anyway. Moving completely out from beneath the flow of heated particles, he studied the details of the charting more closely.

"You have been mosst active. Thiss research would appear to be very thorough."

"It iss, *fssasst!*" Joofik hissed with pardonable pride. "I have checked and rechecked. Tracking the evidence, the only possible conclussion a logical nye can reach iss that the indicated individual native iss not only ressponssible for the atrocitiess againsst our people, it iss *ssolely* ressponssible."

Takuuna gestured understanding. "It sseemss asstonisshing that a ssingle persson, and a native at that, could have successfully planned and implemented both devasstating actss of aggression againsst uss."

The junior bureaucrat enthusiastically agreed. "That iss one thing that hass worked to itss advantage. Until now. Until I began narrowing as opposed to expanding the area of ressearch. A ssingle Vssey wass easy to overlook."

"Certainly a valid, and apparently a rewarding, approach to the problem we have been facing. You are to be commended, Joofik."

"My thankss to you, Honored Administsrator." The delighted subordinate saw the results of all his hard work coming to fruition.

"And you are certain thiss native hass been working

alone? It hass not, for example, received any assisstance, material or otherwisse, from a vissiting alien? A human?"

"A ssoftsskin?" Joofk gestured second-degree bewilderment. "How iss that possible, honored ssir? I have heard talk recently of a human here on Jasst, but only of one."

"Your honesst confussion answerss my quesstion." A composed Takuuna gestured at the subordinate's tablet. "You are entirely ressponssible for thiss line of ressearch, and have conducted it ssolely by yourself?"

Joofik straightened slightly in the wash of heated air. "Truly, honored ssir, I have asked for no help and have received none! No one esse iss aware of what I have been doing. It iss wholly mine, carried out entirely on my own time and out of view or question of any of my cowork-erss."

Takuuna gestured understanding. "Naturally, having done all the work, you desire all the credit. That iss as it sshould be. You have taken sstepss to ensure that it remainss sso?"

The junior administrator gestured with his tablet. As he did so, the images of charts and graphs that had occupied the air between them vanished. "It would be foolish to sstore the relevant information anywhere else lesst it be open to possible access by the curiouss. Think of what thiss will mean to your own division, Ssecondary Administrator! The sspecial unit that hass been created to ssearch for the Vsseyan radicals can be dissbanded, at a considerable ssavings to general adminisstration and to the Imperial budget here on Jasst. Though the now-identified perpetrator doess move around, it sshould be a ssimple matter for a few of your people to locate and capture a ssingle native."

"I concur. In the absence of a large consspiracy among the Vssey, the sspecial unit will no longer be needed. For your information, there *iss* a human active here on Jasst. The factss you have jusst laid before me are more than enough to clear it of any wrongdoing." He moved closer to the junior bureaucrat, who rose proudly at his superior's approach. "Tomorrow you musst come with me to pressent your material to the ssenior adminisstrator, who will undoubtedly resspond as eagerly as myssefl to the fruitts of your demanding effortss.

"But now, it iss quite late. Your revelationss have sspurred me to act on them immediately."

"I am only glad to have been of ssome ssmall sservice," Joofik replied with appropriate modesty.

"Time now for both of uss to get ssome resst." Preparatory to bidding his visitor good night, Takuuna approached and turned his head to the side. Joofik politely did the same, reaching out with his right hand, claws retracted. Takuuna responded in kind, with one small but notable exception.

He did not retract his claws.

14

The highly active AAnn had higher blood pressure than that of the average human and considerably higher than that of the average thranx. As a result, when the suddenly lunging Takuuna tore out the junior bureaucrat's throat, there was a great deal of blood. Though a stunned Joofik instinctively tried to fight back, kicking out and clawing wildly at his attacker with both hands, his initial vulnerability had already sealed the outcome of the contest. He did not die quietly, but die he did.

As the junior worker's life fluids seeped into the sterile sands that comprised the flooring of the lounge, Takuuna moved quickly to the single entranceway. No alarm had been raised, the waiting room beyond was still dim and deserted, and there was no sign that another living being anywhere within the compound was aware of the brief instant of shocking violence that had occurred in the relaxation zone. Returning to the still-bleeding body, a thoughtful Takuuna picked up the dying Joofik's personal work tablet. After carefully tucking it away among his own belongings, he pondered how best to deal with the corpse.

The in-built mechanisms with which the self-cleaning, self-sanitizing lounge was equipped would deal as efficiently with the copious amount of blood as it would with any other volume of spilled liquid. Within a few time-

226

parts, it would once again be as dry and sanitary as when the administrator had first entered it. The physical remnants of the innocent subordinate who had been on the verge of crashing down in ruins everything Takuuna had worked to build up presented a greater problem. It was highly unlikely the administrator would be able to smuggle so sizable a burden out past the night watch, all of whom had been placed on heightened alert ever since the first of the incidents against the AAnn presence.

That meant that the body would have to remain within the administrative compound. That was not a potentially grave problem. What mattered was how, where, and under what circumstances it would eventually be found. Takuuna was confident he could find a solution to the conundrum. Setting his mind to the task, it was not long before he did so.

Hauling the body from the lounge, he placed it on a small cart used for transporting local supplies and covered it with an assortment of items taken from the lounge area that were unlikely to arouse suspicion in anyone who might happen to see them. Returning briefly, he restored the lounge itself to as natural an appearance as possible. The lounge machinery was already beginning to clean up the mess he had left behind.

Guiding the cart through the dimly lit night corridors of the administrative compound, he made his way to the destination he had chosen. It was only by good fortune that he knew the personal code-key that unlocked the door of the workplace he had chosen. Once inside, he settled on a storage closet as the temporary resting place of the meddlesome junior administrator. Removing the corpse from the cart, he dumped it unceremoniously inside. That done, he exited the location, but not before reentering the locking code on the doorway to seal the workplace behind him. The cart he returned to the location where he had found it.

Then, much relieved in mind and soul, he left the administration center and made his way back to the private apartment. After spending a few busy timeparts planning out the next day's activities, he then retired contentedly to his sandy divan, where he entered without turning or tossing into a sleep that was calm, sound, and without remorse.

Arriving at the compound the following morning and preparing to pass through Security, he remarked to the last guard who was checking him through that the workers striding back and forth in the main corridor appeared to be in an unusually garrulous mood.

"You have not yet heard the news, then, Honored Administrator?" the guard asked, punctuating the query with a third-degree gesture of personal unease.

"Apparently not," Takuuna replied, though he had more than a slight suspicion as to the nature of the news the guard was about to impart.

The sturdily built younger nye's reply was a hiss-filled mixture of indignation and disbelief. "A good nye wass found murdered. Right here, inside the compound." His disbelief was plain.

"Murdered, truly?"

"Truly." The guard added a gesture of second-degree astonishment.

"Doess the Authority have any idea who might be ressponssible? Vsseyan extremisstss, perhapss?"

A simple, unrated gesture of negativity. "I undersstand that they are holding a ressearcher named Geelin for quesstioning, as the body of the unfortunate wass found in her place of work. I hear that the female vigorously professess her innocence, and that her reactionss appear to be clouded by bewilderment. Thosse sseeking the truth of the tragedy are as yet unconvinced."

Takuuna voiced and gestured sadness. "It iss regrettable to think that while attempting to pressent a more civilized example to our primitive hossts we can sstill ssuffer such foolisshness among ourselves."

As he passed the administrator through, the guard gesticulated glum agreement.

Takuuna was not so cold that he did not feel a twinge of guilt for what he had done. Regrettably, he'd had no choice. Saddled with a body in need of quick disposal, he had proceeded as expeditiously as circumstances had allowed. One could wish that the resourceful and intelligent Geelin would be able to extricate herself from the awkward situation into which he had cast her. He hoped so. He would enjoy mating with her again. If not, well, the list of females available to someone with his present status was extensive. He did not expect to lack for company. He would move on.

But before he could continue to expand upon his personal as well as his professional life, there was a certain small snag that needed to be dealt with, a persistent irritation, like a scale parasite, that needed to be removed. To accomplish the necessary excision he requisitioned a force of six armed troopers and a suitable aircar. In proceeding, he was exceeding his mandate from the Authority and thereby risking censure. He was prepared to deal with the potential consequences, gambling they would not be too severe. In any event, while his superiors deliberated the matter of possible punishment, the human, his story of survival, and any accusations he might be prepared to level would be rendered moot.

Takuuna was confident in his ability to survive the aftermath of his actions. If the worst threatened to befall, he could always remind them of his irreplaceable brilliance by ordering the arrest of the one Vssey now known to be involved in the violent acts that had been perpetrated against the AAnn presence. The Administrator did not want to do that since it would mean the end of his special unit and the unique status that came from heading it. But the lever was there, if needed, and he could always push it.

Besides, how severely would any fellow nye really want to punish him for the killing of a human?

Gathering his small strike force, he departed Skokosas in high spirits and with the requisitioned aircar operating under a privacy seal, the latter a precaution so that no one could, should they suspect his intent, get in contact with him until he returned. His penitence over the framing of his mating partner Geelin receded as steadily as each new patch of Jastian landscape flew past beneath the aircar.

Softly hissing sorrow, a mournful Yuuvab DDMWWLG let her eyes linger as they roamed over the remnants of her mating partner's short life. There wasn't much. Work attire, casual attire, personal entertainment blocs, the well-strummed, thick-stringed tharp with which he used to serenade her prior and subsequent to their ritual skirmishing, and very little else. As transients in a non-Imperial world, there to be more. There was no reason for Authority staff brought with them only the minimum deemed necessary to manage life. Joofik had been no exception.

Of similar mind, taste, and hopes, they had considered making permanent their traditional intermittent mating. Now that had been reduced to dream ashes, perhaps by the awful individual Geelin, who continued to steadfastly deny any involvement in the junior administrator's death. It did not matter whether the other female was responsible or not, Yuuvab reflected. Her mating partner was dead.

Riffling through his belongings, she looked for anything that especially reminded her of him. As principal, though not exclusive, mating partner of record, she legally had first choice. No one would deny her that. As already noted, there was little to choose from. Sorting through the small stock of entertainment cubes, she picked out a couple that they had enjoyed together. Little enough to remind one of a dead companion.

She was about to leave when she remembered the special compartment. It was a secret place, Joofik had told her. Sharing knowledge of it with her had been a sign of his true commitment. At the remembrance, she hissed so long and hard that she abraded her tongue against her front teeth.

Located behind a small illumination plate and designed to look like a backup power supply, the small private container held very little. Some semi-valuable items of personal adornment, which she immediately and without reservation pocketed in her carry-pouch; a few examples of dried Jastian flora, which she ignored; and a single entertainment cube. No, she corrected herself as she examined the nail-shaving–sized storage device: a data cube. She took it as well.

Looking around as she prepared to leave the apartment chamber for the last time, her gaze fell once more on the unfortunate Joofik's cube translator. It being a cheaper model than her own, and older, she had chosen to leave it for the next certified scavenger. But it provided an excuse not to depart just yet.

Seating herself before the player and settling her tail in the chair slot behind her, she slipped the data cube into the compact player. The information it contained was security-coded, of course, but she knew the code well. She and Joofik had shared much. Images appeared in the air before her, as fleeting as the memory of her lost friend.

There was a diary. She would save that for reading later, when she was emotionally better equipped to deal with such lost intimacy. There were details of personal life that did not fit within a diary's parameters. There were credit account records, tending, as they did with the majority of transients, to the positive. Could she access them? It was certainly worth a try. The boost to her account would be most welcome.

And then, squeezed in among the other recorded inconsequentialities, there was a singular file boldly designated "Vsseyan Activities Directed Against the Imperial Presence on Jast—a Solution." She nearly thought to put it aside, too. On a whim, she decided to skim the initial scribings—and found she could not stop.

Extraordinary! Why had she not yet heard anything about this development, either via internal communications, media, or from friends? Could it be that it was not yet widely disseminated among the administration staff? Could it be that Joofik had been killed before he had been able to deliver the data she was studying by the subdued light of his ceiling? If the latter, it was an oversight that screamed to be rectified—information of importance to every AAnn on Jast. It was her responsibility to pass it along, to see that it reached those in a position to both appreciate the data and take appropriate action on its behalf. Her sharp-toothed Joofik would earn his promotion, even if it would have to be delivered posthumously. As she rose from the chair to remove the information cube from the player, she knew exactly where to go with the information he had so carefully guarded. Only one person was properly positioned to review the material and act on it without hesitation.

The head of the special unit charged with dealing with the threat of the Vsseyan radicals—Secondary Administrator Takuuna VBXLLW.

Given the sensitive nature of the data and the care Joofik had taken to keep it confidential—no doubt to prevent others (including, properly, herself) from benefiting from the fruits of his labor—she determined to submit the information in person. Exiting and resealing the apartment chamber behind her, she strode purposefully in the direction of Administration Central. Once out in a main corridor, she utilized her tablet's communicator to directly access Special Unit Chief Takuuna. There was only one problem.

His office insisted the administrator was out of Skokosas on important covert business and would be completely out of contact until the moment of his return.

Halting in the corridor, tail switching indecisively, she debated with herself how best to proceed. Other nye walked briskly around her, politely ignoring her private contemplation. Probably she ought to wait for the administrator's return. But the data cube, resting in the carry-pouch slung over her right shoulder and across her chest, burned to release the vital information it contained.

I know, she decided finally. I will compromise, and in so doing will gain the greatest possible benefit for poor Joofik, *tilassk*.

She would leave an appropriate message for the absent unit leader, together with the detailed report that had been assembled by her late, lamented mating partner. He would be able to retrieve it as soon as he emerged from the privacy shell beneath which he was currently laboring. Simultaneously, she would forward the data to every other relevant department and sector she could think of, including that of senior administrator Keliichu. If any or all of them thought Joofik's conclusions in need of immediate action, they would be able to respond accordingly and at their own pace.

Increasingly confident she had done the right thing for

the Empire, for Joofik's reputation, and for herself, she began compiling a list of addresses of departments she thought might find the conclusions reached by her late favorite male of more than passing interest.

At first, a bewildered Flinx found himself struggling to keep up with the restless Chraluuc. But the AAnn were sprinters, not distance runners, and as she slowed he found himself loping alongside as she led the way down the familiar trail. Pip, naturally, had no difficulty shadowing them both from above.

"Why are we running? Where are we going?" He was breathing hard, the folds of his custom-tailored robe streaming out around him.

She explained between sibilant intakes of breath. "We have received an official transmission from an incoming aircar requessting that we hold you for 'quesstioning.' The requesst came from the same fixated official who tried to take you in for quesstioning earlier. As you know, we denied that requesst. There is concern that thiss time the official may try to remove you from the groundss by force if he cannot do sso by documentation." Ignoring a wide bend in the descending switchback trail, she scrambled straight downward, making her own shortcut. Flinx followed, his ribbed sandals slipping and sliding on the inconsiderate sandstone. Folding her wings, Pip rocketed effortlessly past them.

"What can be the reason for this official's obsession with me?" Flinx was genuinely perplexed.

Chraluuc managed a second-degree gesture of disdain. "He thinkss you are ssomehow involved in the violent actionss that have been perpetrated againsst our pressence here on Jasst."

"That's crazy!" Flinx leaned backward slightly as he followed her into the familiar side canyon. "How could I give assistance to anyone outside the Tier even if I wanted to? There would be a record of transmissions, of shipments, of—"

"Calm yourself. Truly, your fellow artissans know that. It iss only thiss one official who sseemss not to. I have been given permission to conceal you until he hass departed. As they did previously, the Elders of the Ssemilionn will deal with him."

They were in the canyon of The Confection. It loomed ahead of them now, the vast concentric rings of shimmering applied art filling the gap between natural arch and canyon bottom with extravagant grace and glimmer. As always, he was overwhelmed by the baroque alien splendor of the communal artistic effort. His own small contribution, added only a week ago, spiraled outward from the lower left corner. It seemed pitifully inadequate compared with the towering contributions made by senior sculptors of open space such as the great Haagaz and florid Yiivada.

"Thiss way." She led him to the small but comfortable shelter where those preoccupied by their work on The Confection could spend the night or take cover from the occasional bad weather that swept over the plateau. It was equipped with its own climate-control system as well as food and hygienic facilities.

Once inside, she drew water from the dispenser; tepid for herself, as cold as the unit could manage for him. While they sat and sipped and gazed out one of the two wide windows at the indefatigable spectacle that was The Confection, Flinx wondered why one local administrator was so convinced he could somehow be playing a part in the violent actions that had been directed at the AAnn presence on this world. It made no sense; none whatsoever. All he was trying to do was live peaceably among sentients of similar inclination if different appearance while trying to regain his lost memories. He was no threat to anyone. For reasons known probably only to him, this solitary official thought otherwise.

Try as he might, he could not reconcile the mania this particular AAnn felt with the reality that Flinx knew to be true.

Takuuna's frustration knew no bounds. Initially polite, then formal, he had at last been reduced to ranting and raving and threatening—all to no avail. The senile leaders of this misbegotten Tier of reclusive ascetics had refused absolutely to turn the human over to him. That had left him no choice but to order a search of the premises. In response, his efficient troopers had methodically combed the compound. Their search had uncovered nothing but angry stares and whispered insults.

Could the softskin have recovered its memory and left? It seemed unlikely. No vehicle had been tracked leaving the vicinity of the complex. Would the human, if warned of the approach of Takuuna's aircar, be so foolish as to set out on foot across the intimidating Smuldaar Plateau? That, too, seemed difficult to countenance. Intense contemplation left the administrator with one conclusion: his quarry was still here, somewhere. Was still being sheltered and protected by the ill-advised artisans.

But in the absence of specific information there was nothing more he could do. He had already exceeded his authority by coming here in force, not to mention ordering the search. No doubt he would hear about that later, in response to the official complaint the doddering Elders had declared their intention to file with the Authority. That complaint he could, and would, deal with out of necessity. What galled him was the knowledge that he would have to do so without having accomplished that for which he had risked status and position.

The day was growing late. Re-forming his small troop, he prepared to take his ungracious leave of the compound, the sight of whose neatly groomed grounds and structures he was rapidly coming to hate as well as merely despise. It was on the way out the main entrance that he was approached by a single nye clad in robes of dark blue tinged with silver.

"Your pardon, Respected Administrator. I am Yeerkun."

"Truly honored," Takuuna barely grunted in response. He was anxious to be away from this place that had stymied his intentions not once now, but twice.

"You seek the ssoftsskin who dwellss among uss."

Takuuna halted abruptly enough to kick dust from beneath his sandals as he turned sharply on the artisan who had fallen into step next to him. "That iss hardly a secret among your Tier."

Yeerkun glanced back toward the compound. No one was following them, no one was watching. Whether the administrator's withdrawal was being tracked or not, he could not tell. It did not matter. He had long since determined to carry out his intent.

"Until thiss one fell in among uss, I had never seen a ssoftsskin in the flessh. I knew they were alliess of our enemiess the thranx, and that therefore they are our enemiess as well. But I decided to resserve judgment for myself. After seeing the human, and being around it for ssome time now, I have done that."

"I ssee." Takuuna had resumed walking. "And that judgment iss, tssasst?"

"I do not like it." The artist executed a sharp, first-degree gesture of distaste mixed with contempt. "I do not like the way it lookss, I do not like the way it ssmells. I do not like the ssound of itss voice, or the dissgussting rippling of itss pulpy flesh, or the flatness of itss face."

Takuuna gestured understandingly. "I had desspaired of ever encountering a ssound and mature attitude in thiss forlorn, issolated place. What do you intend to do about your disslike, most valued Yeerkun?"

The AAnn hissed surreptitiously. "I will take you to where the creature hass been hidden."

The administrator managed a stealthy glance backwards. The entrance to and the exterior of the compound were deserted. Since the Tier had known of his coming, it stood to reason they would monitor his departure. He kept walking toward the waiting aircar. As he did so, he sidled closer to the subofficer in charge of the half-dozen troopers.

"Veteran Chaadikik, who iss your besst sshot?"

The subofficer motioned one of the troopers to join them. Acknowledging the arrival with a non-degree gesture, Takuuna maintained the pace as he spoke.

"When we reach the aircar, Trooper Qeengat will join me on the other sside. Ssubofficer Chaadikik, you and the resst of your group will depart. Halfway back to Sskokossass you will find a ssuitable place and make a camp. Asssoon as my bussiness here iss finisshed, I will contact you for pickup."

Chaadikik did not look happy. "Are you convinced it iss ssafe to do thiss, Administrator?" She gestured meaningfully in the direction of the compound. "Finding their judgment disputed, thesse sso-called artissanss may prove dangerouss as well as petulant."

Takuuna gestured second-degree confidence. "I am not concerned about the Tier. They can make trouble only with wordss, and thosse do not worry me." They were almost to the aircar. "Trooper Qeengat, the honorable Yeerkun and I will conceal ourselves in the undergrowth and rockss on the other sside. Once you have departed, I am ssure the place where the vehicle hass been parked will be forgotten and time will ssoon ssee our obsstinate hermitss returning to their mundane daily tasskss." He glanced at Yeerkun.

"Can we get to the ssoftsskin without being obsserved by your missguided colleaguess?"

Yeerkun gestured self-assurance. "It will require some roundabout hiking, Honored Administrator, but there iss a circular trail that sshould give uss unsseen access."

"Excellent!" They were almost to the aircar. "I want you to know, valued Yeerkun, that your effortss on behalf of the Authority will not be overlooked."

The artist hissed tersely. "I am not doing thiss because I sseek advancement, Administrator. The removal of the alien from our midsst will be reward enough for myself and thosse otherss who quietly sshare my sentiment."

Takuuna was most pleased.

There were plenty of places to secrete themselves on the far side of the aircar's shielding bulk. After it had departed, they waited for a long timepart before moving. Following in Yeerkun's wake, they loped a good distance to the south of the complex before the artist felt secure in turning west once again. From there they began to descend a series of narrow, hard-to-discern switchback trails that carried them farther and farther into the depths of a certain canyon.

Nearing their destination, they had to hunker down as two other members of the Tier hurried past on their way back to the compound. Yeerkun was concerned that they might have been seen, but Takuuna was not worried.

"If we are as closse to the place where the human iss sstaying as you ssay, it will not matter. We will conclude the bussiness before anyone can interfere."

Rising from where they had concealed themselves, Yeerkun led them forward. But he added a gesture of third-degree uncertainty. "Thosse two who jusst passed here will have communicatorss with them. The AAnn sstaying with the human will be ssimilarly equipped. They could notify her of our pressence."

"*If they ssaw us.*"

"Truly—if." Yeerkun hurried onward, plunging down the side trail as rapidly as he dared.

Takuuna glanced over at the trooper. He was a stolid type and a typically admirable Imperial soldier: forthright, obedient, well trained, short on original thinking. "You remember, Honorable Trooper Qeengat, what we discussed earlier? Your insstructionss?"

"Truly, Honorable Administsrator." He had already unlimbered the slim, shimmering rifle that heretofore had been secured against his back.

"No time musst be wastted. Do not pay any attention to any wordss that may be sspoken. The ssoftsskinss have clever tonguess, and thiss one iss cleverer than mosst."

"He will not have the chance to lick hiss eye." Trooper Qeengat spoke coolly, with complete assurance.

It was enough for Takuuna. If Yeerkun let on that he understood the administrator's intentions, he chose not to comment on them. More likely, he had not overheard. It would not matter if he had, Takuuna reflected. His principal intent in coming for the human was to ensure that it would never have the opportunity to tell the story of its abandonment in the Jastian wilderness. The administrator had long since determined not to rely on the prospect that the softskin would never recover its memories.

He was going to make sure that no one else would, either.

15

So spectacular, so overwhelming, was the sight of The Confection when Takuuna and his companions entered the main canyon that he momentarily forgot his purpose in coming. Both he and Trooper Qeengat were unable to keep themselves from lingering to stare at the immense enterprise. Reflected beauty nearly blinded them—but not so severely that they failed to see the small shelter that had been built into the far canyon wall.

"They are in there, Honorable Administrator." For the last several minutes, Yeerkun had been growing more and more nervous. "As I am ssure you musst understand, desspite my feelingss toward the ssoftsskin, I do not wissh to rissk my possition within the Tier." He was already backing up. "Therefore, with your permission, I sshould very much dessire to—"

"Truly, truly." The administrator waved the vacillating artist away. No longer in need of his services, Takuuna magnanimously allowed him to depart. This Yeerkun did so gratefully, pivoting and hurrying back up the trail they had just descended, tail extended out behind him for balance, his powerful legs carrying him higher up the canyon with every stride.

Though they worked their way closer and closer to the refuge, there was no sign their presence had been detected by those sheltering inside. Takuuna began to wonder, and

241

to worry, that he might have been deceived by the dithering Yeerkun. He would not put anything past these eccentric hermits. Might the pair huddling inside have been warned of his coming, perhaps by the two artists he and his companions had nearly encountered earlier? If so, could they be armed? Impatient though he was to get the business over with, Takuuna restrained himself.

"Position yourself, Trooper Qeengat—and be ready." The soldier complied. Resting his rifle in a notch between two rocks, he sighted it carefully on the entrance to the shelter. Only when he was ready did Takuuna stand, form a characteristic calling-horn shape with his left hand, and call out to those below.

"The ssoftsskin who callss himsself Flinx! Thiss iss Ssenior Ssecondary Administtrator Takuuna VBXLLW! I bring with me the full authorization of the Imperial Authority annexed to the independent world Jasst. I am empowered to detain for quesstioning any and all thosse individualss ssusspected of harboring or contributing to the detriment of thosse AAnn who are living and working on thiss world." He paused for breath.

"I am ordering you to ssurrender yourrsself to my custtody—now! Truly, make no abrupt motionss or threatening movementss as you come out." Finished, he remained standing in clear view of the shelter across the canyon.

Both human and AAnn sheltering in the building below had heard the words that echoed off the canyon walls. Rising, Flinx started for the door. "This is a waste of time. This official is never going to let me rest until I answer his questions." Raising his voice, he shouted toward one of the partially opened windows, "Be content, truly! I'm coming out!"

The clawed hand that gripped his right arm was forceful, but not strong enough to hold him back. He gazed down into glistening, penetrating eyes. "You sshould not go with him. I have met thiss nye. He meanss to do you ill, and did not sstrike me as the type to allow reasson to get in the way of hiss preconceived notionss."

"He just wants to talk." Flinx grinned, careful not to show his teeth. "I may not remember how to do a lot, but I can still talk. Given time together, I'm sure I can disabuse him of these false assumptions of his."

Chraluuc wavered. "At least let me try to reasson with him before you ssurrender yoursself. Perhapss we may come to an accommodation that will not require you to travel beyond the boundss of the Tier. It may be that I can perssuade him to conduct his interrogation of you on our premissess."

Pip fluttering nervous wings against his shoulders, Flinx reluctantly agreed. "All right. But I don't want to be the cause of any trouble for you, or for the Tier itself. If I have to, I'll go with this one to learn what he wants of me."

"Agreed." After activating her personal communicator to send a brief message to the Tier's central command explaining their situation, she moved toward the doorway, adding a second-degree gesture of reassurance that was reinforced by the particular twitch of her tail.

On the other side of the canyon, Takuuna saw the old-style door start to swing wide and a figure begin to emerge. "Now—truly!" he yelled tightly, directing his command to his single companion. Without hesitation, Trooper Qeengat fired once.

For such a tiny object, the concussive shell that streaked from the barrel of the rifle packed quite a bit of energy. Striking Chraluuc's left side, it detonated with dreadful force. The impact slammed her back against the wall of the shelter even as it crushed her ribs and compacted several internal organs.

Across the canyon, a shaken Trooper Qeengat saw that

he had shot not some renegade suspect alien but a fellow AAnn. Jaws agape, teeth flashing, he stared at what he had done while hissing like a broken water pipe.

"You told me to sshoot! You told me to sshoot!" He repeated the obvious over and over, as if by the force of sheer repetition he could somehow undo what he had done.

"He ssaid he wass coming out. The ssoftsskin ssaid he wass coming out." This was bad, very bad, a confounded Takuuna thought frantically. His mind raced. Could he somehow blame it on the human? The weight of the pistol he always carried with him in his chest pouch pressed heavily against his sternum. Could he shoot the trooper and then the human, plant his pistol on the latter, and somehow blame the entire incident on the softskin? Questions would undoubtedly be raised as to how the human, resident among the Tier, had managed to obtain and conceal an AAnn handweapon for so long. To his annoyance, every viable explanation he strove to construct kept running into a roadblock of reason.

Reaching out through the gap between open door and solid wall, a traumatized Flinx had managed to drag the seriously wounded Chraluuc back inside the protection of the shelter. Only when he turned her gently onto her back on the dry, padded floor inside did the true extent of her injuries become visible. Between arms and prominent hip, her entire left side had been caved in. There was so much blood, slightly paler than human and lightly tinged with green, that it was difficult to tell exactly what had been damaged and what had survived the impact of the shell. Her eyes were already beginning to glaze over, the double eyelids spasming in repeated nictitation. Alarmed and upset at the emotions raging through her master, Pip hovered overhead, circling the room repeatedly like a trapped bat.

"Chraluuc," he whispered as he fumbled for her communicator. "I will call for help. Truly."

Her long tongue emerged. Slipping between her front bottom canines, it lolled listlessly against her chest. "Truly," she hissed back feebly, "there iss no time." Trembling uncontrollably, one hand reached upward toward his face. He flinched in surprise as the middle claw drew a slight, downward-curving cut against his left cheek. Reaching up, he felt blood of his own, redder and darker than hers.

"There. I have marked you. It iss all I would ever have been able to do, anyway—but it iss ssomething. It iss all I can leave with you—artisst. When you create, think of me. Our sskinnss are sscaled and tough, our eyes vertical instead of round, and our backssidess not flat—but we are not monssterss, Flinx." A deep, gagging sound snapped out of her throat, past sharp teeth. The vertical pupils widened. Muscles locked.

The swiftness of her death shocked him. First pain, then fury, roared through him. Voices echoed through his mind. His skull throbbed. He wanted to scream. Darkness roared inside his head. Something snapped. At the same time, unawares, he projected.

Outside, across the canyon, the sky behind Takuuna's pupils and those of the despondent trooper standing next to him grew dark, as if the sun of Jast were rapidly setting inside their eyelids. Both found themselves gripped by a sudden, overwhelming fear. Screaming hysterically, Qeengat staggered backwards, firing his rifle at the sky as if the concussive shells could bring down the clouds. Staggering away from the maddened trooper, Takuuna swung wildly at unseen horrors that were only in his mind. Spinning, pivoting, flailing, he neglected to mind his footing. His right foot stepped on a loose stone, the stone went out from under him, and his feet followed. His head entered into a disagreement with a different rock and, as is the norm in such arguments, flesh and bone lost.

It was quiet again in the canyon. At the far end, The Confection glistened and danced as it partnered with the rays of the setting sun. Yellow turned to gold, white to silver, and every color was heightened, mainlining on sunshine.

After a while, a tall, lone figure emerged slowly from the shelter. It had no scales. Even late in the day, the sun here was very warm, Flinx reflected. Released from the confines of the shelter, Pip shot skyward and commenced a slow, patrolling spiral, searching for the danger that had earlier been active but was now quiescent. Gradually, her anxiety eased. Her master's already had.

Flinx remembered.

Remembered what had happened to him subsequent to the forgetting. Remembered pretty much everything, in fact. It was as if he had been unconscious while awake, sleepwalking with his eyes open. The only thing he was not sure of was how long he had been that way, living among the Tier. Chraluuc could have told him, he knew. Chraluuc, who was thoroughly AAnn but not even slightly, as she had urgently insisted, a monster. Reaching up, he fingered the curving gash on his left cheek. The wound was still wet. Though it stung, he did not mind it.

A signature, he knew, was a personal thing.

He felt something moist slide down his cheeks. Not blood this time. Tears for a lizard.

Whoever had shot her would not shoot him. Not now. He was oddly certain of that. At the instant of the most profound shock, he had done—something. Something he had done before; an instinctive reaction, a singular defense of self. It would keep him from being shot. Pip's continued calm provided further assurance. She continued to circle overhead, composed and unconcerned. A scan of the canyon showed nothing moving; only the fading evening light that glinted off The Confection, vast and impressive as ever. He had contributed to that, he knew. So had the ill-fated she-AAnn Chraluuc. His friend.

Turning, he squinted up the trail that led back to the Tier compound. They would want to know, would need to know, what had happened to her. They would know soon. He readied himself. With his singular abilities now on full alert, he sensed them coming. Members of the Tier—and others.

Let them, he thought forcefully. Perceiving her master's emotions, Pip dove down to rejoin him. For the first time in a long while, they were both ready for whatever might come.

There were troopers with guns, but they had not come for the softskin. As their leader explained to a somber Flinx, certain discrepancies had been noted in the recent activities of Special Unit Leader Takuuna VBXLLW. Accusations had been made and inferences drawn. As a result, the secondary administrator was wanted for questioning by the Imperial Authority. Concerning Flinx, since no orders had been issued pertaining to a softskin, they had no interest in detaining him.

Their inquiries would have to wait, as Special Unit Leader Takuuna VBXLLW was in no condition to respond to questions. Or, for that matter, to talk. Hissing incoherently, he was led away by the medtech who accompanied the unit of heavily armed troopers. Having been rendered comatose, the administrator's short-term companion, a certain Trooper Qeengat, was in even worse condition. Since he had fired the fatal shot, he had received a slightly stronger dose of whatever idiosyncratic response it was that Flinx had reflexively projected onto both AAnn.

The several members of the Tier who had accompanied

and guided the unit of troopers took charge of the limp body of the artist Chraluuc. They did so with resolve and the quiet dignity that comes from living apart from one's own kind. Watching them carry her away, up the trail, Flinx wondered what would be the nature of her final leave-going. The sudden return of his memory did not help. He found that he knew nothing of AAnn funeral practices.

Some of the newly arrived troopers observed with unconcealed astonishment the surprising sight of several of their own kind consoling a human. When explanations were not forthcoming, they concocted their own; some of them as unconventional as what they were seeing. They were still talking about it as they led and carried their two impaired fellow nye away.

Upon his return to the compound, a grieving but recovered Flinx was allowed to utilize the Tier's communications facilities. It did not take long for him to contact the *Teacher* (which, after all, was busily searching for him). After establishing his precise location, the ship contacted the roving shuttle. It in turn put itself on a rapidly descending downward course for the Tier's compound.

Once again, having no instructions to the contrary, the commander of the AAnn force that had been sent out to bring the administrator Takuuna back to Skokosas ignored the activities of the resident human. Any qualms he held about allowing a softskin to travel freely were assuaged by the reassurances of members of the Tier that this particular remarkable human, at least, posed no threat to the Imperial interests on Jast.

Nothing more than a tourist, they informed the officer, the softskin just wanted to go home. In contrast to everything else they told him and his subofficers, that last was at least partially a lie. Flinx had no home. But he saw little utility in complicating the conflicted officer's confusion.

While it might not be a home in the traditional sense, the sight of the *Teacher*'s shuttle waiting for him on the Tier's landing strip still aroused warm feelings of familiarity within Flinx. For reasons he could not identify, that warmth seemed slightly tinged with green. Reflecting back on his experiences on this world and on everything that had happened to him, he was struck by the profound realization that he had yet again cheated Death. Exiting the formal entrance to the Tier's compound, he found himself wondering not for the first time when Death was going to get tired of being hornswoggled.

The Ssaiinn Xeerelu accompanied him partway. "Though there remain a few who feel otherwisse, friend Flinx, the majority of uss, often to our own ssurprisse, are ssorry to ssee you go."

I'm not, Flinx thought as Pip shifted position on his left shoulder and neck. What he said was, "I'm afraid I'm bound to a different calling. Besides, artists, like their art, should never linger too long over the same venture."

"Truly," Xeerelu agreed sagely. "Sstill, you are alwayss welcome here. You will alwayss be lissted on our rollss as a full member of the Tier." The Elder added a second-degree gesture of mild enjoyment. "The only one of your kind, inssofar as I perssonally am aware, to be sso accounted among the nye."

"I take it as an honor," Flinx replied honestly. "Chraluuc—Chraluuc wanted me to be a bridge between our species. An all-too-narrow bridge, I'm afraid."

"A bridge nonetheless," she hissed thoughtfully. "One that perhapss, ssomeday, otherss can usse to cross. A bridge may be narrow, but it only needss to be wide enough for two to meet in the middle and clutch throatss." So saying, she turned her head sideways and extended one hand toward Flinx's neck. Each lightly, briefly, grasped the other's throat before releasing their respective grips.

"Good eating, Flinx LLVVRXX. Think of uss the next time a work of art pleasuress your ssensses. You have left ssomething of yoursself here among uss, and we view it favorably."

"You people saved my life," Flinx replied simply. "It was an effort worthy of a high Tier." Turning, he lengthened his stride as he headed for the waiting shuttle.

Xeerelu watched the softskin go. As always, it was an unsettling sight. No tail twitching typically from side to side, no relaxed side-to-side swaying with each step, no slight bobbing of the head. For all its body's slackness, the stride of the softskin was surprisingly stiff. Strange creatures—though far more like the AAnn than the detested thranx. A pity about that alliance, she mused.

Not for the first time, Xeerelu felt that if politics were left to the artists, the galaxy would be a more congenial place.

Takuna blinked. He had stopped babbling incoherently some time ago. His body rocked ever so slightly to an unmistakable sense of movement. He was lying on his back, on a medical platform, ranged on either side by several monitoring devices. In response to his restored awareness, a medtech materialized. Hovering above him, yellow eyes blinking actively, the tech checked the readout he held in one hand.

"How are you feeling, Secondary Administrator Takuna?"

The figure on the platform struggled to recall what had happened. He had been crouching behind some rocks, waiting for the human to emerge from its hiding place. It had done so and—no, that was not right. He remembered now. The human had declared that he was coming out, but the figure that had come forward had been that of the AAnn who had been with him—and Trooper Qeengat had shot her. At his, Takuuna's, urging that he shoot her quickly. There had been a moment of shock, of furious cogitation over what to do next, and then—and then . . .

Madness had descended.

The administrator shivered as he remembered. An overpowering terror had taken control of him. Fear arising out of nothingness. He could not fathom it then, and he could not explain it now. It had flooded his mind, overwhelming rationality, thought, everything. Thinking back on it, he reflected that it was a wonder he had not thrown himself over a cliff and dashed himself to bits. If a suitable cliff had been handy, he did not doubt that he would have done exactly that. As for his companion . . .

He looked to both sides. There was no sign of Trooper Qeengat.

When queried, the medtech looked uncomfortable. "The medication that hass resstored your mind hass thuss far not proven as effective on the trooper in quesstion. He iss sstill being treated, truly. It iss hoped that when we reach Sskokossass and he iss placed in an advanced medical facility, hiss mental acuity and balance can be returned to normal. Someday. It may be that he received a sstronger dosse of whatever it wass that affected the both of you." The medtech's unease gave way to curiosity.

"What wass it that unssettled you sso powerfully, anyway, Administrator?"

Takuuna struggled with the question. "I honesstly cannot ssay, valued technician. But I promisse you that I will ponder on it, and prepare a ssuitably relevant report as ssoon as anything comess to mind."

The medtech moved to check a readout on a monitoring instrument. "You are lucky you sstill have a mind, Adminisstrator. For a while I wass doubtful that we would be able to bring you back—from wherever it wass you had been ssent. Trooper Qeengat hass not been sso fortunate."

And with any luck, he never would be, Takuna mused. It would be most convenient if the trooper would be thoughtful enough to remain out of mind permanently. That way, there would be no one to contradict the story the administrator was already beginning to concoct. Dangerous softskin sheltered by naïve Tier of reclusive artists while collaborating with delusional, renegade female artisan. Suspicion combined with abusive verbal threats forced him and his companion to defend themselves, albeit a bit hastily, resulting in a tragic but accidental shooting. Yes, that might work. With neither brainsick Trooper Qeengat nor the dead female able to contradict his story, he could be very persuasive. The human's version of events he would deal with later.

The human. The dammable softskin. Where was it now, and what was it saying, and to whom? He forced himself not to panic. There was nothing he could do about that—yet.

An officer Takuuna did not recognize appeared. Ominously, he did not offer either an introduction or voice concern for the prone AAnn's condition. "Adminisstrator Takuuna VBXLLW, by order of the Imperial Authority on Jasst, I have been compelled to place you under aresst." He did not add any gesture at all.

" 'Aresst'?" Feigning confusion, seeking sympathy, Takuuna blinked up at the officer. "On what charge, Captain?"

"Nothing sspecific." The officer was visibly unhappy at having to deliver such news to one who was clearly unwell. "I wass told that there are thosse who wissh to quesstion you about eventss ssurounding the death of another nye, a junior functionary named Joofik."

So that was it. Takuuna thought rapidly. Somehow, somewhere, he had overlooked something. Suspicions had been raised. He was concerned, but far from flustered. Questions, suspicions, no matter how palpable, he could deal with. He had been doing so throughout his entire career. Accusations could be countered by the "success" of his visit to the Tier. A potentially treacherous female nye had been dealt with, albeit more severely than intended.

As for the human, it was plain that it was somehow dangerous, just as he had been insisting all along. Evidence of this was to be found in his own present condition, not to mention that of poor, unfortunate Trooper Qeengat. Though he as yet had no proof that the human was directly responsible for what had happened to them there in the canyon, in the absence of argument to the contrary Takuuna knew he could certainly make a case for it. It did not matter if he was believed; only that his accusations were given consideration. With allegations and insinuations, he would turn any investigation into Joofik's death away from himself. Besides, the fact that he *had* suffered injury would automatically gain him sympathy. Why, if he played it right, he might even come out of this with his position strengthened. There might even be a commendation.

Lying on his back on the medical platform, he contemplated both the transport's ceiling and his immediate future with mounting confidence. One of the strike team's Vsseyan support staff appeared and bubbled deferentially to the medtech, announcing that they had already entered the outer limits of municipal Skokosas and would soon be passing Security on their way into the heart of the Imperial Compound. The medtech acknowledged the native with an absent wave of one hand.

"No time musst be wassted," Takuna told the Vssey importantly. "As ssoon as we arrive, I have ssignificant tesstimony to communicate to the ssenior adminisstrator, and my ssserious injuriess require the attention of experienced medical sstaff."

Utilizing several tentacles, the native gestured deferentially. "I assure the honorable adminisstrator that no time will be waste', and that with any luck his hurting will soon be at an en'."

Relaxing on the cradling platform, Takuna hissed his approval. If only all Vssey were as respectful and servile as this one, the Authority would not be faced with any trouble on Jast. As his head troubled him less, he felt magnanimous.

"May I have your name, sservant, sso that I may commend your attitude to the Department of Ancillary Native Personnel as ssoon as I am able to do sso?"

"Certainly, Honore' Adminisstrator. But no commendation is necessary. Such phenomena, like everything else, are transitory. I am Qyl-Elussab, gladly at your service until the impending termination of this journey." Pivoting on its silent pad-feet, the Vssey departed for another part of the aircar.

For a moment, something about the native's name seemed to tickle a memory deep within the administrator's mind. Something briefly glimpsed and shunted aside. Absurd, he decided. Where could he possibly have encountered the name of a Vsseyan employee of the Authority? Increasingly at ease, Takuna instantly forgot about the submissive native. It did not occur to him precisely where and when he had previously encountered the Vssey's name until the aircar had passed through Security and was deep inside the Imperial compound. Only as the vehicle was slowing toward its parking station did he finally recall it as part of the late, ill-fated Joofik's eager presentation. Something about a single Vssey radical, exceedingly intelligent, subtle, and clever in its ability to wager solitary war against the AAnn presence on Jast. A Vssey whom Joofik had managed to isolate and identify, whose name was . . .

Heedless of the monitoring equipment that cocooned him, of the sensors that were attached to his body, Secondary Administrator Takuuna sat up with a start, just as the aircar and, as the Vsseyan had quietly put it, "everything else" terminated loudly—and violently—deep within the heart of the AAnn Authority's transportation annex. . . .

In the ship's relaxation chamber, with green growing things and running water and familiar smells embracing him in a congenial web of comforting familiarities, Flinx sat sipping a cold drink as the *Teacher* apologized for not having been able to find him.

"You were completely out of touch, Flinx. When my instruments lost the signal from your communicator, they could find nothing to replace it."

"That's all right." He watched approvingly as Pip chased a projection of an Alaspinian degath through the tidily manicured foliage that backed up against the little waterfall and pool. It was one of her favorite toys. "For a while there, I was completely out of touch with myself."

The ship voice was still for a while. That suited Flinx perfectly, as he luxuriated once more in familiar surroundings.

"How was your vacation?" it finally inquired.

Unable to marshal a suitable reply, Flinx responded as best he could. "Somewhere between the looming galactic crisis Bran Tse-Mallory, the Eint Truzenzuzex, and I are trying to think of a way to deal with simply being dead."

For a second time the ship went silent. "Ah," it finally acknowledged. "Sarcasm. It is good to see that you are feeling well."

"I'm not feeling well," Flinx shot back, feeling like being argumentative for the hell of it. "Truly," he added with a hint of sadness.

"Is there anything I can do?" the ship inquired with its usual synthetic solicitousness.

"Yes. Get me away from here. Back to the Commonwealth. No more exotic destinations. But no place too urbane," he added hastily, mindful of the fact that Commonwealth authorities were undoubtedly still looking for him. "And let's initiate another external hull configuration."

"Another one!" Flinx ignored the ship's apparent exasperation. It could not any more get exasperated than it could get tired. It was simply making use of its idiomatic verbal programming.

"Yes. If we're going back into the Commonwealth, we need to take precautions. We don't want to get hurt, or have to hurt anybody else." After a moment's pause, he added, "I'll help with drafting the reconfiguration this time. I'm feeling a little—creative."

Hurt. Wherever he went, whatever he tried to do, it followed him like a cloud. Not so bad if he could restrict it, limit it, to himself. Sorrowfully, that was hardly ever the case. Why was it that even though all he only ever wanted to do was help, everyone he came in contact with, especially representatives of the opposite gender, always seemed to end up getting hurt?

As the *Teacher* made the jump to space-plus, his stomach lurching one way and the ship another as it accelerated sharply in the general direction of the distant

Commonwealth, it occurred to him that perhaps, when it came down to the matter of interpersonal relations, species like the Vssey had the best of it.

You can't hurt a member of the opposite sex if you're both of them.

Read on for an exciting excerpt from

RUNNING FROM THE DEITY

the next Pip & Flinx Adventure
by Alan Dean Foster

At first thought, you'd think it would be easy to find a missing planet. Even a methane dwarf. Except that the missing tenth world of the outlying Imperial AAnn system of Pyrassis was not a world, but an immense automated weapons platform of the long-extinct race who called themselves the Tar-Aiym.

Actually, Flinx mused as he held out his arms and let the magnetically charged droplets of water swirl around him and scrub his lanky naked form, one would think it would be even simpler to find a planet-sized weapons platform than a small planet itself. The only problem was that in the absence of standing orders to guide its revived behavior, the monstrous ancient device had gone looking for some. Since to the best of current knowledge the last of those beings who might be capable of issuing such directives had died half a million years earlier, more or less, the prospects of said intelligent weapons platform stumbling across relevant instructions on how it ought to proceed were slight indeed. Flinx suspected that it would do no good, should he somehow actually succeed in tracking down his galactically perambulating quarry, to point out that the species it was built to fight, the Hur'rikku, were as dead and gone as the massive machine's original Tar-Aiym builders.

Find it first, he told himself as he did a slow turn beneath the recycled water spray from the shower. Semantics follow function.

He did not need to pivot for purposes of cleanliness since the water beads automatically enveloped him in their attentive aqueous embrace. They avoided only the special shower mask that shielded his mouth and nose. Without such a mask, someone making use of such a shower conceivably could drown—though it was an easy enough matter simply to step sideways and clear of the open-sided, freestanding facility.

"Are you finished yet?" The voice of the *Teacher*'s ship-mind reached him through the stimulating vertical bath.

"Almost. Why? Are you going to suggest that after I finish bathing I take another 'vacation'?"

"It is interesting how sardonicism tends to shed efficacy over time," the ship-mind replied tartly. Having suggested that Flinx spend a while resting and recuperating on the out-of-the-way world of Jast, only to see him nearly murdered by one of the expatriate AAnn officials residing on that world, the AI was understandably disinclined to discuss the subject. Knowing this, Flinx lost few opportunities to bring it up.

"I take your point, by which I assume that you're not going to make such a suggestion. Good."

As he stepped out of the shower, the ready and waiting dryer scanned his dripping body. Preprogrammed to his specified level of individual comfort, it set about evaporating from his skin the water and the dirt it had englobed. Standing there, alone in his personal hygienic facilities within the ship, Flinx contemplated his immediate future and regarded it as fraught with uncertainty, danger, and confusion.

Not that it had ever been otherwise.

Some days he chose to dress while at other times he

moved about the *Teacher*'s interior quite naked. As the only human on board, there was no need to concern himself with violating nudity taboos. Pip certainly did not mind. Rising from the resting place where she had dozed in utter indifference to her master's peculiar habit of immersing himself in gravity-defying liquid, she landed on his bare right shoulder and settled down. Her slender serpentine shape was warm against his freshly scoured skin.

Pulling on lightweight pants and a feathery comfort shirt, he made his way to the *Teacher*'s bridge. Around him, the product of the Ulru-Ujurrian's creative engineering genius functioned smoothly. It would have been dead silent inside the ship, except that dead silence smacked too much of death itself. So at present, and in response to his latest request, the hush was broken by the soft sounds of a Sek-takenabdel cantata. Like many of his kind, Flinx was quite fond of the often atonal yet oddly soothing traditional thranx music, which in this particular composition sounded like nothing less than lullabies sung by angry, but muted, electrified cimbaloms.

As the ship sped at unnatural velocity through the nebulosity of higher mathematics colloquially known as space-plus, Flinx settled into the single command chair to gaze moodily through the sweeping, curved forward port. Though shifted over into the ultraviolet by the ship's KK-drive posigravity field, the view of the distorted universe surrounding him was, as always, still spectacularly beautiful. Pulsars and novae illuminated nebulae while distant galaxies vied for prominence with nearby suns.

Meanwhile, out beyond it all, in the direction of the constellation Boötes, something unimaginably vast and malevolent was coming out of a region known as the Great Emptiness, threatening not merely the Commonwealth and civilization, but everything within his field of view. His mental field of view, he reminded himself.

Hence the need, however hopeless the notion of fighting something so immense and alien, to find allies. Such as, just possibly, the primeval weapons platform that had for millennia masqueraded as the tenth planet of the system known as Pyrassis.

Thinking of it made him want to go stand and soak beneath another shower.

A reaction as ineffectual as it was childish, he knew. He could no more wash away the distinct memory of the evil he knew was out there than he could that of his troubled childhood, his subsequent erratic maturation, and the pressure to succeed that had been placed on him by his good friends and mentors Bran Tse-Mallory and the Eint Truzenzuzex. Just as with his unstable, if escalating and potentially fatal Talent, he could not wish such things away.

He stared out at the universe and the universe stared right back, indifferent. Exactly how *was* he supposed to go about finding the wandering planet-sized Tar-Aiym device? The brilliant Truzenzuzex and the insightful Tse-Mallory had been unable to give him much advice. Since he was the only one who had experienced (or suffered, he corrected himself) mental contact with the machine, it was hoped that if he deliberately went looking for it he might make such contact with it again. Strike up a casual conversation with an all-powerful alien artifact, it was supposed.

And, he mused, in the unlikely event that he did? How to convince such a relic to participate in the defense of the galaxy. Nothing of overweening importance—just your average galaxy, in which he, and everyone he knew, happened to live. Reposing in the chair, he shook his head dolefully though there were none present to note the gesture save Pip and ship.

"I don't see how I can do what Bran and Tru asked," he

muttered aloud. He did not need to explain himself. Shipmind knew.

"If you cannot, then no one can," it replied unhelpfully. As befitted its programming, it was doing its best to be supportive.

"A distinct and even likely possibility," he murmured to no one and nothing in particular. He glanced in the direction of the main readout. "We're still on course—if you can call heading in a general direction hundreds of parsecs in extent a 'course.'"

As usual, the *Teacher* sounded more relaxed when responding to specifics of ship operation than it did when trying to understand the often unfathomable complexities of human thought and behavior.

"We have re-entered the Commonwealth on intent to cross vector three-five-four, accelerating in space-plus on course to leave Commonwealth boundaries beyond Almaggee space, subsequent to entering the Sagittarius Arm and the region collectively known as the Blight."

The Blight, Flinx thought. Home to long-vanished species among whom were the ancient Tar-Aiym and Hur'rikku. The Blight: an immense swath of space once flourishing with inhabited worlds much of which had been rendered dead and sterile by the photonic plague unleashed by the Tar-Aiym on their ancient Hur'rikku enemies half a million years ago. Like those who had hastily and unwisely propounded it, the all-destroying plague had long since consumed itself, leaving in its wake only empty skies gazing forlornly down on dead worlds. Here and there, in a few spatial corners miraculously passed over by the plague, life had survived. Life, and memories of the all-consuming horror that had inexplicably skipped over them. No wonder the inhabitants of such isolated yet fortunate systems gazed up at the night sky with fear instead of expectation, and clung tightly to their isolated home systems.

Somewhere within that immense and largely vacant chunk of cosmos, the re-energized Tar-Aiym weapons platform had gone searching for instructions. Hunting for those who had made it. That there were none such to be found anywhere any longer was not sufficient to discourage it from looking. Such was the way of the machine mind. A mind he somehow had to make contact with once again. A mind he had somehow to persuade.

A hard task it was going to be, if he continued to have trouble convincing himself that the enterprise he was engaged in had not even the remotest chance of success.

When applied to most people, the expression *have an open mind* was merely rhetorical. Not so with Flinx. In fact, for much of his life he had prayed for the ability to have one that was closed. Intermittently and uncontrollably exposed to the emotions of any and every sentient around him, he threatened to drown in a sea of sentiment and sensation whenever he visited a developed world. Feelings flooded in on him in endless waves of exhilaration, despair, hope, remorse, anger, love, and everything in between. With each passing year he seemed to become more sensitive, more alert to those inner expressions of thinking beings. Not long ago, he had unexpectedly acquired the ability to project as well as receive emotions. This capability had proven useful in his search for the truth of his origins as well as in escaping those who intended him harm.

Yet for all his escalating skills, he had yet to learn how to master them. Defined by their erraticism, he had long ago decided that they might forever be beyond his control. That did not keep him from trying. Not only because a Talent that was wild was of far less usefulness than one that could be managed, but because the severe headaches he had suffered from since adolescence continued to grow more frequent, and more intense. His ability might be his savior—as well as that of billions of other sentient beings. It might also kill him. He had no choice but to continue wrestling with it, and with what he was, because he was special.

He would have given up everything just to be normal.

Sensing her master's melancholy, Pip rose from her resting place on his shoulder, the deep-throated humming of her wings louder than the ambient music that was being played by the *Teacher*. Circling him twice, she settled down on his other shoulder, wings furled tightly against her slim, brightly colored body. Wrapping herself around the back of his neck, she squeezed gently and affectionately, trying to reassure him. Reaching up with his left hand, he absently stroked the back of her head. Small slitted eyes closed in contentment. Alaspinian minidrags did not purr, but the strength of the empathetic bond between him and his scaly companion managed to convey something like the emotional equivalent.

Leaning back in the command chair, Flinx closed his own eyes and tried to open his unique mind further, to reach outward in all directions. Though he could readily identify the target he sought, he could not have defined with precision the exact nature of what it was that he was searching for. But, like the caressing hand of a beautiful woman, he would know it when he felt it. Out, out, away from the ship, away from himself, he searched. His field of perception was an expanding balloon. But no matter how much he relaxed, even with Pip's aid he sensed nothing. Only emptiness.

Occasionally, as the *Teacher* drove onward through the outer reaches of the Commonwealth, his Talent was tickled by sparks of sentience. A flash of feeling from distant Tipendemos and, later, stronger bursts of emotion out of

Almaggee. Then, more nothingness as he left the region of developed systems and sped through space-plus toward the Blight.

There were worlds in that vast section of the Sagittarius Arm that had once been inhabited, and worlds that were habitable still. No doubt someday, as the human and thranx population continued to expand in every direction, those worlds would once again resound to the voices of sentience. But not for a while yet. The Commonwealth itself encompassed an enormous section of space replete with hundreds of worlds yet to be settled or even explored by robotic probes. However enticing, the ancient worlds of the Blight would have to wait.

In its search for those who had built it, the wandering Tar-Aiym weapons platform would have hundreds of square parsecs in which to roam without encountering intelligent life of any kind. Making contact with anything in so vast a place seemed impossible. What swayed Flinx to try was the imploring of those wiser than himself. That, and the fact that on more than one occasion in his short life he had already achieved the impossible.

Having more or less resolved in his own mind to at least attempt the search, the last thing he expected as he entered the Blight was to have his resolution temporarily countermanded by his own ship.

He was taking his ease, as he so often did, in the central lounge. With its malleable waterfalls and pond, its fountain that sent heavy water trickling down and light water floating upward as decorative bubbles, it was far and away the most relaxing part of the unique vessel. Hailing from many worlds, the lush greenery that now packed every corner of the carefully maintained chamber filled it with wondrous scents and extra oxygen. Of course, he could have achieved a similar effect by simply directing the ship-mind to alter the composition of the internal atmosphere. But artificially regenerated oxygen lacked the subtle smells that accompanied air exhaled by growing things. Merely reclining among the running water and miniature forest helped him to unwind, and allowed his mind to roam free of anxiety and headaches. Green, he reflected, was good for the soul.

Nearby, Pip was pursuing something through the underbrush. It was harmless, or it would not be on board the ship. It was also confined to the lounge area. Chasing such harmless bits of decorative ambulatory life gave her something to do.

Unlike me, he thought.

"There is a problem."

Reluctantly, he bestirred himself from daydreaming of warm beaches on a recently visited world, and the passionate company he had kept there. "If you're trying to astonish me with revelation, you need to choose a less recurrent subject."

Ignoring the cynicism, the *Teacher* continued. "You are not the only one who suffers from stress, Philip Lynx."

Frowning, he rolled over on the supportive lounge. "Don't tell me that *you're* having mental problems. That's supposed to be my area of expertise."

"Mechanicals, however sophisticated, are fortunately immune to such intermittent cognitive plagues. My current situation involves stress of a purely physical nature. That does not render it any less serious or in need of attention. Quite the contrary."

Mildly alarmed now, Flinx sat up straight and set his cold drink aside. "You know how I hate understatement. Tell me straight: what's wrong?"

"We have done a great deal of traveling together, Flinx. In all that time I have endeavored to protect and care for you to the best of my abilities, according to the programming installed within myself by my builders."

"And an admirable job you've done of it, too." Flinx waited uncertainly for whatever was coming.

"We have crossed and recrossed vast sections of space. Because of a singular adaptation of KK-drive technology exclusive to my drive system, I have been able to set down on worlds and moons that would otherwise require visitation in the usual manner, via suborbital shuttle. On your behalf, I have run and I have fought.

"Now internal sensors have detected a disquieting deterioration in certain portions of my makeup. These need to be repaired. I am afraid that continuing on our present course and search without attending to these needs could result in structural failure, eventually of a catastrophic nature."

Flinx knew whereof the ship spoke. KK-drive starships did not fall slowly to pieces, did not wear away like ancient ships of the sea. Bits and parts did not flake off the exterior, exposing gaps and cracks, and still remain functional. Boats traveling on liquid oceans could sustain themselves with such damage and continue to function. So could vehicles traveling on land. But a starship had to be maintained whole and intact, or disintegrate entirely. Tortured metaphors notwithstanding, there was no middle ground in space, to which the doomed crew of the famously lost *Carryon* could no doubt attest.

He took a deep breath. "What do you recommend?"

"We can reverse course and return to the Commonwealth, where repair facilities are widely available and where I judge it should be possible to effect them without arousing overmuch unwanted attention."

Return, Flinx reflected. Go back, risk being discovered by Commonwealth authorities, or members of the Order of Null, or who knew what else, while the *Teacher*, his home and refuge, was laid up in an orbital repair facility somewhere, leaving him no means of flight from possible trouble. Not to mention, once repairs were completed, having to begin this probably vainglorious quest all over again.

"I deduce by your silence that this proposed course of action leaves you less than enthused."

Irritated, Flinx spoke without looking up from the green-and-blue ground cover that gave the floor of the lounge the look of a well-manicured meadow. "What did I just say about understatement?"

"Usefully," the ship-mind went on, "there is an alternative possibility."

"Alternative?" Now Flinx did look up, focusing his gaze on one of the unobtrusive visual pickups scattered around the lounge. "How can there be an alternative?"

Sounding pleased with itself—although it was nothing more than a subset of its conditional programming—the ship-mind continued.

"The structural repairs and reinforcements I need to effect are within the capability of my integrated maintenance faculties. I am convinced that I can carry out the requisite maintenance without outside assistance. Provided, of course, that a location is found that will support my weight while simultaneously making available certain essential raw materials. These consist primarily of carbon and titanium, two quite common elements, that need to be worked under terrestrial-type atmosphere and gravity. It should be possible to locate such a world here within the Blight. This would obviate the need for us to return to the Commonwealth, a course of action I infer from your reaction to my previous suggestion that you would clearly prefer to avoid."

"You infer correctly." Flinx was much relieved. With luck, they would not have to subject themselves to Commonwealth scrutiny, nor retrace the parsecs they had already covered. He did not doubt that the *Teacher* could successfully carry out the necessary repair work. If it was in the least bit uncertain, it would never have put forth the proposal.

For just a moment, he considered instructing the ship to press on ahead and ignore the required repairs. What was the worst that could happen? That the ship would fragment and he would die? In space-plus, the convergent disintegration would occur in less than the blink of an eye. It would all be over and done with: the burden of responsibility, the endless worrying, his confused concerns for Clarity Held, the recurrent head-splitting headaches—all forever finished, and him with them.

Then he remembered what the ever-gruff but affectionate Mother Mastiff had always told him, even when he was a pre-adolescent, about dying.

"Just remember one thing about death, boy," she'd growl softly, in between spitting something better left unidentified into a receptacle in the corner of the small kitchen. "Once you decided to be dead, you don't get to change your mind if you don't like the consequences."

And, he reminded himself, there was Clarity to think of.

A new thought caused him to break out in the slight, subtle grin that always teased and bemused those fortunate enough to gaze upon it. Once again he eyed a pickup concealed among the foliage that enveloped him. "I don't suppose you would by any chance already happen to have located a suitable nearby world?"

"As a matter of fact," ship-mind replied unexpectedly, "there are virtually no systems in the general, let alone immediate, spatial vicinity that fit all of the obligatory needs."

Flinx frowned slightly. "You said *virtually*. Go on."

"There is one. That is, it should prove suitable if the single isolated and relatively old record referring to its location, existence, and physical makeup is of sufficient accuracy."

The sole human on board the expansive, softly humming starship nodded knowingly to himself. "Then we ought to head there, don't you think?"

"I do. Unfortunately, I cannot do that unless you specifically grant permission for me to do so."

"And why is that?" Something small and bright yellow darted between a pair of solohonga trees, energetically pursued by the blur of blue-and-pink wings and body that was Pip.

"Because," ship-mind intoned solemnly, "while the extant situation for a system lying within the Blight is unusual, it unfortunately for our purposes is not unprecedented. This is because the world in question is inhabited."

Even as they changed course to head for the system where the *Teacher* would attempt to carry out repairs to itself, Flinx brooded on whether or not he had made the right decision in authorizing access. Arrawd, as the depressingly inadequate old records indicated it was called by its nonhuman inhabitants, was a Commonwealth-equivalent Class IVb world. Knowing that presented him with an ethical dilemma of a kind he had never before been forced to face.

Class IVb sentients existed at a pre-steam or lower level of technology, usually accompanied by similarly primitive political and social structures. The study of such societies was permitted only after applicants, nearly always scientific and educational bodies, submitted and had their intentions rigorously screened and passed by peer review and the appropriate authorities. Even with suitable safeguards in place, orbital observation was permitted only under advanced camouflage and from strictly regulated distances. Surface study was outright forbidden, actual contact with the species under examination punishable by revocation of academic and scientific accreditation and, in extreme cases, selective mindwipe of the offending individuals.

The *Teacher* was unequivocal in stating its needs. In order to obtain the raw materials to effect the necessary repairs to its structure, it had to set down on Arrawd itself. As for any contact, Flinx determined to hold his natural and inveterate curiosity in check. He would stay inside the disguised ship and wait out the delay while essential renovations were completed.

It had been a long time since the single Commonwealth survey vessel that had filed the only report on Arrawd had visited its isolated system. Though not exceptionally far from Commonwealth space, it lay well within the boundaries of the Blight. As was typical of such remote, inhabited worlds, there were no other populated systems nearby. The likelihood of the *Teacher* encountering another Commonwealth vessel in such a region was more than remote. That comforting improbability did not make his intended visit any less illegal.

His alternative was to reverse course and return to the nearest developed Commonwealth world, there to continue concealing his identity and that of his vessel while the obligatory repairs were surreptitiously carried out. Flinx had never been one to backtrack. Perhaps it was because he was more conscious than most of the absolute preciousness of time.

Also, once a thief, always a thief. In this instance, he would filch an illegal stopover. Somehow it struck him as less unlawful than stealing goods or money. Just a brief, if illicit, visit. Then he would depart, he and his swiftly repaired ship stealing away just as though they had never been there, leaving any natives none the wiser or Commonwealth authorities any the angrier.

So it was with the most righteous and honorable intentions that he entered the Arrawd system, flew past a ringed world that generated unexpectedly powerful pangs of homesickness, and allowed his suitably cloaked vessel to settle into orbit high above the fourth world of the local sun. It was there and then that his virtuous intentions unexpectedly began to unravel.

For one thing, Arrawd was astonishingly beautiful.

Even from orbit, the surface was achingly tempting. In the space immediately in front of him, images of the world below materialized and shifted at his beck and call. There were rainstorms but no hurricanes, seas but no oceans, dry land regions but only unassuming deserts. Capillary-like, rivers threaded their way through rolling plains and dense forests. Jungles matched icecaps in moderation. According to the *Teacher*'s sensors, the atmosphere was almost painfully human-normal while the gravity was sufficiently less to make an athlete of all but the most incapacitated visitor. He could not only survive unprotected on Arrawd's surface; he would have to take care not to let himself go.

As for the local dominant species that carefully crafted government regulations were designed to shield from the potentially unsettling effects of superior Commonwealth technology, there was little enough information on the Dwarra. Since the robotic probe that had discovered and studied their world was prohibited from setting down on its surface, all measurements, readings, approximations, evaluations, and opinions of that unfamiliar species were necessarily fragmentary and incomplete.

The last time he had been compelled to call upon the *Teacher*'s prodigious archives to provide him with a portrayal of a soon-to-be-visited alien race, he had been forced to wrap his perceptions around the completely alien (and not a little grotesque) Vssey from the distant world of Jast. So it was with some relief that he found himself gazing upon body shapes that were considerably less outlandish as the ship called them forth from its files. Even the recorded analysis of their primary language was simple and straightforward.

The Dwarra were bipedal, bisymmetrical, and bisexual, like himself. No more reproducing via spores or budding, like the Vssey. Aside from a distinctive slenderness that bordered on the anorexic, their most distinguishing physical characteristic consisted of a pair of short, whip-like antennae that protruded from their flat, back-sloping foreheads. Concerning the possible function of these prominent appendages, the relevant archive was disappointingly uninformative. For all Flinx was able to find out, their purpose might be nothing more than decorative—or they might be equally capable of sending and receiving radio signals. Though the vaguely humanoid Dwarra displayed ample evidence of sexual dimorphism, both genders appeared to sport antennae of equal length and diameter. He had to smile. The fleshy gray protrusions lent their owners something of the appearance of emaciated sprites.

- Waif-like bodies suited to the lighter gravity boasted two upper arms that divided halfway along their length into two separate forearms. Instead of hands and fingers, each forearm tapered until it split again into a pair of flexible gray flanges that looked oddly clumsy and flipper-like but were doubtless capable of sufficient manipulation with which to raise a civilization. Legs were characterized by a similarly subdivided arrangement. Two legs and two arms giving way to four feet and eight hand-finger equivalents made for a disconcertingly busy physical appearance. Fortunately, hearing organs and eyes were not similarly partitioned. As in humans, the former were small and positioned on the sides of the narrow head, while the eyes were wide, round, and set in deep, muscular sockets in the center of the equally round face. A single small air intake located just above the mouth slit and set flush with the gray skin of the hairless face completed the alien visage.

In place of body hair or scales, flattened fingernail-sized flaps of skin that ranged in hue from light gray to an almost metallic silver covered the visible parts of the slim body. Varying in length from one to three centimeters, they flapped like leaves in the breeze when the projection demonstrated the Dwarra's ungainly but satisfactorily motile gait. Females tended to be slightly smaller than males. According to the sparse records, the Dwarra gave birth to young who remained encased in a nourishing sac of gelatinous material until they were approximately a year old, at which point a second birthing ritual took place to celebrate the emergence of the infant from its mother's insides and manual transfer to its nurturing pouch, where it remained for an additional year before finally being asked to stand erect on its eight wobbly podal flanges.

As he finished perusing the limited information and waved off the floating, three-dimensional imagery, he decided that perhaps the inhabitants of looming, scenic Arrawd were not as much like himself as he had first thought.

Upon arrival, conducting leisurely observations from high orbit, the *Teacher* was able to reconfirm the available historical data on the state of Dwarran civilization. It was impossible to tell what, if any, advances the locals had made since the time the robot probe had carried out its survey, but there was no question that the alien civilization spreading across the world below remained at a low-tech level of scientific accomplishment. There were cities, but they were unexceptional in size and even under high resolution exhibited nothing in the way of explosive technological development. If there were factories, they were fueled by nothing more exotic than the simplest of hydrocarbons. Though roadways were present in abundance, none appeared to be paved with any material more advanced than stone.

Harbors displayed a more sophisticated appearance, boasting among other recognizable components ingenious slipways for the handling and repair of large vessels. Evidence for extensive commerce was present in the form of extensive built-up areas and warehousing complexes. The seas of Arrawd, many in number and unassuming in extent, would be highly conducive to waterborne transportation. The smaller the body of water, the less ferocious were likely to be any prevailing storms, though the lighter gravity would permit higher waves. Mountain ranges further reduced the efficacy of land-based transportation and would tend to cause the locals to focus even more intensively on waterborne shipping. Even so, further observation revealed the presence of nothing more elaborate or advanced than large sailing craft.

Unfortunately for his purposes, while there were no great, sprawling conurbations, all indicators pointed to a sizable and largely dispersed population. When the *Teacher* finally announced that it had located an area appropriate to its needs, Flinx decided that he'd had enough of staring blankly from orbit. The small peninsula the ship had chosen was reasonably far from the nearest community of any size, distant from even a small harbor, and rippling with titanium-rich sand dunes. There was also ample carbon locked up nearby in the form of an extensive and untouched deposit of fossilized plant growth. No indicators of urban population, no signs of commerce, no agriculture. A better spot might be found, but it would take more time to search.

"I concur," he told the ship-mind. "Take us down as fast as practical. At the slightest sign of reaction from the native population, return to orbit and we'll try again on another continent."

"I will be as subtle as possible," the ship-mind replied. A slight lurch indicated that the *Teacher* had already commenced its owner-approved descent.

Of course, what it was doing was not only highly illegal, but almost universally thought to be impossible. By their very nature, KK-drive craft were not supposed to be able to come within a specified number of planetary diameters of any rocky world without causing destruction on the ground and damage to the ship. Only the Ulru-Ujurrians, who had fashioned the *Teacher* as a gift to Flinx, had been able to find a solution to the problem, which continued to bedevil the physicists and engineers of all other space-going species.

Not that the Ulru-Ujurrians could properly be called space-going, Flinx mused as the ship continued to drop surfaceward. More like otherwhere-going.

The touchdown of the *Teacher* would have enormously impressed anyone on the ground—had there been anyone around to witness it. Executed under cover of night, as far as Flinx could tell the massive shape terminating in its coruscant Caplis projector came to rest in near silence among the thirty-meter-high dunes of the bucolic peninsula unnoticed by any living thing save for a pair of nesting amphibians. What little noise the ship generated was masked by a nocturnal onshore breeze, with the result that even the two jet-black, half-meter-long creatures hardly stirred in their burrow.

For several long minutes, an edgy Flinx paced the confines of the command cabin while the ship-mind made note of and absorbed everything about its immediate surroundings, from the chemical composition of the gentle sea nearby (less salty than terrestrial oceans, its tidal shift hardly affected by the three small moons in the sky) to the efforts of a number of surprisingly mobile nearby plants to uproot themselves and move away from the *Teacher's* imposing bulk. Walking up to the curving foreport, he gazed down the length of the ship's service arm toward the now dark disc of the KK-drive generating fan. His craft was as exposed, obvious, and unnatural a part of the landscape as a thranx clan meeting in the arctic.

"How much longer?" The ship-mind was sufficiently intuitive that he did not have to specify the subject of his query.

"Working," the *Teacher* replied succinctly. "I do not foresee a lengthy study period. The immediate surroundings are simple and straightforward and will be easy to mimic."

"Then how about simply and straightforwardly concealing us?" Responding to her master's uncharacteristic irritability, Pip looked up from her resting place on the forward console.

"Processing." The *Teacher* could be talkative when the environment was relaxed, and equally concise when the situation demanded it. "Observe."

Once again, Flinx turned his attention toward the bow of the ship. It was no longer there. In its place was a narrow, low dune that terminated in a higher barchan of mineral-rich sand. The programming and complex projection mechanics that enabled the *Teacher* to alter the appearance of its exterior to resemble anything from a contract freighter to a small warship also allowed it to impersonate more mundane surroundings. Gazing at the forward part of his vessel, a relieved Flinx had no doubt that the larger habitable section that formed his home now also blended effectively into its immediate surroundings.

Not far off to the left, a placid sea glistened invitingly in Arrawd's dim, tripartite moonlight. After weeks spent cooped up on board, the thought of a nocturnal swim in tepid salt water was tempting. No doubt his presence in such waters, however, would prove equally enticing to whatever predators roamed the perhaps deceptively sluggish shallows. Taking a reckless plunge in an alien sea was a good way to meet one's maker in advance of one's designated time. He would wait until morning, see what developed, have the *Teacher* run a bioscan out to depth, and then decide if his present locale was safe enough for him to take the plunge.

Seduced by the serene, moonlit surroundings of solid ground, he had already set aside his promise not to emerge from the ship.

"How soon before you can begin acquiring necessary raw materials and commence repairs?"

"I already have," the ship informed him. Somewhere deep within its self-maintaining mass, faint mechanical noises sifted upward into the living quarters.

Flinx gestured toward the console. Obediently, Pip rose on thrumming, chromatic wings and glided over to settle on his shoulders. "That's great. If I'm not up, wake me at sunrise."

The ship responded affirmatively, even though it knew the request was unnecessary. The ability of its human's biological clock to reset itself almost immediately to whatever new world Flinx happened to find himself on was one that never ceased to amaze the multi-faceted artificial mind. Flinx called it "making myself at home."

Perhaps, ship-mind thought to itself, the human had developed this unusual ability to make himself at home wherever he happened to be because he had never really had such a place of his own.

Looking for more of today's best science fiction and fantasy novels? Explore Del Rey Online

Visit www.delreybooks.com

the portal to all the information and resources available from Del Rey, and find:

• A complete online catalog of Del Rey titles
• Sample chapters from every new book
• Special features on selected authors and books

Sign up for the Del Rey Internet Newsletter (DRIN)

a free monthly publication e-mailed to subscribers, and receive:

• Information on new releases and upcoming titles
• The latest news and announcements from our publishing offices
• Essays and interviews with authors and editors
• Author tour and event updates
• The opportunity to receive an advance edition of one of our books through our readers' review program
• A chance to win free books

To subscribe to the DRIN:

Send a blank e-mail to join-ibd-dist@list.randomhouse.com or sign up at www.delreybooks.com

The DRIN is also available at no charge for your PDA devices— go to www.randomhouse.com/partners/avantgo for more information, or visit www.avantgo.com and search for the Books@Random channel.

DEL REY